THE MUTUAL
UFO NETWORK

THE MUTUAL UFO NETWORK

STORIES

LEE MARTIN

DZANC BOOKS

DZANC
BOOKS

5220 Dexter Ann Arbor Rd.
Ann Arbor, MI 48103
www.dzancbooks.org

Library of Congress Cataloging-in-Publication Data

Names: Martin, Lee, 1955- author.
Title: The mutual UFO network / Lee Martin.
Description: Ann Arbor, MI : Dzanc Books, 2017.
Identifiers: LCCN 2017044833 | ISBN 9781945814495
Classification: LCC PS3563.A724927 A6 2017 | DDC 813/.54--dc23
LC record available at https://lccn.loc.gov/2017044833

First Edition: June 2018
Cover design by The Frontispiece
Interior design by Leslie Vedder

Printed in the United States of America

10   9   8   7   6   5   4   3   2   1

CONTENTS

For Cathy

THE MUTUAL
UFO NETWORK

THE LAST TIME I SAW MY FATHER, HE WAS IN OUR GARDEN TYING PEA vines to bamboo stakes. The vines, he told me, needed something to latch onto, something to climb; otherwise, they would snake along the ground and tangle and make a mess, and the one thing he didn't need, then, was a mess. "You know what I'm saying, don't you, Nate?"

"Right," I said. "Keeping things in line."

"Check." He winked at me. "All our ducks in a row."

It was October. The scorching heat of summer had eased, and the fall rains had come. Each morning, we woke to drizzle, to the sound of water dripping from the eaves. The leaves on the red oaks were turning brown, as was the grass, everything fading to that camel's dun that was Texas in autumn, only an occasional burst of red from a Bradford pear or a spritz of green from my father's fall planting to give the world any color at all.

The pea vines would have another month before the first frost. "You'll be back before then," my father said, "and we'll put everything down for the winter."

I was going to visit my mother in Virginia, where she'd moved when she and my father separated. I was going because I couldn't bear to be with him even though, in the spring, I'd made the decision to stay.

"You don't have to love him," my mother had told me. "There's no law."

But the truth was I did love him—at least, that's what I called the ache that stuck in my throat every time I saw him, when he thought he was alone, tip his head and cover his face with his hands. Or each morning when I came into the kitchen and saw a place set for me at the breakfast table. A cereal bowl and juice glass and coffee cup, all turned upside down to keep out the dust. A cloth napkin rolled and held with a wooden ring. Most mornings, there would be a note held down with a spoon. APPLES IN THE FRIDGE, it might say in my father's small, labored handwriting. PAPER SAYS RAIN. DON'T GET CAUGHT IN THE WET.

Sometimes I stood at the window, hidden by the thick folds of the drapes, and watched him on the lawn, picking stray bits of cypress mulch from the grass or the carpet juniper that ran along our front walk. He got down on his hands and knees and crawled, plucking up any shaving or scrap that had washed out from our flowerbeds. Then he got to his feet and stood there, hands on his hips, surveying the lawn until he saw something he'd missed. Often, he kept at it until dusk came, and I had to go to the door and call to him.

"Dad," I'd say, "it's almost dark."

He'd be on his knees again, bent over as if he were praying, and his voice, when he answered, sounded so far away. "Just a while longer," he'd tell me. "I'm getting everything ship-shape."

How could I not love him, when he was trying so hard to bring our lives back to normal?

Then one day our neighbor, Mr. Laskey, said to me, "Nathan, I see your old man crawling around on the grass. The last three days I've seen him. Did he lose something?"

Mr. Laskey, a retired chef, was the only one in the neighborhood who'd still speak to us. I told him about the mulch and how my father liked to keep it off the grass. "He's particular," I said. "He wants everything to be just right."

"A soufflé I can understand," Mr. Laskey said. "But mulch—how long is life?"

That evening, my mother called, and as soon as I heard her voice, as shy as a girl's, I knew I'd do whatever she asked.

"Come out here and see the mountains," she said. "You can't imagine how beautiful the leaves are. Stunning. I've made a room for you. And there's a good college. You could start next term…well, I'm not asking." For a long time, I didn't say anything. The phone lines were full of static, and I could hear the fuzzy echoes of other people's conversations. "Nate, Nate, Nate," my mother finally said with a sigh. "Did I do wrong? When I left your father?"

"Don't ask me that," I said.

"You can make a mistake and go back and change it," she told me. "You don't know that when you're young."

The pea vines were only a few inches tall—no more than half a foot—and staking them was a delicate job. First, my father had to push the bamboo sticks into the ground, close to the vines, but not so close that the sticks would damage the roots that were claiming a hold. Then he had to tie the vines to the stakes. His fat fingers fumbled with the slender shoots and the strips of nylon he'd cut from some of my mother's old pantyhose. He had to lean each vine over so he could tie it to a stake without pulling the roots from the ground. He used nylon, he said, because it was flexible and wouldn't choke the vines. It would give them the little bit of support they needed while still allowing them to grow.

"Do you want me to help you?" I said. "I've got time."

"No, I don't want you to help me." He was crouched down, his head bowed, the straw of his gardening hat darkening from the drizzle. "I believe I'm quite capable of doing this job."

But he was having a rough go of it. Each time he tried to tie the vine to the stake, the nylon got wrapped around his fingers or the vine slipped away from him. I crouched down beside him and smelled the wet dirt and heard the grunts of his breath.

"Just let me hold the vine," I said.

I reached out and took the pea vine, and when my father tried to knock my hand away, the vine came out of the ground. I felt its roots, the thin white fingers, loosen their hold, and then there was the most incredible lightness at the end of my arm, and my father's lips quivered with an uncertain smile. He looked like he was waiting for a punch line, not sure whether the joke was going to be funny.

"I'm sorry," I told him.

"Sure," he said, his grin vanishing. "Now you say it. Right when you're on your way out the door."

The trouble started that winter when I went out at night and hid myself close to windows—crouched down behind shrubbery or heat pumps—so I could watch our neighbors in the warm light of their homes.

I never saw anything that they would have been ashamed for me to see. I can honestly say that: no quarrels, no lovemaking, no quirky habits. I told them that later, when I went from door to door, confessing what I'd done and explaining how I'd meant no harm or insult. I'd only wanted to be close to them. But, of course, by then, it didn't matter what I said. I was criminal.

Mostly I saw them watching TV, eating sandwiches at the kitchen counter, rinsing dishes in the sink. Mrs. Poe liked to crochet. Miss Nance read the evening newspaper. Mr. Dean built model airplanes. Miss Stevens marked her students' lessons and ornamented them with bright stickers or gold stars.

Mr. Laskey was my favorite. He cooked. I watched him in his kitchen, a long white apron tied around his neck. Even outside, I could smell oregano and tomato sauce, cinnamon and nutmeg. Or at least I convinced myself I could, eager as I was to breathe in the scents, take in the sights of settled, honest living.

In my own home, my parents operated a mail-order business called The Mutual UFO Network. My father transferred computer-generated images to videotape and created illusions of spaceships streaking across the night sky. He took out ads in magazines and sold his videotapes to customers around the world who wanted proof that what they'd suspected all along was indeed true: there were visitors from other planets, and they were watching us.

"We help people see what they want to see," my father told me once. "What's the harm in that?"

"It's a hoax," I told him.

"Hoax, schmoax," he said. "It's commerce."

Then the unexpected happened. My mother began to wonder whether it might be true that we weren't alone in the universe. "All these people," she said, waving a sheaf of order forms. "It's something to think about."

She'd read about a laboratory in Phoenix that, since the late seventies, had been testing photographs and videotapes to see if they were hoaxes, natural phenomena, or something unexplainable. Nearly three hundred fell into the last category, the mysterious and the possible, and suddenly that was enough for my mother. My father's trickery, his blips of light across the screen, had already seduced her.

"Lunatics," he said. "Good god, Lib."

"I suppose that's what you'd think about me if I ever came home and told you I'd seen a spaceship."

"Let's be reasonable," my father told her.

But my mother just arched an eyebrow and stared at him, and I began to wonder what would happen if someone you thought you knew slipped away into another world. How far would love carry you if you wanted to follow? What if that person turned out to be you?

"I just don't think we should rule anything out," my mother said.

A few nights later, before I could see it coming, Miss Stevens turned off her kitchen light and saw my face at her window. What must I have looked like to her? It makes me ashamed to imagine. Then she screamed, and I ran, ran through the cold night, the air rushing up into my face, ran until Mr. Dean, dropping his garbage bag at the curb, stopped me, his arms wrapping around my chest. His hands smelled of airplane glue. "Nate," he said with a laugh. "What in the world's the deal?"

What I wanted to say was that I loved them, loved them all, the people I wished my family could be. But porch lights were coming on all along the street, and Miss Stevens was in her yard, shouting, "That's him, that's him, that's him." And all I could do was stand there and let Mr. Dean hold me.

How many times had I done this, my father wanted to know after Mr. Dean convinced Miss Stevens not to call the police and I was home, my secret revealed. How many houses?

"We'll never be able to face these people again." My father ran his hand through his hair, took a deep breath, and shook his head. "Jesus, Nate. What were you thinking?"

I was thinking how nice it had been every time I looked through a window and saw my neighbors' ordinary lives, and how sad, too, to always be outside the light that enclosed them and kept them from seeing me. Night after night, I'd come home and found my father editing videotape, tracing his finger across a monitor's screen. "There," he'd say, tapping the screen with the point of his fingernail. "Now tell me, Nate. Doesn't that look like the real McCoy?"

My mother, by this time, was already gone but hadn't admitted it. She spent her evenings on our deck, a jacket hugged closed over her chest. She put her feet up on the railing, tipped back her head, and scanned the sky. One night, I joined her and watched the flashing red lights on an airplane. "If you ask me," she said, "it's selfish to think we might be the only life in the universe." It was cold, and I could see her breath. "It's such a big place, Nate. How do we know?"

"Do you really believe it?" I said. "All this stuff about UFOs?"

"I don't believe it the way I believe in love," she said. "But it's an interesting prospect."

She'd always been a woman on the lookout for the rare and unusual. That's how she found my father, who at the time, 1976, had been selling Bicentennial rocks on college campuses. "He had this suitcase," my mother told me. "And it was full of rocks, just plain rocks. Nothing painted on them. No American flag or eagle, not even the date. 'They're just rocks,' I said to him. 'Why would anyone buy a rock?' 'Not rocks,' he said. 'Bicentennial rocks. Years from now, when you look at this rock, you'll think, 1976, and then you'll remember everything.' He had this way about him, even then. Your father has always been very sincere."

He'd always been a shyster, and like all good shysters, he believed every lie he told. "We're going to figure this out," he finally said the night Mr. Dean brought me home. "Don't worry, Nate. We're going to be all right."

But it was too late. My nightly peeks into my neighbors' windows had given my mother a glimpse of escape. "Tell me," she said later, when she came into my room and sat on my bed. "Tell me what you saw."

I'd decided to drive myself to the airport and leave my car in long-term parking because I couldn't face the prospect of sitting on a plane knowing my father was standing behind the wide spread of glass in the terminal watching the takeoff, watching until the plane had climbed above the cloud cover and disappeared. "I stood right there," he'd told me after I flew to California with my high school band to march in the Rose Parade. "I kept watching until I couldn't see you anymore."

This time, before I left, he hugged me in the garden. He threw his arms around me and pressed me to him. My forehead hit the brim of his hat and it tumbled to the ground.

"It's not your fault," he said. "What's happening to your mother and me. We're just putting a little air between us. You know. Taking a rest. I fully expect she'll come back soon."

I drew away from him and saw his face, wet now from the rain. "She's all set up in Virginia," I said. "She sells timeshares at a resort village."

"You tell her I've changed," he said, and his voice was a whisper. "You tell her, Nate, and she'll come back. It was all that UFO crap that caused the problem, but, hey, I was just trying to make a buck on the side. I didn't give anyone anything they didn't deserve."

At the airport, a man was selling books. He was cruising through my boarding area, dragging a canvas duffle bag behind him. The bag kept bumping into people's carry-ons, kept whacking their shins. "Sorry," the man kept saying. He was a young British man with a winning smile. "Terribly sorry." The books, he told people, were collections of stories, each volume focused on a different subject. He had travel stories, wedding stories, brother stories, war stories.

"Each one of them true," he said. "Not a word made up. This is the real stuff. People just like you."

The young man was wearing an emerald-green polo shirt and a pair of khaki slacks that still had creases in them from being folded in the store. The tassels on his loafers—those, too, shiny and new—slapped against the tops of his feet as he made his way up and down the aisles of plastic chairs.

"What about you, mate?" he said to me. He leaned over and put his face close to mine. I smelled the strong citrus scent of his cologne. "Something to read on the plane?" I hesitated just long enough to give him the chance to keep talking. "What's your cup of tea? Adventure? Romance?" He jostled my arm with his elbow and winked. "Erotica?"

Sitting across from me was a man who kept chewing his fingernails. He bit them off and spit them onto the floor. He was a skinny man with a gold tooth, and every time he gnawed at a fingernail, that tooth—an incisor—caught the light and twinkled. The woman who was with him, a woman with no hair—just a shadow of fuzz—and a very soft voice, said, "Would you calm down? Would you just calm down? Planes go up and then they land. Hundreds of them every day. It's perfectly safe."

The nail-biter, this guy with the gold tooth and a few scraggly whiskers on his chin, put his hand on the woman's head. He palmed it like it was a melon and squeezed. The woman tried to pull away. She tried to stand up, but the nail-biter kept pressing down with his hand, a hand that looked like it wasn't even his. It was so broad and the fingers were so long. It looked like something made out of plastic, a fake hand, but I knew it was, as my father would have said, "the real McCoy," by the way the woman grimaced and bit down on her lower lip. "You are," she said in that soft voice of hers. "You are." I knew, from the way she said it, that this was a regular occurrence, something she had to endure with the nail-biter. She had such a lovely face, her skin smooth and glowing, that it was easy to forget she had no hair. It was something about her eyes, I decided. They were eager eyes, wide open and trusting, the kind of eyes my father must have imagined on every sucker in the world. She looked like she could get on a plane, without a thought of crashing, go anywhere in the world, and feel at home. Whoever she was, and whatever her story was with the nail-biter, I felt certain she didn't deserve the way he was treating her. It made me think of all the people who'd sent in their money for my father's fake videos.

"Do you have any plane crash stories?" I said to the British man.

"Wouldn't sell many of those, now would I?" he said. Then he slung his duffle bag over his shoulder and moved to another gate.

The nail-biter lifted his hand from the woman's head, and I could see his fingerprints, their red smudges, rimming the front of her skull. She opened her eyes even wider and bunched up the skin on her forehead as if she wanted something to click back into place. The nail-biter put his hands on his knees and leaned forward. "You said that on purpose, didn't you, Chicken Little? That stuff about plane crashes. You wanted it to get under my skin."

"Pardon?" I said. "Are you talking to me?"

"That's right, chickee. You hear anyone else squawking about the sky falling?"

The nail-biter's long fingers were trembling, skittering about on his knees. The woman reached over and put her hands on top of those trembling fingers, pressing down to hold them still. "Jinx," she said. "Don't."

Jinx, the nail-biter, moved his left hand out from under the woman's. He held it up between them. "It's all right, Yum-Yum. Everything's square." He patted the empty seat beside him. "Come over here, chickee," he said to me. His chin was trembling now, breaking up into goose flesh around his sad whiskers. "I want to tell you something."

Suddenly, he seemed like such an easy mark, and I was ashamed of how I'd spooked him. I'd known exactly what to say, and now there he was, looking like he might cry. That was the last thing I needed to see because then I'd start thinking about my father, on his knees in his garden, putting the pea vine I'd ripped free back in the ground, pulling soil up around it with his hands, hoping its roots would take hold. If

I looked at that picture too long—if I saw my father's faith—I knew I might never get on my plane.

"Here's a true story," Jinx said to me when I was finally sitting beside him. "I'm scared."

His honesty won me. "The plane?" I asked.

"He thinks it's going to crash," Yum-Yum said.

"They rarely do," I told him.

"I know." He nodded. "But when they do…oh, doctor."

Yum-Yum was patting his knee. "Have you taken the ginger yet?"

"No, I haven't done that."

"Ginger capsules," she explained to me. "For air sickness. They're a natural alternative to Dramamine."

"I'll go find a water fountain." Jinx looked behind him, up and down the concourse. "That's what I'll do."

While he was gone, I remembered how, when I was a kid, my parents and I drove from Texas to Virginia every summer to see my grandparents—my mother's folks, who owned a farm in the Shenandoah Valley. In East Tennessee, the climb and drop of the mountains made me car sick, and I had to sit in the front seat with my father. He called me The Navigator. "Mister Navigator," he always said, "you're riding shotgun. It's up to you to keep us on track."

My mother took my place in the backseat, and soon she dozed off, and my father said, "She's out like a light. Now it's just you and me."

I always wondered whether she resented my delicate sense of balance—the simple act of moving through space left me dizzy—and the way it exiled her to the backseat. But when we came down from the mountains into the lush valley, she reached over the seat, put her arms around my neck, and gave me a hug. "Nate," she said once, "your mother's a fool. Tell me. Why did I ever leave something so green?"

"Maybe I had something to do with it," my father said.

"Yes," my mother told him in a flat voice. "For better or worse, you did."

Outside the terminal, the rain was slicking the tarmac. Though it was early afternoon, the landing strip lights were distinct. Way off, on the other side of a chain-link fence, two longhorn cows huddled together beneath a mesquite tree.

"His first time?" I said to Yum-Yum.

She got down on her knees and began picking up the bits of fingernails Jinx had spit onto the carpet. She held them in her palm. "We wouldn't go if we didn't have to," she said, and it was as if she wanted to apologize for their presence and the way our lives had intersected.

"Emergency?" I said.

She moved to a trash can so she could get rid of the fingernails. "That's another story," she said.

At that moment, there was a commotion behind us. It was two security guards, their two-way radios squawking. They held the British bookseller; each had a good grip up in one of his armpits, jerking him up onto the balls of his feet, crinkling the leather of his new loafers. His polo shirt had jerked free from his trousers. The roll of flesh around his waist was very white.

"I don't care if you've got the Ten Commandments on Moses's tablets," one of the guards said. He was a man with a gray moustache and pink bulbs for cheeks. "You can't sell them here."

What were the truest words I knew? That's what I wondered then. What could I say if I ever came to a moment where the rest of life depended on what I said?

"Yum-Yum." She turned, startled to hear me use her nickname. The lid of the trash container slammed shut. "I'll take you wherever you want to go," I said. "Right now. You and me. Before Jinx comes back."

She scraped the fingers of one hand across the palm of the other as if Jinx's nail clippings had worked their way under her skin like splinters and she couldn't get them out.

"Your flight," she said.

"We could leave," I told her. "I know that's what you want to do."

The British bookseller was still putting up a fuss. "The truth, I tell you, gents. All true. This whole bloody life."

"You think it's easy," Yum-Yum said to me. Her fingers were curled down now, and I imagined her nails digging into her palm.

My mother had done it. She'd walked away. "You find your chance," I told Yum-Yum, "and you take it."

She turned and looked out over the tarmac, through the rain, to the horizon. A jet was touching down on the runway; another was climbing. She tipped back her head and watched the plane until it slipped into the cloud cover and vanished.

I heard a woman saying my name over the PA system, and it felt so strange to hear it, then, at the moment when Yum-Yum and I were in the midst of spinning a secret plan.

"That's me," I said.

"See?" She lifted her slight shoulders and let them fall with a sigh. "There are ways. He'd find me. He always does."

It was my father calling. I picked up the courtesy phone and heard him say my name. "Nate," he said, "what are you doing?"

"I was talking to a woman." I could see Jinx, back from the water fountain, looking at the spot where his fingernail clippings had been. "She's with this guy. I think he's mean to her."

Jinx kicked at the carpet with the toe of his boot. "Do I embarrass you?" he said to Yum-Yum, who was sitting down now, her hands folded in her lap.

"I was never mean to your mother," my father said. I could hear the whir of his computer in the background, the sleek glide of tape through his editing machine. "You know that, don't you, Nate?"

Jinx had his hand on Yum-Yum's head again, but this time he was rubbing it, letting his fingers brush the velvet of her hair, and, finally, she leaned into him and closed her eyes.

"No," I told my father. "I don't think you were mean. Not on purpose."

"What was it, then?" I could hear him running the tape backward and forward through the editing machine. "What made her leave? UFOs? What's that to make a life together go kaput?"

The security guards were dragging the British bookseller away. They had handcuffs on him, and he wasn't talking now. One of the guards carried the duffle bag full of books. All those stories. All those people's lives.

Since then, I've wondered, if I'd told my father the truth—if I'd said to him, "You made everything matter a little less"—whether things would have worked out other than the way they did. He'd created too much possibility. He'd made the world so enormous, all my mother and I could do was fall into its space like the blips of light he threw upon a screen. There. There. And then they were gone.

"It was me," I said. "I got caught looking in windows, and everything went wrong after that. No one but Mr. Laskey would talk to us. What kind of life did we have?"

I lied because I remembered how I felt when I'd gone to our neighbors' doors and told them I'd watched them when they'd thought themselves hidden away in their homes. No matter how kind I was, how sorry, I knew they were all thinking back, reliving the nights of that winter. How could they help but catalog everything they'd done and wonder whether I'd seen their worst moments, the moments of anger, gossip, appetite, despair. No matter how I assured them, I knew they'd start to feel guilty about the way they'd lived, and this, for better or worse, was what I couldn't do to my father.

The only neighbor who hadn't felt exposed had been Mr. Laskey. "Nathan," he'd said to me. "All those nights. So cold out there. Please. Why didn't you just come in?"

All the others shrank away from me, my last glimpse of them a face in the vanishing strip of light as a door closed. "Oh, you boy," Mrs. Poe had said. "You wretched boy."

Jinx and Yum-Yum were huddled together. The rain was coming hard now, and everything outside—the tarmac and the planes, the baggage handlers in their orange slickers, the sky itself—wavered and blurred.

"It's not so bad getting caught," my father said. "It can be a start." He took a breath and then let it out. "I did time once. Even your mother doesn't know this. I had this racket going, a little bait-and-switch routine."

His confession, which I believed he meant to make me feel better, less alone, only made me think of myself as more criminal. "Is that what you called to tell me?" I said.

"No, I wanted to tell you I got that pea vine back in the ground. I thought you'd want to know that." For a good while, neither of us said anything. Then he said, "Don't feel sorry for your old man. It wasn't so bad in prison, not in this minimum security joint. It was waiting, mostly, and I had a job, a way to pass the time." He made Braille maps, the raised lines meant to be traced with fingertips. "I did the New York City Subway System," he said. "Disneyland, Yellowstone, the Grand Canyon, the Loop in Chicago."

He went on listing the maps he'd done, and I closed my eyes and followed his chant. I imagined all the places in the world where a person could try to hide. I memorized my father's voice, told myself I'd always remember it.

"All those maps," he said, his words a whisper now, distant and faint. "All those places I couldn't go. Jesus, Nate. All those people who couldn't see."

ACROSS THE STREET

THE IDEA WAS TO LET THEIR ADULT SON LIVE ON HIS OWN. AFTER YEARS of group homes and institutions and finally time spent in their care, his parents—he an inventor, and she a dour, nervous woman—purchased a two-story house on Bay Meadows Court and helped their son move into a subdivision just inside the outer belt with its constant noise of traffic. They lived in one of the city's high-toned suburbs nearly ten miles to the east, a village of stone houses and stone walls and a fall festival on the green, a ritual they had to bypass this year because they were busy with the house that would now be their son's. It was time, the father assured his wife, to let whatever was going to happen run its course.

"He'll be aces," the father said. "Not to worry. He'll be tip-top."

Said the mother, "I'm beyond worry. I mean it. I wash my hands."

The son's name was Jim, a solid name, a name one might expect a fifty-eight-year-old man to have, coming as he did from a generation of Jims and Eds and Bobs and Joes and Steves—good, solid names for good, solid men.

But this Jim, as the neighbors would soon discover, was wobbly. He was, as the neighbors would finally say to each other, "peculiar."

"An odd bird," said Artie Manks. Artie owned a wholesale jewelry business, and his stubby fingers were heavy with rings—gold bands, some with onyx stones—and a Rolex of Everose gold nestled into a tuft of gray hairs on his left wrist. He drove a red MX-5 Miata with a retractable hardtop and was known to come speeding down the cul-de-sac in the evenings with a toot-toot of his horn to let his wife, Glory, know he was home.

Glory worked for a company that sold self-defense products to women. She organized home parties and convinced women to buy pepper sprays, steel batons, throwing stars, kubotans, door braces, and even complete home security systems. Whatever it takes, she told her clientele, to keep you safe. She'd perfected a delivery that made women feel simultaneously afraid and confident. She dressed in business suits, wore sensible shoes, kept her dyed black hair in an upsweep, wore a single strand of elegant pearls around her neck.

At home, though—ah, at home, she was a different gal: relaxed, carefree, on the lookout for the next laugh. She drank Knob Creek bourbon—in moderation, of course—even smoked a little weed from time to time. She was of a generation bred in a time of excess, and she'd never quite got with the program that said she should be a lady of restraint as she aged.

"Artie, you're a card," she was heard to say on more than one occasion. She'd tip back her head and laugh, and the light would make the rhinestones in the frames of her cat-eye glasses sparkle. "You're a cut-up," she'd say. "A scandal." Then she'd swat him across the arm and give him a stern look of disapproval that everyone knew was anything but—was, in fact, unmitigated adoration. "Oh, Artie," she'd say. "You kill me. You really do."

Glory and Artie lived directly across the street from Jim, and it was Glory, that autumn, who finally realized that each Monday, when the green trash Toters were lined up at the ends of driveways up and down the cul-de-sac, no such Toter ever made an appearance at the end of Jim's.

"What do you imagine he does with his trash?" she asked her friend Tippy Duncan, who lived next door. Tippy was a stylist at a salon called Mop. She did Glory's hair and was even kind enough to open the shop during off hours if Glory happened to need a cut or her dye job touched up before a home party. In exchange for her kindness, Glory sometimes gave her free samples of pepper spray, which Tippy accepted with some reluctance. "Golly, I wouldn't know how to use it," she said, "and besides, with Bart around, I always feel super safe." She was the sort of gal who said things like "golly" and "super." She wore cardigan sweaters and corduroy pants from L.L.Bean, and Glory had noticed she had a Jesus fish on the back of her Jeep. A mousy sort who needed more meat on her bones and more gravel in her gut. An easy mark—slight of frame, nearsighted because she refused to wear her glasses and contacts made her squeamish, slope-shouldered, always walking around with her head down. Just the kind of gal who needed to learn how to protect herself.

A sweet gal, though, with a sweet face and fair skin and lustrous brown hair worn in a pageboy cut. She was cute, Glory supposed. Cute and wholesome and appealing in that L.L.Bean sort of way.

Maybe that's what Bart had fallen for, the placid predictability of a faithful and dependable girl.

Bart was a personal trainer at AussieFit, but his real love, Tippy said, was astronomy. Instead of putting people through their paces, he'd much rather be training his telescope on the heavens. "He's a sensitive soul, Glory," Tippy said. "People have no idea." His special interest was optical astronomy, she said, the study of light, but by that point Glory had stopped listening.

"What about the trash?" she asked Tippy again. "It has to go somewhere, right? I tell you, that man is odd."

"Maybe he's just troubled," Tippy said. "Maybe it's like that."

Then one Saturday afternoon in early November, Artie was outside using a leaf blower. He was humming a tune, "Fly Me to the Moon," and he was a million miles away, taking smug pleasure in the perfect nature of his life—a flourishing business, a house he owned free and clear, a wife who was nuts over him. Not a care in the world. Then he felt the tap on his shoulder, and when he turned around he saw Jim mere inches away, his finger about to jab Artie in the center of his chest.

Jim wasn't an imposing man. He was slender and tall with long arms and a narrow face shaded by the bill of a Titleist golf cap. He had a shaggy brown moustache and he wore glasses. A sidepiece had broken off the frames, and he'd fashioned a substitute out of duct tape. A man who looked a little on the down side, but certainly not a man that Artie would fear.

Still, Artie couldn't help but take a few steps back and feel his heart come up into his throat.

"What the hell?" he said.

Jim ran his finger across his own throat and then pointed to the leaf blower. Artie understood that he wanted him to turn it off, which he did.

"My mother is trying to make a call." Jim gestured with his thumb, and Artie, following the invisible line it made behind Jim's ear, saw the mother sitting on the porch, a cell phone to one ear, her finger stuck into the other. "She's trying to have a very important call," Jim said, "and here you are making noise with your rather large instrument."

Artie didn't like Jim's tone, which made him feel that he was a schoolboy in Dutch with a teacher or his father.

"It's a cell phone," Artie said. "She can go anywhere. She can go in your house, for Christ's sake. I've got nothing to do with any of that."

Artie started the leaf blower again and even had the nerve to point it at Jim, revving the engine.

"You hadn't ought to have done that, mister," Jim shouted. "I'm your neighbor."

"That's what he said to me," Artie told Glory when he finally put the leaf blower away and went into the house. "Who the fuck does he think he is?"

Over the next few weeks, a series of strange and unsettling incidents occurred. On more than one night, Glory was jarred from sleep by angry shouts coming from across the street. A last balm of Indian summer had settled over the cul-de-sac, and Glory and Artie slept with their windows open. Glory woke in the middle of the night to Jim shouting, "Fuck this shit. Goddamn the motherfucker." At least that's what she thought she heard, but the words were so strangled, so guttural, she couldn't be sure. She got out of bed and went to the window, where she fingered back the curtain and looked out onto the front porch of the house across the street. Jim was pacing back and forth and throwing his arms about as if he were trying to punch someone. "Fuck it, cocksucker," he said.

He windmilled his arms, throwing haymakers. Then he stopped. His shoulders sagged and he stumbled forward, bracing himself with a hand against one of the porch pillars. He said, in a much softer voice, "Yes, sir. Yes, sir. You can count on me, sir."

Glory was not a delicate woman. How could she be, when she had to recite horror stories of rape and mayhem, all in a direct, restrained manner in order to convince women to plunk down their cash for instruments of self-defense? She was surprised, then, to find herself, as she watched Jim go back to his wild gyrations, beginning to cry a little, feeling this immense sadness swell up in her. She had no way of understanding the connection between Jim's disturbing behavior and the emptiness and dread that now came over her. Here she was, far on the other side of girlhood, sailing through her middle years, comfortable and well-tended, but now, standing at the window watching Jim, she felt a despair she hadn't even known was hers.

She wanted to tell Artie about it, but she knew she didn't dare. She recalled the night of their thirty-fifth wedding anniversary. He gave her a three-stone drop diamond pendant in eighteen-karat white gold, and for just an instant she felt that old quickening of her heart, and she said to him, "If only it could always be like this." But Artie was a man who left emotions to his customers. He said to Glory, "Geez, just wear the necklace."

Three nights running, Glory woke to Jim's rants, but she never went back to the window. She stayed in bed and wrapped her feather pillow around her head to muffle the noise and prayed that soon he'd stop. When he finally did, the silence was just as bad—a sudden, long silence that made her terribly aware of her own breathing and her discontent.

The only time she said anything about what she'd heard and seen was one Wednesday evening when Tippy was doing her hair.

"He must be awfully troubled," Glory said, "to carry on like that. I could feel it in my chest, how troubled he was. Poor man."

Tippy was giving Glory a cut, and she stopped, her scissors' blades open. Glory felt the chill of the steel on her right temple for just an instant. "Poor man?" Tippy said. "I don't know, Glory. Let me tell you what happened last night."

Her sister, Dinah, had stopped by after supper to show Tippy some photos of cakes she was considering for her wedding. It turned into a gab fest, and it was nearly eleven when Dinah got around to leaving. She'd just backed out of Tippy's driveway and was about to drop her Land Rover into low and head out when she heard a noise at her window.

"It was Jim," Tippy said to Glory.

"Jim?" said Glory. "Well, what in the world?"

He was pounding on the glass and shouting—at least Dinah thought he was trying to form words, but all that came out were grunts and yowls. Unlike Tippy, she was a formidable woman of height and girth who skated for the Ohio Roller Girls, and she was nonplussed by Jim's display. She rolled down her window and told him to fuck off before driving away.

"I would have been scared to death," Tippy said, "but not Dinah. Nothing ever bothers her."

"My goodness," said Glory, which was something she remembered her mother saying when she was so stunned she didn't know what else to say. Glory, at least to her best memory, had never used that phrase, and the fact that she had told her how unsettled she was.

"Do you think he's dangerous?" Tippy asked her.

"Oh, Tippy," said Glory. "Of course he's dangerous. Civilized people don't do the things he's doing. I'd give anything to know his story. Doesn't it all just give you the shivers?"

Jim was the valedictorian of the class of 1973 at Upper Arlington High. President of the Science Club, first-team all-state golfer. Nights, as they thought of him left to his own devices, his parents sometimes went back over all that their son had accomplished as a way of convincing themselves, again, that they'd done the right thing leaving him to his own life. They reminded themselves of the time when all had been well, those spring days of the prom, the golf tournament, the scholarship offers. He eventually chose the University of Texas at Austin, where he'd play golf and study mechanical engineering.

"I'll be like you, Dad," he said, and his parents, when they were alone in their room at night, remarked how lucky they were, how blessed. At a time when so many young people were questioning their parents, their teachers, their leaders, and losing themselves to the turmoil around them, here was Jim—their boy, Jim—with his head on straight and all of his life ahead of him. Oh, sure, he could be a little high-strung from time to time, a little too emotional, a little hot-tempered, but what teenager wasn't?

"We're lucky, Miriam," the father said.

The mother's name was Miriam; the father was Thomas, but he went by Tom.

"I know we are, Tom," Miriam said. Then she kissed him goodnight and closed her eyes, and together, they slept the sleep of the blameless and woke to birds singing, a pleasant breeze through the windows, warm sunlight, the sweet smell of lilac.

They went on like that, the way people do when they hold blind faith in the future, until, in late autumn, a call came from Office of the Dean of Students in Austin—the call Miriam would always say marked the beginning of their disgrace.

It might be nothing, an associate dean told them, but, nevertheless, it was a matter of some concern. The parents of a young lady, another UT student, had been to see him, and, yes, what they told him was enough to make him pick up the phone and call Ohio.

"Have you talked with your son lately?" he wanted to know.

"It was a few weeks ago, wasn't it, Tom?" Miriam said over the extension.

After a long silence, Tom said, "A few weeks, maybe, or maybe last month."

It occurred to Miriam, then, that she couldn't really say when they'd last talked to Jim—last week, last month, or had it been longer? She knew a mother should have been devastated to find her only child gone, the house so empty without him, but the truth was she'd been nearly narcotic, blissful and unaware, with the luxury of no longer having to take care of her son. Time just slipped away from her. As for Tom? He was always distracted by some new invention. He barely knew what day it was, even when Jim was at home.

"We should call him," Miriam said to the associate dean, a man with a Texas drawl who kept calling her *ma'am*. "Is that what you're suggesting? That we call Jim?"

"Well, ma'am, I don't directly know if that would be possible." The associate dean paused then, and Miriam heard him take a breath and then let it out. Then he said, "I'd suggest that you and your husband book a flight to Austin. You see, ma'am. Well, this is hard to say, but, ma'am, the police just took your son to the hospital."

"Someone's going to get hurt," Artie said when he came through the door on Wednesday night, the night that Glory came home rattled by Tippy's story about Jim and Dinah. "I swear, Glory." Artie tossed the keys to his Miata into the rimmed bowl on the console table in their entryway. She'd thrown and fired that bowl in her pottery class at a studio in the Short North, and it grated on her last nerve when Artie, no matter how many times she asked him not to, tossed his keys into it with no appreciation of how much the bowl meant to her, the one pretty thing she'd managed to make with her own hands. "That guy is nuts," he said. "Certifiable. Just wait till you hear."

It was well past dark when Artie turned the Miata onto the cul-de-sac. Glory remembered hearing the whine of the engine as he made the turn and then sped up, in a hurry as he always was. *You're going to kill somebody someday,* she was always telling him. *I mean it, Artie. Slow down.*

Did he listen? No, he never did. He reached his hand out to point to the cul-de-sac, and she saw his fingers trembling. She realized, then, that he was sweating. All the color had drained from his usually florid face.

"He was just laying there in the middle of the street. Jesus, Glory, I must've been six inches from his feet when I finally got stopped. Christ-a-loo, I can't get it out of my mind. He was laying there like he was in his own bed."

"My goodness." Glory slipped her arm around Artie's waist and told him to come and sit down. "Sit down, Artie," she said. "You've had a shock."

"Damn right, it was a shock," he said. "I should call the cops."

But he didn't. He drank the glass of water that Glory brought him, and soon the color was back in his cheeks, and he was able to eat the dinner she'd warmed for him. He told her how he honked his horn, and Jim, hearing it, sat up and slowly got to his feet and moved to the side of the street so Artie could pass.

"I put the Miata in the garage," he said, "and when I got out and looked over, he was nowhere to be seen."

Not until later that night. When Glory took out the trash, there he was, Jim, exactly as Artie had said, just lying flat on his back in the middle of the street. It was a cool night, the approach of winter proper more than a hint. Not the sort of night for someone to be lying on the pavement, even if there was a sane reason to do so.

Glory tipped back her head and looked at the sky, wanting to see what Jim was seeing. Stars, bright and distinct here in this neighborhood on the western edge just before housing developments gave way to cornfields and flat land, here where there were no streetlights, no light pollution of any kind except the occasional porch light or the lights on either side of garage doors.

"Jim?" Glory said. "Jim, what are you doing?"

He took his time before he answered. "I like to look at the stars," he said.

She was standing right by him, but his voice sounded far away. He spoke the way someone would inside a church or a hospital—in a whisper, nearly breathless, one born from wonder and awe. It caught Glory by surprise. Such a different sound from the strangled ranting she'd heard late in the night. Now he was calm and content.

"Will you watch with me?" he said. "Just for a while?"

She wanted to, but goodness, what would that look like: Glory stretching out beside the neighborhood crazy to gaze at the stars? Still, it was exactly what she wanted to do—to have that moment of stillness rather than going back into her house where Artie had the TV too loud because he refused to admit that he was losing some of his hearing. Any second now, he might step outside and shout for her. *Glory*, he might say. *Glory, what in the hell?*

What would she tell him? That she could understand what might make Jim want to lie down and look at the stars? Just to get away from the noise, whether it came from someone else or maybe from the voices in your own head.

"They are something, aren't they?" she said to Jim. "The stars."

"We're not alone, you know," he said. "There are other universes. We shouldn't be so arrogant to believe there aren't. Other universes, other dimensions."

Such talk brought Glory back to her own life. "Jim, I think you should get up. It's not safe for you to be out here like this."

"If I keep really, really still, sometimes I can hear them trying to tell me things."

"Who, Jim?"

"Other life forms."

"And what are they trying to tell you?"

"That they're there. That's all. That's everything. Just to let someone know they're there."

Glory heard the storm door of her house open, and she knew Artie would soon be calling to her. Still, she lingered. "Jim, please get up. What you're doing is dangerous."

"Just a while longer," he said.

She stamped her foot. "Jim," she said in a stern voice. "Do you want me to call the police?"

That was enough to get him moving. First, he sat up. Then he came to his knees. Finally, he pushed himself up to his feet.

"I wouldn't want to see you get hurt," she said.

He looked at her for what seemed like a very long time. Then he took a step toward her, and she stepped back.

"I wouldn't want to see you get hurt either," he said.

That's when Artie called out, "Glory, what in the hell?"

As she turned to him, she was already imagining what she'd say, even though she knew it would shame her, would feel like a betrayal of what Jim had chosen to share with her.

"You're right, Artie. Geez. Certifiable."

"Jim," Miriam said when she saw him in Austin. "Jimmy? My God, what have you done?"

He wouldn't answer, wouldn't so much as look at her or at Tom, who stood beside her, his hands stuffed into the pockets of his khaki slacks as if he'd already accepted that there was nothing he could do to make anything better.

Jim wasn't wearing his own clothes. He was wearing light blue hospital scrubs, and he was sitting in a chair by his bed, smoking a cigarette, as he had the right to do in those days. Miriam knew that, but she'd never seen her son smoke and she wished he wouldn't.

"Can't you put that out?" she said. "Can't you talk to your father and me? We came all this way to see you."

The ash on his cigarette had grown perilously long. Miriam tried to take the cigarette, a Pall Mall—the red pack was right there in his other hand—but he jerked it away from her, holding his arm above his head, and the ash tumbled down to the thigh of his scrubs. Miriam had never seen such a look on his face—eyes narrowed, nostrils flaring—a look of pure hatred. That's how Miriam described it later to Tom. *Did you see the way he looked at me?* she said. *Pure hatred in his eyes. Like he'd felt that way about me all his life.*

"Oh, don't be like that, Jim," she said. "Please, Jimmy." She tried to smooth down his hair, which was wild and greasy, but he knocked her hand away. He'd grown a walrus moustache that hung over his lip, and his gaunt face was in need of a razor. "Just tell me it's not true," she said. "Just say that much, and then we can start to fix things."

But he still wouldn't say a word, nor did he the entire time she and Tom were there. Finally, after a week of just sitting with him in his room—at least he'd tolerate that—a doctor told them he'd diagnosed Jim with paranoid schizophrenia.

"He hears voices," the doctor said. He was a tall man with rimless glasses that perched on the end of his nose. His face was fleshy. He rubbed his hand over his mouth and chin. Then he said, "He has delusions. He fears that people mean to do him harm. That was the story with the girl."

"The girl," said Miriam. "Then what she claimed is true?"

"Yes, Mrs. Morrison. I'm afraid it is."

Tom cleared his throat and began to speak in the high-pitched breathless voice he'd had ever since an accident in his lab exposed him to phosphoric acid fumes.

"Will there be criminal charges?" he asked.

"That's a question for the police." The doctor leaned forward in his chair as if to better hear Tom. "I imagine it's up to the girl and her parents. My concern is your son's mental health."

"How in the world did this happen?" Miriam reached out and took Tom's hand. She still wasn't able to say the words, *How did my son become a kidnapper?* "How did this happen to our son?" she said. "He was always such a good boy."

"Often there's a family history of schizophrenia," the doctor said, "but according to you and your husband, that's not applicable in this situation. Sometimes it's poor nutrition or exposure to viruses while in the womb. Sometimes stress." Here, the doctor took off his glasses and folded the temples down and let them rest in his lap. "In your son's case, I'd say it might be an overuse of psychoactive drugs. Hallucinogens, to be more precise. LSD, to be exact."

Tom said, "Are you telling us our son used that drug?"

"I'm afraid so," the doctor said. "He was under the influence of it the night the police brought him here."

"Let's fix this," Tom said. Miriam heard the change in his voice even though it was barely above a whisper. He was the chemist, the engineer, the inventor. He believed in answers. "What are the treatments?"

"Psychotherapy, of course," the doctor said. "Certain antipsychotic medications, electroshock."

Tom got to his feet. Miriam felt his hand slip away from hers, and then he was standing. "As long as the police have no reason to hold him," he said, "we're taking our son back to Ohio."

"I wouldn't advise that, Mr. Morrison." The doctor's voice was stern now. "Your son has a serious mental illness."

"We'll take care of it." Tom looked down at Miriam. "Mother?" he said.

This was the first choice that she'd come to question. The second would come forty years later, when she and Tom decided to leave Jim alone in the house on Bay Meadows Court. She wasn't thinking about all the years ahead of them that day in the doctor's office. She wasn't thinking about the string of hospitals and doctors and the medications and the eruptions of violence and the visits from the police and the shame that would finally force her and Tom to buy the house for Jim and to leave him there.

No, that day in the doctor's office, she was only thinking, *This is my son, who needs me.*

She met Tom's expectant look, her head already beginning to nod. "He's our son," she said, not even looking at the doctor. "We're going to take him home."

"Sometimes I look at him sitting over there on his porch," Tippy said to Bart one night, near Thanksgiving, "and I wonder what he's done. Glory found him lying in the middle of the street last week. Do you think he's a killer?"

They were on their side deck, and Bart had his telescope trained on the northern sky in anticipation of the comet ISON, which was supposed to be visible soon. He was bent over the eyepiece trying to see what he could see.

"A killer?" he said. "Who? Jim? Seriously, Tippy?"

She'd always tried to ignore the fact that he had a way of making her feel small, as if she and everything she said didn't matter. Sometimes, like now, she felt so insignificant when she was with him, so tiny. He might be looking right at her, and she'd have the sense he couldn't see her at all.

"Yes, seriously," she said. "You know what he did that night Dinah was here."

"I know what Dinah told you." He'd never liked Dinah. Tippy knew that without having to ask him. Dinah, the roller derby girl, was too big of a personality for Bart to tolerate. He had to feel like he was the show. "I also know that Dinah likes to embellish," he said. "Something happened and she made a good story out of it. Jim, a killer? Nah, I don't think so. Spend a while talking to him like I have and you'd never make that kind of accusation."

"I wasn't accusing him." Tippy knew her voice was shrinking, and she hated herself for that. "I just said I wondered. I didn't know the two of you were such good pals."

Bart straightened up and turned to look at her. Although the night was cool, he wore cargo shorts and flip-flops. The hood of his black sweatshirt, which said AUSSIE, AUSSIE, AUSSIE in yellow letters, covered his shaved head. She hated it when he looked at her like she didn't have the right to an opinion.

"I talk to him sometimes when you're at work. I go walking by his place, and I say, 'What's up?' and he tells me."

"What do you talk about?"

"Stars mostly, telescopes. He's into astronomy."

"He told Glory he was looking at the stars that night she found him lying in the street."

"That's right. He likes to stargaze."

"But he can't do it lying in the street. That's crazy."

Bart nodded. "I said, 'Dude, what if a car comes?' He said, 'I see its headlights and I get out of the way.' Cause and effect, Tippy. Sounds pretty logical to me."

"Ever heard the word 'premeditated'?" Tippy said. "Sometimes killers know exactly what they're going to do and how they're going to do it. They plan it all out. Logically."

"Not Jim. He's a little odd, but that's all. One look around his house and you'd know there was nothing to be afraid of."

"You've been in his house?"

"Once. He was having a hard time getting his front door unlocked, so I helped him—his key was bent—then he asked me in."

"Asked you in?"

"Why so shocked? He was just being neighborly."

"I guess I never thought of him as the neighborly kind."

Bart said, "Maybe that's what's wrong with the world. Everyone making up their minds about everyone else before they have the facts."

"And the facts are?"

"Geez, Tip. Everyone's a mystery."

"Really?" she said. "All right then, Mr. Know-It-All. Why don't you enlighten me?"

Bart went back to his telescope, and for a while Tippy thought he wouldn't oblige her. Then, bent over the eyepiece, he started to tell the story of the day he went inside Jim's house.

"It was quite a surprise," Bart said. "I can tell you that. Nothing like we'd always pictured."

Tippy had to admit she'd always imagined the inside of Jim's house to be a mess, cluttered and dirty: stacks of newspapers and pizza boxes, dirty dishes and piles of unwashed clothes, nests of rubber bands and bread ties, dust thick on the furniture, mud tracked in on the floors.

"It was pristine," Bart said, and then he went on to describe what he saw. Studio portraits on the walls of the entryway—photos of Jim when he was a boy, some with his parents and some of him alone: Little League baseball, junior high science fair, high school graduation. Golf trophies on display on shelves in the family room. An afghan neatly folded over the arm of the couch. Countertops bare except for a ceramic teapot and a vase of fresh flowers—lilies, Bart recalled—and a bowl of potpourri.

"Totally Martha Stewart," Bart said. "Just like, you know, a family lived there. Not a killer, Tip. Really."

———

When Miriam went to the Giant Eagle to pick up a few things and saw the women's carts stacked high with turkeys, cranberries, dinner rolls, pie crusts, cans of pumpkin filling, whipping cream, she remembered the Thanksgiving meals she used to prepare. Now she had a hand basket with a loaf of whole wheat bread, a jar of Sanka, and a bunch of bananas. The woman she used to be seemed so distant to her. She barely remembered her family's life before that call from Texas.

What was more familiar to her was the feeling of being on the outside, the same feeling she'd had as a girl when her mother had gone away to the hospital because she started to hear voices. It didn't take long for word to get around, and by the time her mother came home, most of the little town where they lived already knew that Daisy Wright had gone around the bend. From that point on, Miriam knew that people were watching them, talking about them, judging them. She knew that there were normal families and then there were families like hers. The shame was so deep and lasting that when the doctor in Austin asked if there'd been any mental illness in her family, she lied and said no, none at all.

This Thanksgiving, she and Tom would drive to Jim's and, if he'd allow it, take him to the MCL Cafeteria where they'd eat, and privately Miriam would give thanks that they'd all survived another year. It would just be the three of them, Miriam praying for a few moments of contentment.

She carried her hand basket toward the checkout line, but stopped when she felt someone behind her grab her sleeve.

"Ma'am, I've been calling after you." Miriam turned and saw a woman she recognized from Bay Meadows Court, the woman who lived across the street from Jim, the one with the black hair and her hands and wrists and ears and neck heavy with jewelry. Her husband was in the business. He drove that little sports car. "I saw you drop this," the woman said. Oh, what was her name? Something that started with a "G." Glenda? Gloria? No, Glory. That was it. The woman's name was Glory.

She was standing there, her hand held out, something so ordinary—a coupon for Cheerios—resting on her palm. Seeing it there, knowing it had fallen from her coat pocket, Miriam felt like an impostor. She wasn't a woman who could pour herself a bowl of Cheerios, sprinkle them with sugar, maybe add some strawberries or sliced peaches, a little milk, and take her time facing another ho-hum day.

Nothing was ho-hum in her life. When she and Tom came to look in on Jim, she shied away from Glory and the other women on the court for fear they'd find out that she was an impostor, someone pretending to be a woman without a care when, really, she was scared to death.

"Thank you," she said to Glory, and she reached out and took the coupon between her fingers.

"Any little bit helps, doesn't it?" Glory said.

Miriam nodded. "The way prices are these days."

"Oh, isn't it the truth?" Glory nodded. She even reached out and touched Miriam on the shoulder. "It's the men who have no idea what it costs to feed a family, but we know, don't we?"

The two of them stood like that for a moment longer before Glory took her hand away. Miriam felt her heart sink at its leaving. How wonderful it felt to be touched like that, to be drawn into this intimacy.

"Yes," she said, "we always know."

She closed her hand around the coupon, trying to hold on, just a moment longer, to the notion that the most pressing issue in her life was the cost of a box of breakfast cereal. She imagined herself being that sort of woman, one who could grouse about the most trivial things because she had no other complaints, because everything else in her life, if not entirely hunky-dory, was at least unremarkable. She pictured herself lying down at night on freshly ironed sheets. She tried to remember what it had been like to wake in the morning with a lightness in her heart.

Then Glory said, "Wait a second. I know you, don't I? Your son lives in my neighborhood."

Just like that, Miriam came back to her life, her real life, the one she tried so hard to hide.

"On Bay Meadows?" she said, as if she were trying to place Glory, as if just that second she'd begun to recognize her. "You live across the street, don't you?"

"Yes," Glory said. "From your son, I mean. I see you visiting from time to time."

"We come by," said Miriam, trying her best not to sound defensive. "We're not so far away. Just in Upper Arlington. Not so far at all."

It was true. She and Tom came by to look at Jim's mail, to see what sorts of bills might need paying, to bring him sacks of fast food from Wendy's or Burger King—it was all he would eat—and to get some sense of his emotional state, to make sure he was taking his Abilify and his Zoloft. He always forgot to put out his garbage. Even though he was clean and tidy, for some reason, he stored his garbage bags in the garage, never quite remembering to put them in the Toter and push it to the curb. After a while, Tom would hire a man to come in his pickup truck and haul the bags to the landfill.

"Jim," Glory said. "That's your son, yes?" She didn't wait for Miriam to offer a confirmation. "I worry about him. Lately, he's been acting strangely."

"There's nothing strange about Jim. Nothing at all."

Already, Miriam was turning, heading back up the aisle.

Glory called to her. "I'm sorry. I didn't mean to pry…" But Miriam didn't want her apology. She'd long ago grown weary of saying she was sorry to people because of Jim, and, therefore, she neither expected nor would accept any kind of apology in return. She remembered a T-shirt that Jim liked to wear. It said, YOU CAN STUFF YOUR SORRIES IN A SACK. Exactly. Sorries never changed anything.

She turned back to face Glory. "Has he hurt anyone?"

"No," Glory said, "but I…"

"All right, then." Miriam cut her off. "All right."

Glory carried the story home to Artie and, at her next hair appointment, to Tippy—the story of something she recalled from months past, when Miriam and Tom were visiting Jim.

"Remember when the ambulance came?" she said to Artie.

"Did it come to this house?" Artie said. "No. Then why in the world would I remember it?"

She'd looked out the front windows one evening and seen the red lights flashing.

"You remember that, don't you, Tippy?" she said.

"I sort of do," Tippy said.

It was Miriam. The ambulance had come for her. She'd slipped on the front steps and fallen. At least that's what Tom told Glory when she saw him at the mailbox the next day and went out to ask him if everything was all right. Oh, yes, he told her. Everything was fine. Just a little slip. Just a little bruising of Miriam's face and a sprained shoulder. An overnight stay in the hospital. Nothing to worry about.

"She had her arm in a sling the next time I saw her," Tippy said. "Sure, I remember."

"I never thought a thing about it until I tried to talk to her about Jim at the Giant Eagle." There was something about the way that Miriam looked at her when she asked her whether Jim had hurt anyone—some dread—that made Glory wonder whether Miriam's injuries had really happened the way that Tom said they did. "She had the look of a woman who's afraid."

"You don't think," Tippy said. "I mean, do you, Glory?"

"I told you someone was going to get hurt," Artie said when she was finally able to make him really listen to what she was saying. "Geez-a-loo."

The night before Thanksgiving, Tippy was at AussieFit working out with Bart. Just some time on the elliptical and then a few light sets of arm curls and lat pulldowns and bench presses. Just enough to keep her muscles toned the way Bart liked.

For some reason, he was pushing her harder than usual. "C'mon, Tip, one more rep. Thanksgiving's tomorrow. Turkey and pumpkin pie. You don't want it to turn to flab."

"Enough," she finally said, refusing to do just one more arm curl. "That's enough."

"C'mon, babe. You can do more. Push yourself."

"I said no."

She slapped her towel down on the weight bench and stormed away. Her heart was pounding inside her chest, and she felt something rising up in her she couldn't quite call anger. It was more embarrassment, she decided, because she'd let her temper get the better of her.

"Jesus, Tip," Bart said in a low voice when he finally came to her. "Let's go home."

On the drive to the house, she tried her best to make small talk, to get beyond the ugly moment at AussieFit and get things back on track. Bart responded in kind, and they filled the drive with comments about the weather (cold with a chance of snow), Dinah's wedding (Tippy was a bridesmaid), and the comet ISON (Bart hoped he'd finally get a glimpse of it).

Then he turned down Saddlehorn Drive and fell in behind a slow-moving Subaru wagon that Tippy knew belonged to Jim. It had a bumper sticker on it, a quote from the Dalai Lama: THE PURPOSE OF OUR LIVES IS TO BE HAPPY. She'd seen that bumper sticker on Jim's car many times, but something about seeing it tonight, after her moment with Bart at AussieFit, put a lump in her throat. She fought back her tears and turned toward her window so Bart wouldn't notice. When was the last time she'd truly been happy? Maybe when she and Bart were first starting out, but that all seemed like a long time ago. Now the days were all the same. She went to work and came home, and Bart spent the nights looking at the sky through his telescope. When had he stopped looking at her, she wondered. When had he stopped seeing her? When had she become only muscles to be made in the image that he manufactured?

And yet she loved him. She couldn't deny that. The thought of a life without him was impossible.

"There's your killer," he said. Then he laughed.

If it were some other night, Tippy knew she might be able to laugh along with him, laugh at herself. But not tonight, not after Glory's story about the time the ambulance came for Miriam, nor after the ugly exchange with Bart at AussieFit. Tonight, she finally said what she'd never known she wanted to say.

"Look at you," she said. "So smug. You think you know everything, don't you?"

"I was just having some fun." Bart sounded wounded. "Jesus, Tip. Can't you take a joke?"

"I don't think it's funny," she said. They drove the rest of the way home, creeping behind Jim's slow-moving Subaru with the Dalai Lama bumper sticker, and they didn't say a word.

Down the street, Artie was saying plenty. "I mean it, Glory. I'm going to find his parents and I'm going to ask them what's what."

"Don't, Artie," Glory said. She was standing at the window in the dark, looking out at Jim's house across the street. The porch light was on, as was a light in an upstairs window. All of his upstairs windows were half covered with paper, so she could only see the light in the top half. "Just leave them alone. I mean it, Artie. Something tells me they've had enough to deal with."

"But, Glory, is he the sort we want living across from us? He's dangerous. We have a right to know why he's living there alone. All his neighbors have a right to know what to expect."

"Artie, I said don't."

At that moment, in Upper Arlington, Miriam was sitting in the dark in her living room. She was alone because Tom, as was his habit most evenings, was in his basement lab working on something new. He invented apparatuses that were used by welders. That was as much as Miriam understood. He made things to help people hold other things together even while everything in his own life was fractured.

At least, that's the way she chose to think about it on nights like this, when she was alone, worrying over what she might have done differently. Of course she should have admitted to her mother's mental illness, and maybe, yes, she should have left Jim in Austin and let the doctors there do what they could for him. But all of that was ancient history. Miriam tried to believe that much was true. She spent her evenings arguing with herself, second-guessing each decision and then coming up with rationales that assured her she'd done exactly what any mother would have done to make sure her son was near to her.

She got stuck, though, when she recalled the day when Jim, in a fit of rage, pushed her down the stairs. Lucky she hadn't broken her neck. Lucky she'd only sprained her shoulder and got some marks on her face. She couldn't make sense of it, though, the memory of Jim's face twisted in anger, the growl of his voice just before he reached out and pushed her. At the emergency room, she knew she'd reached the bottom of something. She knew she was weary with loving her son. She'd wanted him to have a home. All along, that's what she'd wished for him, that he have a home and a family.

"Jimmy, you understand what you've done, don't you?" she asked him when she came back from the hospital.

He nodded his head. He was contrite. He looked lost the way he had when he was a boy and he did something to disappoint her.

"I'm sorry," he said. "I didn't mean to hurt you."

What had they argued about? The paper he'd taped over the bottom half of the upstairs windows. "Do you want the neighbors to think you have something to hide?" she said.

"I don't want anyone looking in."

"What are you afraid they'll see?"

"My heart. The inside of my head. My soul. They can't have that, Mother. I won't let them."

"Now you're being ridiculous," she said, and she started ripping down the paper. She was thinking about all that while Tom was in the basement. Finally, he came upstairs. Miriam was sitting in the dark. He turned on a light and found her in the living room.

"What are you doing?" he asked.

"Tomorrow's Thanksgiving," she said.

"Have you told Jim?"

She nodded. "He doesn't want to go to MCL with us."

"Oh?" Tom said. "I'd quite hoped he might."

"I told him we'd come by later," Miriam said. "We'll bring him some food. I don't know what else to do."

The only person not talking was Jim, because he had no one to talk to. He'd been to the Burger King drive-through, and he'd told the girl working there that he hoped she'd have a Happy Thanksgiving, and she'd smiled and said, "Same to you."

Now he made the slow drive home, trying to let that moment last, that brief instant when he felt normal. The voices in his head were still tonight, and in that stillness he listened. He heard his life the way it used to be. His father's voice deep and full, because this was before his accident, saying to him, "Get up, Jim. Get up, Jimmy Boy. It's Thanksgiving." His mother humming in the kitchen, something bright and cheery, and the sounds of platters and dishes and the oven door opening and then closing and the beaters on her blender whirring. Then his father's voice asking the blessing, "Our Lord, we pray..." And later a football game on the television and Jim talking on the telephone to his friend who lived three streets over because he still had friends then. He wasn't sick yet. He hadn't gone to Austin and fallen in love with a girl. He hadn't reached the point where he wasn't going to class and he was about to lose his scholarship and his golf coach hadn't yet told him he was mighty disappointed in his game—"Can't you concentrate, Jim? Good Lord sakes alive, boy."—and the girl hadn't told him that she was sorry, but she couldn't love him back—"I just can't, Jim," she said that night in his dorm room. "You can't make me feel something that I don't."

But he tried. He pleaded and wept and wouldn't let her leave. At some point, he had his arms around her trying to get her to stop screaming—"Please, Betsy. Please." Then he was hearing the voice in his head, telling him to stop her before she hurt him more, to put his hands around her throat and squeeze. "I can't do that," he said. "I can't." But she wouldn't stop, and he watched his hand move to her face and start to slip down to her neck. Then the door broke open, and there were boys in his room, and one of them pulled him away, and Betsy was sobbing, and sometime later there were policemen and the hospital and his mother was there and she was saying, "Jimmy? My God, what have you done?"

Now Jim turned down Bay Meadows Court. All of the voices were quiet. He was able to remember everything without shame. He hadn't meant to hurt Betsy. He'd only meant to love her. The same was true for his mother, who was an old woman now. The same was true for himself. He'd never meant to hurt Jim. He'd only meant to love him.

He decided then to make a list of everything he was thankful for, starting with the years he'd had outside of institutions, his mother's undying love, his father's calm acceptance, this house, this night, this neighborhood, the girl at the drive-through window. Perhaps there would be blessings and blessings to come.

A car went down the court. He looked in his rearview mirror and saw that it was the young couple who lived at the end of the cul-de-sac. The man who had a telescope, the woman whose guest had startled him not long ago when he'd been starwatching. He needed to apologize for that.

He got out of his car and took a few steps down the sidewalk. Then he saw that the man and woman, who were out of their car now and standing in the driveway, were arguing.

The man said, "Jesus, Tip."

"Happy Thanksgiving," the woman said in a way that made it clear she didn't mean it. She brushed by the man, bumping his shoulder with hers. The man reached his hand out for her, but she was gone.

It was a thing that pained Jim to see. He knew now wasn't the time to try to apologize. Now was the time to let them be alone. He hoped tomorrow would be a better day for them because he liked the young couple. He liked the way the man talked to him about stars. He liked the sound of the woman's laugh. He wanted them to be happy. He wanted everyone to be happy. He didn't want anyone to feel the way he felt so much of the time.

The girl at the Burger King drive-through had smiled at him. She'd wished him a Happy Thanksgiving. All through the night, even in his dreams, he tried to remember that.

––––––––

Tippy slept in on Thanksgiving. She heard Bart downstairs in the kitchen, banging cabinet doors, hunting up something for breakfast, and she rolled over and went back to sleep. When she finally came downstairs, it was nearly eleven. She saw the sheets and blankets in a wad on the couch where he'd slept after their argument.

Now he looked sheepish, leaning against the counter, eating a bowl of cereal, still in his AussieFit T-shirt and his sweatpants. He hadn't shaved and his face was slack. He looked at her with such a sadness in his eyes that she couldn't help but say she was sorry.

"Me, too, Tip," he said. He set the cereal bowl on the counter and gathered her up in his arms. "I hate it when we fight."

She closed her eyes and let him hold her, remembering how every moment of every day had felt like this when they were first starting out. Now she wondered whether there was too much between them for it to ever feel like that again. Maybe that's what life did to you, she thought. Takes you away from the people you were once upon a time.

"Guess we better hustle," she finally said. They were due at Dinah's for a family dinner at noon. "I'm surprised Dinah hasn't been calling."

Bart looked at her, and the sadness was still in his eyes. "Where *are* we, Tip?"

She didn't answer for quite a while, so long that she had to tell the truth since it was evident in the silence.

"I don't know," she said.

Bart nodded once. He didn't say anything else, and like that something was sealed between them, though Tippy couldn't say what. She only knew the shiver that passed through her as she wondered whether it was the beginning of something or the end.

Down the cul-de-sac at Artie and Glory's, Artie had found the number for Thomas Morrison on Waltham Road in Upper Arlington.

Glory was in the kitchen, cooking, and the first inkling she had that Artie had disobeyed her and made his call, even when she'd made it very clear that she preferred he didn't, came when she went into the living room to ask him what time he wanted to eat. It would just be the two of them this Thanksgiving. A snowstorm in the west had stranded their son in Denver; their daughter was serving in the Peace Corps in Senegal. Glory saw Artie standing at the front window, his back to her, his cell phone to his ear.

"Is that right?" he said. "Well, I think maybe it *is* my business. I live right across the street, you know. He threatened my wife, said he wouldn't want to see her get hurt. Doesn't that sound like a threat to you, Mrs. Morrison?"

"Artie," Glory said. "For heaven's sake."

He waved his arm to hush her and went on talking. "Perhaps I should speak with your husband. Maybe he'll understand why I'm worried. He surely knows what it is to want to protect his wife." He stopped talking and listened for a while. Glory said again, "Artie, I mean it." Then he said to Mrs. Morrison. "I see. Well, then, maybe I should just speak with the police."

"Artie, that's enough."

"I'll be fucked," he said. He took his phone away from his ear and stared at it in disbelief. "She hung up on me."

Glory swatted his arm. "What did you expect? Really, Artie, where's your decency?"

"I'm just looking out for you," he said.

"I don't need you to look out for me." She started taking off her jewelry and throwing it at him, first a bracelet, then her earrings, then the three-stone drop diamond pendant he'd given her for their anniversary. He crossed his arms in front of his face and stooped over to try to escape. "Damn it, Artie, I need you…" She didn't know how to finish the sentence. "I need you…" She failed again. "I need you," she said a third time, still with no idea of exactly what she needed him to do.

She wouldn't know that until evening. They ate their Thanksgiving meal. Artie watched football games. Glory worked on a jigsaw puzzle. The house grew so dim that she had to switch on a light. Then it was dark, and when she glanced up at the window, all she saw was her own reflection, an aging woman, a woman who'd left her best years behind her, holding a puzzle piece between her fingers, a woman working on a jigsaw puzzle on Thanksgiving.

Then someone was knocking on the front door, not a gentle knocking, but a loud pounding. Three, four, five, six hard knocks in succession before Glory could get into the living room. Artie was there before her. He said to her, "Knock, knock. Who's there? Geez-a-loo. Ever hear of a doorbell?"

He flung open the door, and Jim stepped across the threshold with such force that his head bumped into Artie's.

"You," Jim said. His Titleist cap was crooked on his head, and he was breathing hard. He kept jabbing his finger into Artie's chest. "You had no right to call my mother. You shouldn't have done that. You leave her alone. You leave me alone. I can hurt you if I choose. Don't you understand that? Is that what you want? Well, is it? No, I don't think it is."

The bill of Jim's Titleist cap was frayed, and a sharp edge had gouged into the skin above Artie's eyebrow. It was bleeding a little.

"You can't come in here like this." Artie had his handkerchief out of his pocket and he pressed it to his brow. He bent at the waist, his other hand on his knee. "Who do you think you are?"

Jim took Artie by the arm, pulling his hand away from his head. Glory saw the blood on the handkerchief.

"Don't ever call my mother again," Jim said. Then he turned and walked out the door.

Glory hurried to close it. She set the deadbolt. Her heart was pounding in her chest.

"Are you all right?" she asked Artie.

He was dabbing his brow with his handkerchief again. "I could have him arrested," he said.

"Oh, let it go, Artie. Let these people have their privacy."

She went back to her puzzle, but soon Artie came to her, and he said, "What say we go for a drive? Just to be out of the house. Just to be around people."

Glory laid down the puzzle piece she'd been holding. "What

people? Everyone's with someone else. It's Thanksgiving."

"The stores are open at the mall tonight." Artie snapped his fingers. "We'll watch people shop."

"Have we become like that, Artie? Do we have to pretend we have places to go and people to see? Have we become that irrelevant to each other?"

"Glory, can't you see I'm trying to tell you I'm sorry?"

So they went. At least they tried to. They got into Artie's Miata, and he hit the garage door opener and started the car and put it into reverse and backed out onto the driveway all the way to the street, tapping the opener again to put the garage door back down, and then Glory happened to glance in her sideview mirror, and she called out, "Artie! Artie! For God's sake, stop!"

It was Jim, lying on his back in the street, illuminated finally by the Miata's taillights as it got close to him.

"Oh, geez-a-loo." Artie put the Miata into neutral and set the parking brake. "I told you, Glory. Didn't I tell you? I could've killed him."

Just then, a car turned down Bay Meadows, a car coming too fast. The headlights swept over Jim, but he didn't move.

"Oh, good Lord," said Glory, as she pushed open her door and for the umpteenth time cursed Artie's squat car that made getting out of it such a chore. She waved her arms back and forth over her head. "Stop," she said, shouting because the car, a white SUV, was getting closer, and still Jim wasn't moving. "Stop," she said again, and she saw that it was Tippy and Bart in the SUV. He was driving, but his face was turned away from the road toward Tippy, who was pointing her finger at him. It came to Glory, then, that they were fighting, and distracted, they had no idea what was about to happen.

That's when Glory stepped out into the street. She didn't stop to think about what she was doing. She just did it. She put herself between Jim and the speeding SUV.

Miriam was driving the old Volvo, the 1973 model that she and Tom had bought for Jim when he graduated from high school. She'd never been able to part with it. She was driving behind a white SUV that was going much too fast. Tom sat in the passenger seat, a Burger King bag on his lap—a double cheeseburger, onion rings, a chocolate fudge sundae, and a Coke ICEE. For Jim.

"Reckless people," Miriam said under her breath. "Foolish, reckless people."

Then the brake lights on the SUV came on, and she heard the tires squealing on the pavement, and she saw the heads of the man and woman inside jerk forward and then back, and she realized they'd come to a stop in front of Jim's house.

"Tom?" she said.

"Pull over," he told her in his high-pitched whisper, filled now with as much urgency as he could muster. "For God's sake, pull over."

When Bart's SUV finally came to a stop, its front bumper was touching Glory's legs and Tippy was screaming.

Artie ran to Glory and threw his arms around her. "Oh, Jesus," he kept saying, rocking her back and forth.

Tippy threw open her door and jumped down from the SUV. "Glory," she was screaming again and again. "Glory, Glory, Glory."

Bart got out of the SUV and was so overcome with what had almost happened that he could barely get a breath. He bent over, his hands on his knees, and tried to draw air into his lungs.

Miriam was out of the Volvo and hurrying, as best as her arthritic knees would allow, to see what the alarm was all about. Tom was slower. He still had the Burger King sack in his hands.

"Mother," he said to Miriam. "Oh, Mother."

She came along the side of the SUV and saw Jim lying in the street, these people wailing around him. She paid them no mind, for she was a mother and this was her son, and, no matter that she and Tom had left him to fend for himself, he was hers, would always be hers, to tend to.

"Jim?" She bent over as best as she could, trying to look into his eyes. She thought the SUV must have hit him and sent him sprawling. She looked for signs of injury. "Jimmy? What are you doing down there?" she finally asked.

"I'm waiting for the comet," Jim said. "I want to see its bright light."

"The comet?" she said.

Bart was leaning against the front fender of his SUV now. "The comet ISON," he said. "The comet of the century."

"Traveling at 845,000 miles per hour tonight," Jim said. His voice was dreamy and sounded far away from Miriam, who did her best to hear what he was saying, something about the comet catapulting around the sun. "We'll see it," he said, "if it survives the heat and doesn't burn up. It's something we'll never see again. A bundle of ice and dust, three miles in diameter, hurtling through space toward the sun. It's…" He tried to find the words to finish his sentence, but they escaped him. "It's just so wonderful," he finally said. "It's…"

Miriam felt that he was on the brink of saying something that would make all the difference, something that would forgive them all: Tom and her for moving him to this house, the man across the street who had been so rude to her on the phone, and the young couple whose bickering had nearly led to disaster. But then Tom arrived and, when Jim saw him, he stopped talking.

"Jim, do you know where you are?" Tom said.

Everyone had stopped talking now. Glory and Artie and Tippy and Bart waited to see what Jim might say. Glory was finally getting around to realizing how frightened she was and how foolish she'd been, but at the same time she was sensing something glowing at the edge of her fear and her stupidity, some beacon calling her, telling her she could do whatever she wanted to do. She might even leave Artie, probably not tonight, but some night she'd pack a bag, she'd tell him goodbye. Artie marveled over how brave she'd been. He was still holding her in his arms. He remembered the first time he saw her. It was at a high school basketball game. He couldn't stop looking at her, and when she finally caught him, her eyes told him they were about to start a glorious adventure.

And Tippy and Bart had found each other, and what had seemed so important only minutes before—a silly fight about the fact that Bart had insisted on leaving Dinah's early to rush home to his telescope—seemed small and inconsequential now. They had years and years ahead of them, enough time to disappoint and redeem each other many times over.

"Jim?" Tom said again.

Jim's voice, when he finally spoke, was so calm and clear, as if he weren't lying in the middle of the street, as if he hadn't almost been killed, as if he were as peaceful as he'd been in quite some time, which he was. It was Thanksgiving, and his parents were there, and he was alive, and, at least for the time, he suffered no torment.

"I'm in my neighborhood," he said. "I'm in my neighborhood, and these are my neighbors."

As if summoned, as if Jim had created each of them, the neighbors began to speak. They were able to tell Miriam and Tom the story of how, throughout the autumn, it had been Jim's habit to come out at night to lie down in the street to gaze up at the stars. Working together, each adding to the story, they were able to tell it in a way that didn't pass judgment on Jim or on Miriam and Tom. Even Artie was subdued. He offered Jim his hand, and Jim took it, and Artie helped him to stand. Tippy and Glory brushed the dust from his back with gentle sweeps of their hands, and Miriam struggled to hold back her tears, so overwhelmed she was by the sight of them treating her son with kindness and concern.

"I didn't mean to disturb anyone," Jim said, and his voice was so apologetic, so injured with the thought that he'd caused them alarm, that for a while no one knew quite what to say.

Then Bart stepped forward to suggest that everyone come down to their house and sit on the deck. He'd light a fire in the fire pit, he said, and he'd help them all take a look through his telescope, and like that they'd keep watch for the comet—the comet of the century, he reminded them.

"Nothing like it as long as we live," he said.

One by one, they looked up at the sky. They stood in the middle of the street and looked up, as if waiting for some blessing to find them, these neighbors, glad for now to be where they were, in each other's company, on Thanksgiving, the way people were meant to be.

LOVE FIELD

ONE NIGHT, THE BABY DIED, AND A FEW DAYS LATER, THE MOTHER, Mrs. Silver, came to Belle's house and said, "I want to talk to you."

Belle had been fearing this moment, because on the evening the baby died, before she had known anything about it, she had put a card in the mail to the Silvers. CONGRATULATIONS ON YOUR BEAUTIFUL BABY. She had known the card would be hurtful to the Silvers. The baby had come home from the hospital with jaundice, and it was obvious, even without that taint, that she was unattractive. Then Belle had heard the news of the baby's death, and she had felt stupid and mean. Ordinarily, she wouldn't have been so ugly, but so much had already happened before she decided to send the card.

The story started earlier that summer when, each evening, she tied back the lace sheers at her front door, eager for a glimpse of the Silvers' first daughter, Naomi. "Sweet Naomi," she often whispered. "Funny little Naomi." She loved to say the name, her mouth rounding with the long "o" and then puckering with a kiss to the "m" as gently as the dusk curtained everything with its soft light. Belle welcomed the gaslights' yellow blooms on the lawns, the silvery ropes of water arcing from sprinklers, the last red of the sky shrinking in the west.

Then, with a flourish that delighted her, Naomi appeared. One evening, she came in a bathing suit, her round little tummy pooching out, her feet covered with rubber flippers that slapped the street.

Another time, when it was raining, she came on roller blades, a black umbrella held over her head.

With Naomi, it was always something. Privately, Mrs. Silver had told Belle that Naomi, who for eight years had been an only child, was having trouble getting used to the fact that she would soon have a little brother or sister. Sometimes Belle went to backyard cookouts at the Silvers' house, and there she saw Naomi bouncing on a trampoline, tooting a toy horn she clamped between her lips. "Oh, that's Naomi," her father said once, with a shake of his head. She went down the slide into their swimming pool, a bowling ball held in her lap. She stuck her arms out to her sides and spun round and round in her driveway, shouting something she must have heard on a television program. "My fellow Americans," she said. "I am an idiot."

"You're a pistol," Belle said to her once.

"That's me," said Naomi. "I'm a pistol-packin' mama."

She came to noodle around with the piano, the baby grand Belle had bought for her granddaughter, Irene. But Irene was in Hawaii now, and there was that baby grand, its mahogany cabinet gleaming. "So she'll play here," Belle had told Naomi's father when he mentioned, at one of the cookouts, that Naomi had begun taking lessons, but, after putting in the swimming pool that summer, not to mention the fact that a new baby was on the way, he wasn't keen about springing for a piano, especially given that this was Naomi he was talking about, Naomi who flitted about from one thing to another like a bee, delirious as it drank from this flower, and this, and this. "Your little Naomi," Belle had said. "You send her to me."

She came each evening at eight thirty, saving the piano like a last piece of candy, a treat at the end of the day. After water balloon fights, bicycle trips, swimming shenanigans, soccer games, she came smelling of chlorine and raspberry-scented sun block, and, when she was finally there, she gave Belle a hug, her cheek pressing into Belle's stomach— latched onto her, she did, as if she were dizzy with all the exertion of her day and wanted now nothing more than these few moments with Belle, alone in this house where the old Regulator clock on the fireplace mantle ticked off the minutes and the water garden in the atrium babbled and the piano waited to sound its splendid tones.

In her own home, Naomi told Belle, after the baby had come, there was too often the noise of her crying. "Wah, wah, wah," Naomi said, opening her mouth wide and scrunching up her face in imitation of her new sister, Marie. "All the time. Wah, wah, wah. Please, just shoot me."

"She's getting used to being in the world," Belle said. Marie had only been home a matter of days. "I bet you fussed and fussed when you were that small."

"Oh, no," said Naomi, with a grown-up earnestness. "I never cried."

Belle could almost believe it. Naomi seemed so convinced she could tame whatever was before her, it was easy to imagine her untouched by misery or distress even as she first settled into life. Nothing daunted her. Belle had seen her fall on her roller blades, go scraping over the street, and get up laughing. Once, during a thunderstorm, Naomi had sneaked out of the house to collect hail stones, and one of them, as big as a golf ball, had thumped her in the head hard enough to knock her to her knees, but she was up in a flash, shaking her fist at the heavens, shouting something Belle couldn't quite make out, but which sounded to her like, "Try it again. I dare you. Just you try."

Oh, Naomi was full of the most outrageous stunts. She put firecrackers in clay flowerpots to see whether they would shatter. She climbed onto her roof one day, pretended someone had shot her, and fell backward, arms akimbo, onto an old mattress she had dragged out to the lawn.

The planet could barely hold her. At any moment, she seemed ready to escape its natural laws. But then she sat at the baby grand, and suddenly she was timid. She pecked at the keys, her fingers barely disturbing them, and the notes were faint in Belle's ears, so faint they reminded her of the emptiness of the house now that Irene had gone. She encouraged Naomi to play with more gusto. "A little zip, please, darling," she said. "Don't worry. You won't hurt it."

Irene had played like a house on fire; she had banged the keys with stunning chords and runs, had shot them with one finger the way

Chico Marx did in the movies. She played ragtime, classical, jazz. Day and night, she had filled the house with music. Then, in the winter, she had gone off to Hawaii instead of finishing her performance degree at the university. "Oh, Gran," she said. "I'm ready for a change."

What could Belle tell her? She was merely her grandmother, the one who had given her a place to live while she went to school so her father, Belle's son, could save money on her room and board. He had lost so much on oil investments. Belle had even bought the baby grand with the last of her husband's life insurance money so she could entice Irene into her home. "We'll be roomies," Belle had told her. "You'll have the piano, a room of your own, home-cooked meals. None of that cafeteria junk. You'll be on easy street."

In the end, it hadn't been enough. Irene had gone away with a boy who told her there were humpback whales off the west coast of Maui whose mating calls sounded like notes played on a bass flute. She thought it would be marvelous to record them. "I'll always be able to play the piano," she had said, "but how many chances will I have like this?" Though Belle wished her smooth sailing, she couldn't help but feel betrayed.

She was glad to give Naomi the use of the baby grand, and later, when she had finished practicing, her favorite snack, a concoction called "Dirt and Worms" that Belle had seen Naomi's mother prepare, a mix of chocolate pudding and crumbled-up Oreo cookies and strings of gelatin candy that wiggled like fishing lures.

"Like this," Naomi said, as she showed Belle how to grub down into the pudding with her fingers, pull out a worm, tilt back her head, and drop it in her mouth. "Gulp it down," Naomi said. "Just let it slide down your gullet."

"Goodness," said Belle. "I'll choke."

Naomi shook her head. "No, you won't. And even if you do, I know the Heimlich maneuver." She stood behind Belle, wrapped her arms around her waist, and squeezed, her little fist driving into the soft flesh just below Belle's ribs. "Just like that," said Naomi. "You'll pop it right out."

When she finally left Belle's and started walking down the street toward home, she sang a song Belle had taught her, the same silly song Belle had taught Irene when she had been that age, "Mairzy Doats." Belle held the door open so she could listen to Naomi's voice drifting out of the dark, a thin, dreamy voice, as hushed as the notes she played on the baby grand. "Mairzy doats and dozy doats and liddle lamzy divey. A kiddlely divey, too, wouldn't you?" As the voice faded in the distance, Belle ached for the hours to pass so Naomi would come again.

Then, one night, she failed to appear. Belle waited by the door as the Regulator clock ticked and ticked. Eight thirty passed, and then it was nine, and all she saw was the dusk turn to dark, and as it did, she became aggravated with Naomi, who had, she assumed, lost interest in the piano and forsaken her.

Well, as her father said, that was Naomi. Belle untied her lace sheers and let them fall across the glass in her front door. She turned back to her house, such a cavernous house now that she was alone. Her husband, when he had retired and built the house forty miles up the freeway from Dallas, had insisted on the two stories, the rooms and rooms and rooms they would need if their grandchildren came to live with them, as surely they would when it was time for them to attend the university. But all of them had gone to schools out of state, except Irene, who, like Naomi, had turned out to be a flibbertigibbet. Off chasing whales. The idea. As practical as the notion that their grandchildren would one day fill their house. Belle tried not to blame her husband, but there were times, when she felt the space of the house about to swallow her, that she couldn't help but resent him for dying—a heart attack while mowing their expansive lawn—and leaving her with so many rooms and so many days to wander through them.

It was nearly nine thirty when the doorbell rang. Belle peeked out through the lace sheers and saw Naomi on the step, about to press the bell again with her nose. She held her hands behind her back and leaned over. Belle opened the door, and Naomi jumped back with a scream.

"Lollapalooza," she said. "How about a little warning? I was just getting ready to ring the bell, Belle." Naomi giggled. "Get it? The Belle bell?"

At any other time, Belle would have thought Naomi's play on words endearing, but on this night, when she had waited and waited, she only found it irritating. "Don't be fresh," she said. "You're late."

"It was her fault," Naomi said. She pointed back in the direction of her house, and Belle saw that she had wrapped each of her fingers with rubber bands. The bands were scissoring into her flesh, cutting off the flow of blood and turning her fingertips the color of pencil erasers.

"Whose fault?" Belle squinted out into the darkness, looking off to where Naomi was pointing. "Who are you talking about?"

"Yellow Baby," said Naomi. The doctors had told the Silvers to make sure the new baby got plenty of sun, plenty of vitamin D. "We kept her out by the pool until the sun went down, but she still wouldn't go to sleep. I sang and sang to her." Naomi gave Belle a shy smile. "She likes it when I sing to her."

"What did you sing?"

"The song you taught me."

"Mairzy Doats?"

"Most of the time it conks her right out. But tonight." Naomi rolled her eyes. "Oh, brother. She made me so mad I pinched her. Hard. Right on her fat old leg."

"Oh, you didn't do that?" Belle felt certain Naomi was exaggerating. "Tell me you didn't."

"I didn't," said Naomi.

"I knew you were playing the devil." Belle took Naomi's hand and led her to the baby grand. She sat beside her on the piano bench. "What will you play for me tonight? 'Twinkle, Twinkle'?"

"All right," said Naomi in a meek voice, and she began pecking at the keys.

Such a mouse, Belle thought. What was it about the baby grand that spooked her? "I can barely hear you," Belle said. "Can't you, please, give it more zing?"

Naomi lifted her hands from the keyboard. Her fingers, still wrapped in the rubber bands, were trembling. "Aren't I pressing hard?" she said. "I thought I was."

"You can't feel a thing." Belle felt her irritation return. "Look at your fingers. Take off those rubber bands."

"Oh, I can't do that," Naomi said. "If I do, Yellow Baby will wake up."

"That's nonsense." Perhaps, on some other night, Belle might have thought Naomi's superstition charming, but tonight the hocus-pocus with the rubber bands was merely a further annoyance. "That's just a game you've made up. How can you play the piano with your fingers like that?"

"I can't play the piano at all." Naomi put her hands over her eyes. "I'm rotten."

It was true that Naomi's playing, even though she had only begun her lessons, lacked the confidence it would need if she hoped to continue with it.

"You can't be afraid," Belle said. "The piano knows when you're afraid and it won't give you anything. Maybe you need to let it know who's boss."

"Like this?" Naomi brought her hands down on the keyboard, and the jumbled notes, the most forceful she had ever played, rang out with a vitality that delighted Belle.

"That's it," she said. "Yes, if that's what it takes."

Naomi was shaking her hands as if they were on fire and she was desperate to put out the flames. "That hurt," she said. "I mean it really hurt. Yowza-wowza. I'm going home."

She tried to get up from the piano bench, but Belle grabbed her arm and pulled her back down. "You'll be all right. It's those rubber bands. Here, let me get them off you."

Belle tried to roll the rubber bands off Naomi's fingertips, and Naomi began to yowl. "Stop it," she said.

She tried to wriggle away, but Belle had her own finger between Naomi's and one of the rubber bands and it stretched out until it snapped.

Naomi's hand flew up to her eye. "You've hit me," she said. She jumped up and ran out of the house. By the time Belle made it to the door, Naomi was running down the street. "I'm blind!" she was shouting. "I'm blind!" And though Belle wanted to follow to make sure Naomi was all right, she saw neighbors opening doors, stepping out to see what the fuss was, and she couldn't bear the thought of passing by them, feeling their questioning eyes upon her, hearing herself saying to them, with a wave of her hand, "Oh, you know Naomi."

The next morning, early, she called Naomi's house, and Naomi's father answered in his subdued baritone that Belle always imagined might be the voice of God. Mr. Silver held an endowed chair in Peace Studies at the university. It was his job, in his research, to figure out why groups went to war. Whenever Belle listened to him, she got the impression that he could tame any unruly force with merely a word. Any force except Naomi, for whom he had no answer.

"She has a scratch on her cornea," he told Belle. "Nothing serious. We'll keep it covered for a while."

"So she'll be all right?" Belle had spent the night imagining she had maimed Naomi forever.

"A scratch," said Mr. Silver. "She'll be Naomi in no time."

The musical lilt of the phrase, "Naomi in no time," reminded Belle of the baby grand and how she had encouraged the girl to play with more pizazz. "She had rubber bands wrapped around her fingers," she said to Mr. Silver. "I was only trying to get them off."

For a while, Mr. Silver didn't say anything. Belle could hear the baby cooing in the background. She could hear the chirr of the swimming pool filters, and she imagined Mr. Silver on the cordless phone, sitting by the pool, the baby snuggled against him. Finally, he said—and his voice was even more quiet than usual when he spoke— "That isn't exactly the way Naomi tells it."

"No?" said Belle. "What, then?"

"She says you got angry with her." Again there were only the sounds of the baby and the pool filters and then a thread of static on the phone as Mr. Silver cleared his throat. "She says you tried to slap her, and your fingernail scraped across her eye."

Now it was Belle who could barely find her voice. "And you believe her? You believe I'd do that?"

"In my work," Mr. Silver said, "I know that the truth is always somewhere between stories. One party says this, one party says that. What do we know? Only that we have trouble, and almost always each side is partly to blame."

"Those rubber bands," Belle said again.

"Who's to say why Naomi does what she does?" Mr. Silver chuckled. "Don't worry. She won't bother you anymore."

"If I could just talk with her."

"I don't think she wants to do that. At least not now."

"Just a few moments."

"Belle, I'm afraid I must insist."

She heard just the slightest tone of irritation in Mr. Silver's voice, and in that instant she knew what she had become, the old woman in the neighborhood whose granddaughter had left her alone, an object of pity, a burdensome test of the compassion of those who lived around her. She feared Mr. Silver would soon end their conversation. The thought of not being able to speak with Naomi—she wanted so badly to ask her why she had lied—while the rumor that she had tried to slap her spread through the neighborhood, left her desperate, and all she could think to do was to tell a lie of her own. "Naomi's right," she said. "I lost my temper. I feel just awful. Please, I must see her to apologize."

But already, Mr. Silver had hung up, and all Belle heard was the hum of the phone line, which seemed to mock her admission to a crime she hadn't committed, all for the chance that she might once again see Naomi.

Belle, if she had to admit the truth, had never quite taken to motherhood. She had never gotten used to the feel of a baby squirming in her arms, the heft of it slung against her hip, and somehow, she feared that her children had sensed her discomfort, knew it even now that they were grown. She thought it must be particularly true for Irene's father, who had left home as soon as he had been old enough to join the Army. Now, though he lived in Houston, he rarely made the trip north to visit. He telephoned from time to time to let her know, in brief conversations, that he was well. Irene was as bad, throwing away her music studies for some wild expedition to Hawaii. Belle began to wonder whether the fault was hers. Did some lack in her, some inability to give herself wholly to people, end up driving them away?

The night Irene packed her duffle for her trip to Hawaii, she suddenly turned from her dresser and threw her arms around Belle's neck. Belle stood there, surprised, afraid to return the hug, knowing that if she did, she would never want to let go. "Do you have enough undergarments?" she finally said, cringing at the prim sound of the words.

One day, not long after Naomi's accusation, a letter came from Irene, along with a cassette recording she had made of the humpback whales. When Belle played the tape and heard the whales' calls, she felt something collapse inside her, some notion she had manufactured that it didn't matter a stitch to her what Naomi claimed. What was the word of a child to her, who had managed without Miss Naomi Silver and would do so again?

When Belle listened to the whales' urgent calls, she knew she was a fraud. In their groans and trills, and their bellows that rose to screams—what Irene, in her letter, called the "ascending phrases"—Belle heard her own need, and she nearly wept. She thought of all the nights she had stood at her door saying, "Naomi, Naomi." She imagined the first sailors to hear the whales' calls and how the cries must have pierced them to the quick, made the pitch and sway of their ship—this world at sea they had come to trust—seem foreign and perilous.

"The bellows are called bells," Irene wrote. "Like when a deer bays. He bells. Sort of a trumpeting sound."

The association of the sounds with her name stunned her, and it seemed then as if the whales were calling her, "Belle, Belle, Belle."

She imagined Irene and her boyfriend on the boat they had rented, their underwater microphones dropped over the side, their headphones in place as they listened to the swell of the ocean and then the whales' cries. Eavesdroppers, they were, listening to pleas and shrieks and whimpers, stealing this ancient and intimate language not meant for human ears.

Sometimes, Irene went on to say, the whales swam up onto the shore and stranded themselves on dry land. The theory was that they navigated by using the geomagnetic field of the Earth, and when that field fluctuated, as it often did, they continued to follow a field of constant strength, a geomagnetic contour, no matter where it threatened to lead them. Often, a beached whale, when towed back to the sea, would again swim to the shore, convinced it was moving in the right direction.

Belle's husband had been a geologist for an oil company, and he had explained to her the plates of the Earth's crust and mantle and how they drifted at various speeds and in different directions. At one time, there had been a single supercontinent, Pangaea, before massive blocks of the Earth's surface separated. Some converged again; some slid past one another. The world of the here and now was only a fleeting manifestation of a grander reality. The land beneath their feet had started somewhere else. Perhaps two hundred million years ago the North Texas plains had been part of what was now Africa. Even as they spoke, he told her, they were drifting westward at one to three centimeters per year. "In the big picture," he said, "we're all moving."

Now she thought of the whales and their calls going out through the oceans of a drifting Earth. Most of their songs, Irene said, were audible to other whales nearly twenty miles away, and some of the low-frequency moans and snores could range over a hundred miles. Belle thought of Naomi and how she was only three houses away, but still the distance seemed too great for either one of them to close.

That night, and for several nights thereafter, her husband came to her in her dreams. Always, he was young. His black hair gleamed, and his broad chest flared up from his narrow waist. And in these dreams, she, too, was young. They were back in their old house in Dallas, not far from the airport, Love Field. When jets took off, teacups rattled in the china cabinet, picture frames tilted on the walls, the trapdoor to the attic rose and fell and banged against its frame as if spirits were tromping across the ceiling joists. "It's like someone just walked across my grave," she used to say to her husband, her hand at her throat. "Oh, don't complain," he would tell her, with a wink. "How can we go wrong when we live so close to Love?" It became a dear joke between them. "We're in the Love Field," they teased. "Oh, baby. We've landed in Love."

Now she lived in a neighborhood surrounded by pasture fields where longhorn cattle grazed and the blue sky stretched off to the horizon. Some evenings, she walked to the farthest reach of the subdivision and saw the land the way it had been before people had come to claim it: scrub trees and clay soil cracking from drought and grass turning to tinder—dry and burnt—under the blazing sun. How vast Texas must have seemed to the first settlers. So much room, a person could disappear if he wanted to, and perhaps no one would ever know.

One afternoon, though the heat was almost more than she could bear, she went for a walk so she could pass the Silvers' house in hopes of seeing Naomi playing in the yard.

And there she was. She was sitting on the grass, her head bowed as she tried to lace up her sneaker. She was having a hard time of it. Her hair had fallen over her face, and she was poking the shoelace at the eyelet with no success. Finally, she let the lace drop from her hand. Her shoulders wobbled, and Belle knew she was trying hard not to cry.

Then Naomi looked up, and Belle saw the gauze patch over her left eye, held in place with strips of tape stuck to her forehead and cheekbone. At first, Belle could hardly bear the sight of Naomi, stymied, when she had always breezed through the world. Then Belle felt a stronger part of her drift toward Naomi's need. She was, after all the crazy stunts, a child who needed someone now to help her.

"That old shoelace is being a pill, isn't it?" Belle said.

Naomi nodded her head, and her bottom lip quivered. She picked up the shoelace again and held it out, inviting Belle to take it.

"Slip off your shoe, sweetie," Belle told her, "and I'll lace it for you. If I try to kneel down, I may never get back up."

Naomi kicked off her shoe, picked it up by the lace, and brought it to Belle. "I would have asked my mom to help me," Naomi said, her voice hushed the way it had been when she came to Belle's house to play the piano. "But she's busy with Yellow Baby. She's always busy with Yellow Baby. I could just disappear, and she wouldn't even know."

"Oh, she'd miss you." Belle threaded the shoelace through the eyelet. She thought of Irene so far away in Hawaii. "Just like I've missed you."

"Me?" said Naomi, and Belle could see that her surprise was genuine. She had never known how much Belle loved her.

"I don't know why you lied, sweetie. You know I didn't hit you."

"No, you didn't," Naomi said.

"Will you tell your parents that? Tell them the truth? It was those rubber bands that caused all the trouble."

Naomi bit down on her lip. "I want to," she said, "but I can't. Then they'd know how wicked I am."

Just then, Mrs. Silver came out of the house with Marie in her arms. "Naomi," she said, "your father wants you to come inside now."

"Yes, Mother," Naomi said. Then she snatched her shoe from Belle's hand and dashed across the lawn.

Mrs. Silver owned a candy store. Belle had seen her commercials on television. In them, Mrs. Silver, a lanky woman whose teeth were too big, wore a tutu and tights and a pair of gauzy fairy wings. She carried a magic wand with a glittery star on its end. "At the Sugar Plum Cottage," she always said at the end of the commercials, "where being sweet to you is our business."

Belle walked across the lawn so she could get a closer look at the baby. "So this is the one," she said, letting her voice fall into the singsong rhythm she recalled other women using when they had admired her own baby. "This is the little sweetheart."

"This is Marie," said Mrs. Silver. She matched Belle's tone, an inflection just like the ones she used in her commercials.

Belle peered down at the baby, who was, as Naomi had claimed, fussy. She was crying, her eyes clamped shut, her mouth open wide, her chubby fists waving in the air. "You're trying to tell us something, aren't you, little Marie?" Belle said. She was well aware that she was trying to curry Mrs. Silver's favor so she could broach the subject of Naomi and her lie. "We just can't understand what you're saying. No, we can't."

Marie was, in all honesty, sorely featured. Her head was too big, her eyes set too close together. Even without the yellow tinge to her skin, she was not, though Belle would never have said this to Mrs. Silver, a looker.

"She's...jaundiced," Mrs. Silver said, and the way she hesitated between the two words made it clear to Belle that she knew as well as anyone with two good eyes that her baby was far from handsome.

"Oh, that'll go away," Belle said. "What we need now is to get this sweetheart to stop crying."

And then Belle started to sing. She sang "Mairzy Doats," and the cadence of the song seemed to catch Marie's ear. She toned down her squall to an occasional whimper. "Maybe if I held her," Belle said.

She reached for Marie, and Mrs. Silver took a perceptible step back. There was an awkward moment, then, when Mrs. Silver tried to cover over the fact that she had just snubbed Belle. "Babies," she said, and her voice trembled with a phony laugh. "They're such a handful. I wouldn't want to trouble you."

Belle wanted to feel sorry for Mrs. Silver because she was a nervous woman, not such an eye-catcher herself, who owned a candy store and dressed in a fairy princess costume to make herself feel pretty. Now she had a baby with jaundice and, beyond that, a face that people would remember for the wrong reasons. Belle wanted to offer her sympathy, but she couldn't manage it. Instead, she felt a rage start to rise in her because she knew that, when Mrs. Silver had stepped back from her, she had been announcing that she thought Belle dangerous, a crazy old woman who had nearly blinded Naomi. Let her hold the baby? Not on her life.

That evening, Belle wrote her message in the baby card, underlining the word BEAUTIFUL five times, satisfied with the irony. She had just dropped the card into the mailbox on the corner when she heard a siren's rising keen.

It was dusk, and she saw red light swell and pulse on the trees and houses as an ambulance turned down the street. She waited to see where it would stop.

Naomi's house. Naomi, Belle thought. Something's happened to Naomi.

But it wasn't Naomi at all. It was the baby, Marie. She had fallen into the pool. The word spread up and down the street. The pool. The baby. Marie. It was all anyone knew.

It was nearly dark by the time the paramedics brought her out to the ambulance. As they came hurrying through the Silvers' front yard, Belle saw, just for a moment, the baby's tiny hand, as the man carrying her slipped through the gaslight's glow.

Then Mr. Silver came running, barefoot in his swimming trunks. Mrs. Silver and Naomi dashed out of the house. They all got into the back of the ambulance, and its siren shrieked again as it sped away.

For a moment, Belle stood with her neighbors in the middle of the street, looking at the Silvers' house. They had left the front door open, and she could see the lights burning inside and the slow turn of a ceiling fan.

"I suppose someone should go down there and shut the door," a man said. "And turn off the lights."

"I'll do it," said Belle.

"Oh, I can do it," the man told her.

"No." She stepped forward. "Please."

In the Silvers' house, she went from room to room switching off the lights, letting darkness follow her. Upstairs, in Naomi's room, she noticed that a window was open. The screen had been popped out and was leaning against the wall. She felt the warm night air, smelled the chlorine in the backyard swimming pool. Her hand moved over the light switch, and then the pool lights cast the reflection of the water into the room. It spread over Belle and across the wall behind her. The blue tint of the shuddering light, rising and falling with the gentle motion of the water, caught her by surprise—how delicate it was, how wispy, like threads of smoke lacing the air.

She went to the window to close it. She looked down on the pool and saw a bright orange raft, the kind someone could inflate and float on, turned upside down. It was spinning in a lazy circle as if it had a slow air leak. As it swung around, she caught a glimpse of something settled on the pool's bottom, a dark shape, mysterious in the dim glow from the underwater lights. Then she smelled the scent of raspberries, and, in an instant, she remembered the sunblock Naomi always wore, and she imagined that what she saw on the bottom of the pool was a bowling ball. She pictured Naomi standing at the window, struggling with the ball's weight, balancing it on the sill, and then shoving it out into the air. Perhaps Mr. Silver had been on the float with Marie. He would have looked up just as Naomi yelled. Perhaps she screamed, "Look out below." Then the ball came crashing down into the water, and Mr. Silver, trying to shield Marie, let her slip from his hands, while Naomi looked on, stunned by what she saw.

Or maybe that wasn't how it had happened at all. Maybe, Belle thought, she simply needed to believe that Naomi had finally astonished herself, had wandered so far from the world she had found it again, had found her mother, her father, Marie, even herself, had felt the weight of their living.

One evening, not long after the funeral, Mrs. Silver came to Belle's house, the baby card in her hand. "You saw something in her, didn't you?" she said. "That day when she was crying and you sang to her. You saw something pretty in her."

Standing there with Mrs. Silver, the door open just a crack, Belle thought of her own son, and her husband, and Irene, and even Naomi, who would be a different girl now that she knew loss, who would more than likely remember Belle in the years to come, if she remembered her at all, as the old woman about whom she had lied the summer her baby sister drowned. Belle imagined all of them standing together on the drifting Earth, all of them lifting up their voices, sending out their cries.

"Such a racket," she had always said when the jets had taken off from Love Field and risen with a scream over their house.

Her husband had made the same joke every time, yet she never tired of it. "What can we do?" he had said with a shrug of his shoulders. "So little us. So much Love."

She thought of the joke again as she opened her door wider. "Yes, I saw it," she said to Mrs. Silver. "Your Marie was a beautiful child."

THE LAST CIVILIZED HOUSE

ANCIL

HE FOUND THE TRACKS IN THE SNOW ONE EVENING SHORTLY AFTER New Year's, when he went out to the burn barrel with the trash. The temperature was fifteen, according to the old Prairie Farms thermometer tacked to the doorframe, and the wind was out of the north. It blew in over the empty field that stretched back to the railroad trestle and stung his eyes. He hunched his shoulders, drawing the upturned collar of his barn coat toward his ears. He looked down at the ground—they'd had snow cover since mid-December—and that's when he saw the tracks, where none had been that morning when he'd come out to fill the bird feeders.

The tracks came around the corner of the house and ran in a straight line to the back steps. Ancil knew they weren't his, which he could distinguish by the Cat's Paw heel prints. This set had been made by someone wearing Red Wing boots. Ancil figured it was a man for the tracks were long and wide, the wavy soles of the boots and the Red Wing logo pressed deep into the snow.

"What in the world?" Ancil said to himself.

He lived with his wife, Lucy, on the edge of town, just before the pavement turned to gravel and ran out into the country. Theirs was the last civilized house, he always told people when giving them directions. The last house before the wilderness. The last chance for comfort before crossing the border into lands unknown. The last chance to save yourself, he said with a wink and a laugh. Now he wanted to know who in the world had been snooping around in broad daylight, and, more to the point, why?

The prints came up onto the back stoop. Had the man stood there and tried to look in through the glass in the door, the glass that Lucy kept covered with curtains? Whoever he was, he'd hopped down from the stoop on the side where the double kitchen windows ran along the back wall—the prints were deeper there—and walked around the house, stopping at every window, from bedroom to living room to dining room. To think that someone had looked into the house that afternoon while he and Lucy had been doing their trading in town struck a nerve. It kept gnawing at Ancil as he tracked the prints out to the sidewalk and then into the street, where they disappeared, as if the man had stepped into a car and driven away.

Ancil stood at the side of the street and looked back at his house— such an ordinary house, a wood-frame house with aluminum awnings over the windows and the front stoop—and he tried to imagine that he was this man, up to no good. What would he see if he were to peep through the windows?

The next thing he knew he was standing at the front window looking in. Nothing he saw seemed remarkable to him at all. The fireplace of red brick, generations of family Bibles stacked on the mantle along with the Christmas garland Lucy had yet to take down. The wedding ring quilt on its rack in the corner. The big round braided rug on the hardwood floor, the two reclining chairs where Ancil and Lucy sat most nights watching some nonsense on TV. Lucy's knitting spilling out of her sewing basket on the floor by her chair. The doily on the back of his, dingy from where his hair oil had stained it. Just the marks and signs of all their years together. Nothing much of value that anyone would want to steal. Nothing much of interest.

One dining room wall had a painting of apples in a basket—red and yellow apples that looked so real Ancil could taste them each time he looked at that picture. The dining table, an old oak drop-leaf, had newspapers scattered over it and the mail that he'd carried in from the box just minutes ago: a circular from McKim's IGA, the water bill, and a late Christmas card from Lucy's pen pal in Oklahoma, a woman Ancil knew only through the photo she sent each year at the holidays, a picture of her and her husband. He was in a wheelchair, a skinny man with a pencil moustache. She wore what was obviously a wig—black, lustrous hair down over her shoulders—and she had gaps between her big teeth. Now that was a couple some stranger might take an interest in, but Ancil and Lucy? He didn't think so. They were dry as dust, unremarkable in every way. They'd lived in that house over fifty years, Ancil pulling on his overalls every morning and grabbing his lunch bucket and heading to work on a section gang for the B & O Railroad, Lucy asking him to zip her up, please. He'd always liked that, the way she turned her back to him, her bra strap showing, and he took the zipper tab and ran it up from her waist and then closed the hook and eye at the top where the knobs of her vertebrae raised up beneath her skin.

"Thanks, sweets," she always said, and then blew him a kiss on her way out the door, heading uptown to have coffee with her girlfriends before working behind the counter at Piper's Sundries.

Fifty-five years together, fifty-two of them in this house. Retired now, still in reasonably good health, no scrapes with the law, property taxes always paid on time, lawn tended in the summertime, walks and driveway kept clear in the winter. Good neighbors. Now, as he continued to follow those tracks in the snow—*Red Wing, Red Wing, Red Wing*—Ancil felt at loose ends. Someone had Lucy and him in his sights.

Lucy was in the kitchen getting supper started, so he didn't linger there, only long enough to see her at the sink, peeling potatoes, her back humped up, no longer the straight-backed girl who'd asked him to zip her dress. She was his "old girl," he always said. He was her "old man." They'd had years and years together, so many of them that they'd nearly forgotten the boy and girl they'd once been. But on occasion, he might surprise her with a kiss, and she'd say, "Old man, don't start something you can't finish."

At one time, they'd seen the world together and brought it back in pieces: the music box from Switzerland, the lace table runner from

England, the cuckoo clock from Germany. Decorative plates from Washington, D.C., New York City, Boston, Chicago, the Grand Canyon, Yosemite, San Francisco, Hollywood, Miami Beach hung on the kitchen walls.

What was any of that to make them worth the attentions of a peeping Tom?

Ancil stood at the bedroom window and looked in. It gave him the oddest feeling to see the details of his and Lucy's life together on display. Here were the most intimate things, the ones they never meant for anyone to see: the pint bottle of Crown Royal and the shot glass on his nightstand—just a nip before bed each night to help him sleep. The crumpled tissues on Lucy's stand from where she'd awakened in the night, crying, because an inexplicable sadness came over her. "Well, old man," she told him when he asked, "it's just so hard to say why."

Her collection of porcelain dolls on the shelves. She had a name for each, and sometimes she talked baby talk to them. That always embarrassed him a little, much the way he felt now as he stood there, looking at them the way the peeping Tom must have done.

What else had he seen?

Had he seen Ancil coming to bed in his pajamas, the shirt buttoned to the top button, a white handkerchief folded in the pocket? Had he seen Lucy in her sweatpants and thermal shirt, her heavy breasts loose beneath it? Had he seen their toothless mouths, their cheeks caved in, and the way they slept with their backs turned to each other, he on his side of the bed and she on hers? Had he wondered, as Ancil did now, how they'd ever managed all those years together? No children and now just the two of them to take care of each other, all the way out here on the edge of town in this unremarkable house, a house of last chances.

Only when Ancil thought this thought to himself, he confused a word and it came out "a house of *lost* chances," and all the while he stood at the burn barrel, setting a match to a piece of newspaper in the trash and watching the flames lick up above the rim, he found himself overwhelmed with a great sadness that had something else smoldering at its edges, something he couldn't quite name until he went back inside the house and Lucy asked him what had taken him so long with the trash, and he said he'd been checking the bird feeders.

"You just filled them this morning," she said, and she said it in a voice that was impatient and severe. She stood at the stove, frying potatoes for their supper, and she banged the metal spatula twice on the edge of the pan. "Good God, old man," she said.

He felt it again, that thing that was rimming his sadness, and he knew the name to give it. Rage. A smoldering rage drawn up from somewhere deep inside him, brought there by the man—whoever he was—who had looked through their windows.

That night in bed, Ancil couldn't fall asleep. The Crown Royal hadn't done the trick, and as he tried to decide whether to have another drink, he found himself listening to the noises of the house. With each click of the furnace coming on, each pop of a roof joist contracting in the cold, he imagined that the peeping Tom had returned and was standing outside the bedroom window.

Lucy lay beside him, sound asleep, and it only stoked his anger to know that he couldn't tell her what had him on edge. Someone had come looking to see what he might find, and because he had, Ancil was feeling every regret and sadness of his life with Lucy with a sharpness that left him raw with guilt. He'd never be able to tell her any of that. What would be the use? Here they were, toward the end of their years. What would he gain by saying hurtful things to her now?

Still, she seemed to notice that something was bothering him. The next day, as they ran their errands uptown, she said, "Cat got your tongue?"

They'd just come out of the bank, where they'd deposited their social security checks and kept a little cash for spending money. The teller, a girl Ancil recognized but whose name he couldn't recall, counted out the cash, and then said to Lucy, "Now he can take you out on a date."

"Oh, we're too old," Lucy said. She tapped the bills on the counter to square them and then slipped them into her wallet. "That lovey-dovey stuff is for you young folks. We're done with all of that."

The way she said it so quickly, and in a flat voice with no hint of humor at all, shook Ancil. Again, it was as if a window had opened to their lives, and he felt ashamed to be on display, the young woman knowing the truth: he and Lucy, whoever they'd been in the past, were now nothing more than companions. He knew that should be enough—a blessing—but now that the peeping Tom had come and Ancil had taken a hard look at his years with Lucy, it wasn't. It just wasn't.

So when she asked him if the cat had his tongue, he said, "I can't talk to you right now." He heard the catch in his own voice, that hiccup of air that braced against tears. "I just can't."

"Old man?" Lucy said. "What's wrong?"

The sun was out, but in the miserable cold, the dusting of new snow that had fallen overnight was packed and frozen on the sidewalk. Ancil knew if he tried to tell Lucy what was troubling him, he'd make a mess of things. He could tell her about the footprints in the snow and how he'd followed them and stood at the windows looking in and seen what the peeping Tom had seen and how that had left him feeling empty and sad and angry, but where would that lead them? Only to the truth, which was complicated and well beyond Ancil's ability to express. Even if he could, how would he begin to tell Lucy that as much as he'd loved her all these years, he'd come to regret the life they'd stumbled through together?

"Ancil?" Lucy said, her voice, this time, full of what he himself was feeling, a tremendous fear of what he might say next.

He couldn't look at her. He watched two pickup trucks, their fenders gray with road salt, bump their way over the railroad crossing. Across the street, at Ferguson's Market, Lucy's next stop, a high school boy wearing a red sock hat and a black insulated coat under his white apron came out with a bag of Ice Melt and started scattering it on the walkway. He was singing that song about a tropical heat wave as he worked, just a boy in high spirits on a cold day. The wind was still out of the north, pushing snakes of loose snow in squiggly lines down Main Street.

Ancil knew he and Lucy would have to move soon. They couldn't stay there outside the bank in the cold and the wind much longer.

They'd have to cross the street and do their grocery shopping and make the drive home and eat some lunch and turn on the radio and listen to the local news on WAKO the way they always did, and when it was over, he'd snap off the radio and the silence would settle around them, and there they'd be.

Ancil knew he could stop that from happening. He could stop so much from happening if he'd only say what had been troubling him ever since yesterday, when he'd stood at the bedroom window and taken in what the peeping Tom had seen. *I wish you'd kept the baby. If you'd done that, our lives would be different.*

But because he was a cowardly man, and always had been, he didn't say that. He looked down at his feet, amazed by what he saw. There, imprinted in the crust of snow covering the sidewalk, was a footprint and then another, a trail of prints headed south, each of them saying, *Red Wing.*

"Nothing's wrong," he said to Lucy. He even reached out and patted her on the arm. "You go on to Ferguson's," he said. "You wait for me there when you're done. Go on. I just remembered something I forgot."

He didn't give her a chance to respond. He just started walking. He looked back once and saw that she was still standing there. He lifted his arm to wave at her, and she did the same. Her wave, hesitant and shy as if she were a child, nearly broke his heart and he almost went back—the thought of the two of them apart even for a short time overwhelmed him—but there were those tracks in the snow, and he had to know where they led and who might be waiting at the end of them.

LUCY

What a puzzle he was to her sometimes, even after all these years. What a mystery all men were, really, with their silent hearts. That's what she was thinking as she crossed the street and stepped up onto the sidewalk along Ferguson's Market where the box boy, one of Hattie Mack's towheaded grandsons, was just then finishing up with the Ice Melt.

"Here now, let me help you," he said, offering Lucy his arm. "Wouldn't want you to slip."

"You're just like your granddad," she said. "You're a gentleman just like him."

"Yes, ma'am," the boy said, and she took his arm and let him usher her safely inside the store.

Lucy bowed her head and kept a watchful eye on her feet. She noticed the boy was wearing what appeared to be new boots.

"Were they a Christmas present?" she asked.

"Ma'am?"

"Your boots."

The boy looked down at his feet. He lifted the right one and turned it to the side. "My gramps got them for me."

Lucy nodded. "They look like the ones he always wore."

"You remember what boots he wore?" the boy said, amazed.

"Oh, I'm well acquainted with your granddad. You be sure to tell him Lucy says hello."

Yes, she knew Burton Mack and could have told his grandson things about his grandfather that she wondered if even Hattie knew—like the fact that when he was a younger man he worked summers on the section gang with Ancil. Then when autumn came, he went back to college in Champaign, where he was studying agriculture. Ancil said he'd never heard of such a thing. All that money and time spent learning to be a farmer. Wasn't that something a man knew from doing it?

When Burton finally came back with his diploma and settled into farming with his father, he brought a bride with him. Hattie was the one who insisted on calling him Burton—not Burtie like everyone else—and wearing white gloves and sun hats covered with plastic flowers and sending away to St. Louis for just the right living room set—*it's Danish modern*, she said—and otherwise making a snooty show of herself. At least that's how it appeared to Lucy.

Oh, there was so much she could tell Mrs. Hattie Mack if she took a mind to. She could tell her that she remembered when Burtie Mack was a boy who was just becoming a man. Broad shoulders and bulging arms, Vitalis Hair Tonic, Aqua Velva aftershave, a scent Lucy still recalled from time to time, like she did now as she grabbed a wire shopping cart inside Ferguson's. Oh, yes, she could tell anyone who wanted to know that Burtie always wore Aqua Velva and bought Wilkinson Sword double-edged blades for his safety razor. He liked to eat braunschweiger sandwiches with thick slices of longhorn cheese, and he always put salt in his Schlitz beer. He kept a Camel cigarette behind his left ear, within easy reach when he wanted it, as he often did after their lovemaking. She'd snuggle in close to him, her head on his chest, the two of them in the backseat of his Chevy Impala pulled back into the woods down a Marathon oil lease road, and she'd listen to the steady beat of his heart and let herself believe that they could go on and on like that and Ancil would never know.

Those were the days of autumn, glorious sunny days before the turn to winter, Indian summer days when Burtie would come home from Champaign at the end of the week to help his father with the corn harvest. Fridays were theirs. He'd pick her up in his Impala after lunch and they'd go driving in the country. She'd scoot over next to him on the bench seat like a schoolgirl, and he'd drape his arm over her shoulders. Her Burtie. *Aren't you afraid someone might see us?* he asked her once, and she told him, *Let 'em look.*

He told her she was brazen and she said that suited her just fine. She could still recall her brassy red hair and how it lifted from her shoulders in the warm air that came through the Impala's windows. Sometimes she didn't wear any underthings, so when he slid his hand under her dress, up her bare leg, he'd find her moist and ready. She didn't stop to consider why she needed this. She only knew that she did. On occasion, she felt how much it would hurt Ancil if he ever knew, but she convinced herself he'd never find out.

Then one afternoon, Burtie drove her back into town from the west, sticking to the gravel roads as he always did, past the cow pastures and the old Hadley School and the cornfields where the pickers were going up and down the rows. The air smelled of the corn dust, a smell Lucy would always associate with Burtie.

"Where's this all going?" she asked him. "You and me?"

"Does it have to be going anywhere, Lucy? You're a married woman."

"That doesn't always mean forever," she said.

"You'd leave Ancil?"

"Might."

Burtie slowed down and took a long look at her. "You say that," he said, "but I doubt that you mean it."

"Want to try me?"

"Seems to me I already have," he said with a wink.

"You're horrible." She swatted him across his arm and slid over to the window. She folded her arms over her chest and turned away to watch the telephone poles go by. "You shouldn't have said that," she finally said. "You shouldn't have made us ugly."

"I'm sorry," he said, and she believed him. That was her trouble. She always believed him. "Lucy, I never meant…I mean, I wouldn't want to ever hurt you…aw, hell, Lucy, sometimes I just get too full of myself. Sometimes I can't believe I'm with a woman like you."

They rode in silence, then, the rest of the way to her house. Burtie pulled the Impala into the driveway. They had an old collie dog then, named Dickie, and he came out from behind the garage when he heard the car and started to whine for her.

"There's my Dickie boy," she said. "There's mama's good boy."

Then, before either she or Burtie could realize it, Ancil's truck was pulling into the driveway behind them.

"Oh, good Christ," said Burtie. "It's Ancil."

Lucy didn't miss a beat. She got out of the car and was standing in the yard when Ancil stepped from his truck.

"Look who gave me a ride from uptown," she said in a bright voice.

"Is that Burton?" Ancil said.

"Burtie Mack," said Lucy. "Burtie, come on out here so Ancil can see you."

Ancil shaded his eyes and squinted into the sunlight that Lucy felt warming the back of her neck and her legs. She heard the Impala's door open and then swing shut, and then Burtie was standing beside her.

"Burt, what are you doing here?" Ancil said.

Too much silence went by with no answer from Burtie, so Lucy knew she had to say something.

"I told you," she said. "He gave me a ride." She looked at her wristwatch, a Timex Ancil had given her for her birthday. "My goodness, is it four o'clock already? No, it's only three fifteen. What are you doing home early?"

"I'm sick," Ancil said. "I've been sick all afternoon."

"Mercy, what's wrong?"

"Sick to my stomach."

"Well, let's get you inside." Lucy took him by his arm. "Burtie, I appreciate the ride."

"I'm sorry I don't feel like a visit," Ancil said. "Can you get around my truck?"

"I believe I can," said Burtie.

"All right, then. I thank you for favoring my wife."

And that was that, so Lucy thought. She helped Ancil into the house, and she heard Burtie's Impala moving fast back out into the country. She got Ancil into bed and she made him some nutmeg tea to help settle his stomach. She brought it to him in the bedroom, and she sat on the side of the bed while he drank it.

"It was so hot today. Too hot for October. That sun beat down on me, and I wasn't feeling worth a pinch anyway. What were you doing uptown?"

"I needed some flour from Ferguson's."

"Did you get it?"

She realized, then, that he'd seen her get out of the Impala with nothing in her hands.

"It was a funny thing. They were out."

"Out," said Ancil. "Flour? Whoever heard of a market being out of flour?"

"Something about a shipment that didn't come in." She was trying to think fast. "You done with your tea, baby?"

She took the cup and saucer from him and stood up. She turned toward the door, but he reached out and took her by her wrist.

"Look at me," he said, and there was an edge to his voice that she didn't like.

"You're hurting my wrist," she said.

He let her go then, and she tried to walk away as if nothing had happened, but she knew that something had.

Later that night, as they were falling asleep, he said to her, "Are you in the habit of going to town without your underpants on?"

"What in the world are you talking about?"

"That white dress of yours. The sun behind you in the west this afternoon. A blind man could have seen."

"You're crazy," she said.

"Am I?"

And like that, little by little, over the course of the night and on into the morning and afternoon of the next day, it all came out about Burtie Mack and her.

"Do you love him?" Ancil asked. He was still sick to his stomach and he was in his pajamas and his hair was wild on his head, and she was sorry for the hurt she'd brought him.

"No, no, of course not," she said, even though she knew it was a lie.

ANCIL

The trail of Red Wing prints went along Main Street in front of the bank and Piper's Sundries and the hardware store before turning right and heading west past the Odd Fellows' Lodge and Hazel and Abner's Café, where the tables were starting to fill up with folks trying to get a jump on the lunch crowd. Soon the noon fire whistle would blow, and then store clerks and the workers from the grain elevator and City Hall would come filing in. The door opened as Ancil went by, and he heard the clatter of dishes and silverware and the chatter of voices. Someone said, "My God, that's rich," and Ancil tried to look through the plate-glass window, which was steaming over from the heat inside. The waitresses looked like they were moving underwater. Ancil put his head back down and kept following the tracks.

At the end of the block, they stopped, the last ones turned toward the door of Tubby's Barber Shop. Ancil pushed open the door and stepped inside.

Right away, his eyeglasses fogged over, and he had to take them off. Without them, he couldn't see who was sitting in the chairs along the back wall, nor could he see who was in Tubby's chair.

"Ancil, I've got a few ahead of you," Tubby said in his gravelly voice. "Hope you got time to wait."

"I got time," Ancil said. He took a red bandana from his hip pocket and went to work on his glasses.

Someone had been telling a story, and now he returned to it. "Like I said, it was a Sunday, and Poke Hobbs had just got out of church." The voice sounded familiar, but Ancil couldn't quite place it. "You know how hard Poke is to understand when he talks. Well, he went up to Emma Lawson—you know, Mitt Lawson's widow?—and he says, 'Miss, may I walk you home?' Everyone knows that Emma's a little hard of hearing, and what with the way Poke was mushing up his words, well, she didn't have a chance of getting what he was saying. So she says, 'What's that, Poke?' And he comes at her again. 'I said, may I walk you home?' Still no luck. 'I didn't quite catch that,' Emma said, and Poke says to her—now get this, boys—he says to her, 'Miss, you can kiss my goddamn ass.'" The barber shop exploded with laughter. Ancil heard the hoots and belly laughs and the sound of men clapping their hands and slapping their thighs. Then when it was about to die down, the storyteller—Ancil had figured out it was Pat Best, who helped Charlie Sivert out at the funeral home—said, his voice rising with excitement, "You can bet she heard that. Clear as a bell." And the laughter broke out again.

That was the sort of town it was—Ancil had always known it to be so—a town where everyone's flaws were fair game for the loafers and the busybodies, everybody looking for a chance to feel grateful that their own lives were in order compared to those of their neighbors. To hear that story told on Poke Hobbs, a lonely man mustering up his courage to ask for companionship despite his speech impediment— that story told as a joke—added to the anger that Ancil felt.

He slipped his eyeglasses back on and took a look around the shop. There was Pat Best in his sport coat and tie, his high forehead shiny under the lights, a grin on his face. There was Ellis Roderick from the Texaco station, bent over at the waist from laughing so hard, a cigarette dangling from his fingers, the marks from his comb visible in his oiled hair. And there in the corner, laughing the loudest of them all, was Burton Mack. He was wearing a pair of blue jeans and a green-and-black-checked flannel shirt, the sleeves rolled to show the long-sleeved thermal shirt he had on underneath. He wasn't a boy anymore, but even Ancil had to admit he was still a handsome man—lean face, square jaw, broad shoulders, a man muscled with the work of farming. Burton Mack. He laughed so hard that he kicked a leg up in front of him, and when his boot lifted off the floor, for just an instant, Ancil saw the sole: *Red Wing*.

Three strides took him to where Burton Mack was sitting.

"I don't think that's funny," Ancil said, and everyone in the barber shop, Burton Mack included, fell silent.

Then he said, "What's that, Ancil? I didn't quite catch that."

And the whoops and hoots and guffaws started in again.

Ancil stood there, feeling the heat come into his cheeks. He stood there a long time, letting the men laugh themselves out, and when finally they had and the silence waited for him to fill it, he said to Burton Mack, "I want you to stay away from my house."

For a good while, there was only the sound of the strop slapping as Tubby began to put an edge to a straight razor.

Then Burton Mack said, "Your house? What in the hell would I want at your house?"

Ellis Roderick ground out his cigarette in the smoking stand. Pat Best leaned back in his chair, his posture erect and his face solemn as if he'd suddenly found himself back at work at the funeral home.

Ancil felt certain that they both knew the story of Lucy and Burton Mack. It was no secret in town, particularly after that Saturday night when Ancil found him in the café and said to him loud enough that everyone could hear, "What kind of man tries to steal another man's wife? A lowlife, I'd say. A no-account. Is that the kind of man you want to be?" When Burton wouldn't answer him, wouldn't even look at him, just kept his eyes on his glass of Coca-Cola as he stirred it with the drinking straw, Ancil said, "You'll have to answer for what you've done. There'll come a day when you'll have to answer." Then he turned and walked out of the café, leaving everyone there to tell the story. How many times had it been told over the years? He knew if he'd walked into Tubby's at another time, he might have heard someone telling it to whoever was waiting for a haircut, the story of Burton and Lucy and the night Ancil confronted him, a story of love in ruins.

Now Ancil said, "I might be an old man, but I haven't forgotten. You know I haven't. You come around my house again, and I swear I'll do to you what I should've done all that time ago."

"That's ancient history," Burton Mack said.

"Not to me," said Ancil. "Not by a long shot. I've lived with it every day of my life."

Burton Mack stood up. He was only inches from Ancil. The two of them stood there, neither saying a word. Then Burton, in a soft voice, said, "You're right, Ancil. You're an old man. Time runs out. Life's shorter than we'd want it. Trust me, you should let it go."

Burton reached out and laid his hand on Ancil's shoulder, and that's what finally did it, broke through whatever restraint Ancil had been able to manage. That touch. That gentle voice. That holier-than-thou tone. It was more than he could stand.

He knocked Burton Mack's hand off his shoulder. Then he pushed his forearm into Burton's throat, driving him backward toward the wall, and he held him there, rage giving him the power he'd lacked on that long-ago Saturday night in the café when he'd still been sick to his stomach and weak with the thought of what Lucy had done. Now he was so gone-to-crazy his voice was a noise he didn't recognize. Later, he'd try to remember exactly what he said—at least what he tried to say. Something about pain. Something about trying to make a life beyond the moment when all reason to live went away. Something about standing back and taking a long look at your life. Something about knowing exactly who you were.

The only thing he could remember for sure that he said was, "That baby. That poor baby." But even that was said in a strangled voice, just a bunch of gobbledygook, something to be turned into a joke.

He let his arm drop to his side. He took a few uneasy steps backward and slumped down in a chair, his breath coming fast.

Burton Mack was coughing, sucking air down his windpipe.

Tubby stepped out from around his barber chair with his straight razor. "Everyone just calm down now," he said. "Everyone just take it easy."

"What'd you say, Ancil?" asked Burton when he could find his voice. "I couldn't quite make it out."

But all Ancil could do was shake his head as he got to his feet and headed toward the door.

He heard Burton say with a lisp, "I guess you can just kiss my goddamn ass."

LUCY

And so, in that long-ago day, there came a time when she had to tell Ancil that she was with child. She told him on a winter day when the snow was on the ground, as it was now, and the mercury in the thermometer had dropped below zero. A cold snap. Days and days of it. Days with anguish between them and no way for them to escape each other. Windows iced over on the inside. Ancil kept faucets dripping to save the pipes from freezing. The wind howled down the stovepipe while in the house their voices rose and fell, became silent, then started in again.

"Is it his?" Ancil said. "It is, isn't it?"

"I don't know," she told him, and it was true. She didn't. She and Ancil had been trying to have a baby for some time with no luck. The first time with Burtie, he had no condom, and she wanted him so badly she lied and said she was on the pill. After that, she couldn't bring herself to tell him the truth, and so they went on and on. "Ancil," she said, "what am I to do?"

This was the moment that always came back to her each winter, the moment when she left everything up to him. She stood at the frozen foods case in Ferguson's Market, about to reach for a carton of butter pecan ice cream—Ancil's favorite—and she remembered how lost she'd been, the child taking hold inside her, and how much she needed Ancil to tell her the right thing.

"It's your mistake," he said. "I'll be no part of it."

Which she took to mean he wouldn't allow her to stay if she kept the baby.

She realized then that she wanted to stay. Yes, it was exactly what she wanted. What had ever made her think that a boy like Burtie would have any interest in a life with her? If she went to him, what a shame she'd be, she and the child. Burtie had his college to finish. He had his whole life ahead of him, a life that, she was beginning to see now, would have no place in it for her.

So she did what she needed to do. She found a doctor in St. Louis who for the right price would perform a dilation and curettage and make the baby go away. She asked her sister, Eva, to drive her, Eva who had been dead now for years, Eva who said to her, "Oh, honey, this just breaks my heart."

That evening, when they came back, Ancil was sick with worry. Where had she been? Where had they driven in weather like this?

Eva helped her into bed. She closed the door and went out to face Ancil. Lucy heard their voices.

"Jesus, Eva," Ancil said. "I was ready to call the State Patrol."

His frantic worry soothed Lucy.

"Hush," said Eva. "You've got what you wanted."

Then she went on to tell him exactly where she and Lucy had been.

Lucy waited for Ancil to answer, but for a good while there was only the sound of wind rattling the windowpanes and the whoosh of the gas heating stove as it kicked on.

Finally, he said, "What I wanted? Oh, good Christ." His words came out in a nearly breathless rush, as if all the air had left him. Lucy heard the springs of his chair as he sat down. Then he said, in a shaky voice, "Was he with her? Does he know?"

"It was the two of us. You know he's back at school."

"But does he know?"

"That's something to ask Lucy," Eva said.

And finally he did. He waited until the morning after Eva, who had stayed the night, had gone. The sun was out, and from the bed Lucy could see the long icicles outside the window beginning to drip.

Ancil came into the room and stood by her bed. He said to her, "So it's done."

She couldn't look at him. Everything felt so strange. She knew she was in her own house, in the bed they shared, but all of the things around her—the baby-doll nightie tossed over the back of a chair, the bottles of perfume on the dresser, the combs for her hair, the bottles of lotion—seemed as if they belonged to someone else.

"It was for the best," she said.

"Is that what you decided?"

She turned then and looked at him. He'd spent the night pacing through the house, and once, though Lucy hadn't been sure, she thought she heard him sobbing. His clothes were wrinkled, his hair uncombed. His eyes were wide with fear or amazement or both.

"Wasn't it what you decided, too?" she said.

They looked at each other for a long time before he bit his lip and looked away and his face seemed to fall in on itself, cheeks hollowing with a sudden breath, brow sinking, chin wobbling, before he said, "Does he know?"

"No," she said. "This was our choice, yours and mine."

He took a long, staggered breath. He lifted his chin, drew his shoulders back. Then he gave the slightest nod and said, "Is there something I can bring you?"

She took that as a sign, the first sign that there might be a chance for them. Winter would pass and spring would come, and they would have years and years.

"Some tea," she said. "Some hot tea."

He went out to fetch it, and they went about the business of trying to forget.

ANCIL

What work it had been to get through the days. That's what Ancil recalled as he walked from Tubby's Barber Shop to Ferguson's Market. The grim effort of believing in the future at a time when so much seemed to be lost. He didn't know whether Lucy ever told Burton Mack about the child. He didn't know whether she ever talked to him again, and he couldn't know whether she regretted the decision she made to stay. He only knew he now felt embarrassed over the scene he'd made at Tubby's and ashamed to be a part of this story that he'd given new life to, this story of lives in disarray that would live longer than any of the people involved. The only person he could think to speak of it with was Lucy, who was just then stepping out of the Market, the box boy behind her, two bags of groceries in his arms.

"I can take those," Ancil said, and he reached to grab the bags.

But the boy was insistent. "That's all right, sir," he said. Such a polite and earnest boy. "It's what Mr. Ferguson pays me to do."

What could Ancil do but give in, even though what he really wanted was to be alone with Lucy so he could tell her about the footprints in the snow and the fool thing he did in the barber shop.

"It's the truck down there," he said, and raised his arm to point.

"You drive that silver Explorer?" the boy said. They all started walking toward the truck. "Do you live at the end of Cedar Street in the white house, the last one as you go out of town?"

"That's us," said Lucy. "The last house on your left."

"I was out there yesterday looking for you." At the truck, the boy put his foot on the front bumper, so he could use his knee to boost the grocery bags up in his arms as he adjusted his grip. "I knocked and knocked, but no answer. I even went around looking in windows, hoping I might raise someone."

Ancil looked down at the boy's boot. *Red Wing.*

"What in the hell did you want?" Ancil said. His mistaken assumption about who'd left those footprints filled him with anger. "What was so urgent that you felt you should go around looking in our windows?"

"I just…"

"You just what?" To think he'd raised a ruckus in Tubby's—had actually pressed his forearm into Burton Mack's throat—with no cause other than the bitter history between them left Ancil with little patience for the boy. "Well, what was it?"

"Ancil," Lucy said, "there's no need for that tone."

"It was your change from when you were in the store that day," the boy said. "You walked out without it. Didn't you find it in the envelope I put between your front door and the storm door? I didn't want to leave it like that, but like I said, I couldn't raise anyone."

Ancil had trouble finding his voice. He remembered now, laying the change on the counter while he reached for his keys. Lucy had gone ahead and was already on her way to the truck. He was in a hurry to catch up with her so he could be there to steady her in case she slipped on the ice. He knew now that he'd left the change—a five, two quarters, and a nickel—on the counter, and that had been the start of this sequence of events that had brought them to where they were now.

"Unlock the truck, Ancil," Lucy said, and he did what she told him to do.

Lucy reached into her purse and took out a ten-dollar bill. "You take this," she said to the boy. "Go on. Take it for your trouble. It was a good thing you did."

He put his hand out in front of him and shook his head. "I can't do that, ma'am. No, ma'am. It was no trouble at all."

Lucy looked at him a good while before folding the ten and putting it back into her purse. She reached out, then, and touched him on the cheek, just the way, Ancil thought, that a grandmother would, and the boy let her, as if he sensed somehow that this was what she needed to do and who would he be if he stopped her?

When she finally spoke, her voice had a bit of a quaver in it. "You're a good boy," she said. "Mercy."

"Yes, ma'am," the boy said, and then he was gone, on his way back to the store.

ANCIL AND LUCY

On the drive home, Ancil said to Lucy, "Who was that boy? Who are his people?"

She looked out the window at the snow that had started to fall. "That boy?" she said. She thought Ancil knew, and for a moment, she wondered if he did and only wanted to make her say the name. "That boy is Hattie's grandson."

The truck bumped over the railroad tracks. Then Ancil said, "Hattie Mack?"

"Yes," said Lucy, and then they rode along in silence, leaving Burton's name unspoken.

Ancil had been about to tell her what he'd done in the barber shop, but then she told him who the boy was, and he couldn't bring himself to go on. Sometimes, like now, the past was too much with them, and all Ancil knew to do was to be quiet, to hunker down, and wait.

The snow was slanting down hard from the west, already sticking to the street. He had to turn on the wipers to keep the windshield clear.

"Are your lights on?" Lucy asked.

Ancil reached forward and turned on his running lights. He said, "Lucy?"

He wanted to tell her about his anger, about the way it was always with him, and how it had boiled over in the barber shop. He wanted to tell her that he felt diminished by it all—what a scene he'd made—and that he saw the end of their life together getting closer and how he was glad that they'd managed to hold on. He wanted to say that he'd never stopped loving her, that the thing that had happened with Burton Mack and her had sliced him open, but little by little, day by day, he'd found a way to heal—until he saw those footprints in the snow and he started to wonder what someone looking in would make of the two of them.

Once upon a time, there was a man and a wife and a child that the wife decided she didn't want. He wanted to tell Lucy that if he mourned at all, it was for the fact that he'd led her to believe that this was what he wanted, too. If only he'd said the right things all those years ago, but really, at the time, who knew what those things were. Ancil wondered if she ever knew that he sometimes imagined who that child would have been and how he or she might have changed them in ways both wise and wonderful—taken them outside themselves, perhaps, made them look toward the future rather than so much into the past.

But then Lucy said, "It's slick out. Be careful."

And all Ancil could think to say was, "I will."

Lucy remembered how Burtie's grandson had let her touch his face. How much love had she never had the chance to give, all because a long time ago, Burtie had seemed like the world to her. She wondered if Ancil knew that she sometimes thought back to those days and especially that moment when the doctor in St. Louis asked her one more time if she was sure, and she said yes, yes she was. Did Ancil know how often she wished she could go back and change her mind, to leave that doctor's office and go to Burtie and tell him about the baby she was carrying and to ask him—please, Burtie, oh please—wasn't there a way that they could manage a life together? What did anyone know about what they wanted and what they didn't? What did anyone know about how to live a life?

At the last intersection before the straight shot out of town, a pickup truck with rusted fenders ran a stop sign.

"Watch out," Lucy said.

But Ancil had already seen the truck and he was slowing down, tapping his brakes, trying to keep the Explorer from sliding in the snow. The pickup shot through the intersection just a fraction of a second before the Explorer would have been in its path.

"It's all right," Ancil said.

"My word," said Lucy. "My heart is pounding."

"It's all right, old girl." Ancil reached over and patted her arm. "Don't worry. We're fine."

They drove on, the houses becoming fewer and farther apart as they went, the darkness coming on now—a quiet, cold night, the snow settling in over the houses and the fields. Ahead of him, Ancil could see the porch light that Lucy had thought to leave on, a faint glow in the distance. He drove toward that light, toward the house of last chances, where some bright thing between them—neither Ancil nor Lucy dared anymore to call it love—had almost gone out, but not now, not yet, not quite.

BELLY TALK

One morning, Jackie rode along with his father on his collection route. The day was clear, and all along the blacktop the sun glinted off silo domes. A jet left a white trail across the blue sky. Wheat fields, golden and ripe, stretched off to the horizon, but the newly planted beans and corn were already wanting for rain. The clay soil had cracked and turned as white as plaster.

"Riding high in the crow's nest," Jackie's father said.

"Yo ho ho," said Jackie, because this is what he always said when his father made his remark about the cab of the tank truck being high above the other vehicles on the blacktop. Jackie thought it was fine to be able to see into the cars they met, to be so far above them that he could see the tops of people's heads, even their feet on the floorboards. He made note of their shoes: sneakers, penny loafers, sandals, thongs. He thought each pair more magnificent than the one before it. His own shoes were made by a man in Vincennes, an old German with a leather apron and a red nose. One shoe, the right one, had a higher heel than the left, a thicker sole, because Jackie had been born with his right leg shorter. His shoes, the same kind year after year, were bulky oxfords, black with three pairs of eyelets for the cord laces. "Built to last," the shoemaker always said. "Not some silly shoe for you."

Jackie's father turned off the blacktop, onto the Bethlehem Church Road, and the tank truck bounced over the ruts. Jackie thought of the red letters on the side of the silver tank—MARATHON—the letters painted over the drawing of a runner, a flaming torch held in his hand. Jackie knew, because his father had told him, the story of how the Greeks had defeated the Persians at Marathon and how a runner had carried the news nearly twenty-five miles to Athens. Jackie couldn't imagine what it would be like to run that far. "You know when we drive to Vincennes to buy your shoes?" his father had said once. Jackie had pictured the highway running along muskmelon and watermelon patches in the bottomland, the bridge arcing over the Wabash River, and then the spires of the Old Cathedral rising up as they drove into the city. "That's how far," his father had said, and Jackie marveled at the enormity that could make a man run that distance, his lungs bursting with all he had to tell.

"Yo ho ho," Jackie said again, only this time he said it with his mouth closed and in a muffled voice that made it seem that the words came from a concealed place, the glove compartment, perhaps, or the toolbox on the seat, or the tank itself, full of gasoline, riding behind the cab.

"You crack me up," his father said. "You and that voice."

It was Jackie's talent, ventriloquism. He had learned how to form letters with his tongue, how to say words without moving his lips, only the tongue waggling in the cavity he made inside his mouth. He could imitate a muffled sound and then "throw" it. He made pies talk, drawers, closets, flowerpots. "Listen closely to everything around you," his ventriloquism manual said, "and when you speak, think what you want to hear."

He had learned his fifth-grade classmates' voices and could imitate them perfectly. On occasion, he would make it seem that one of them had said something outrageous right in the middle of class, and the teacher would stop her lesson to scold him. She had long ago learned his trick. Even if someone really did speak out of turn, she would put the blame on Jackie. If he tried to tell her the truth, she wouldn't believe him.

"No one likes a joker, mister," his mother told him. "You better cool your coppers."

He listened closely to what she said, learned that phrase. "Cool your coppers." He said it while drinking water one night at the supper table, a new trick he had perfected. "Cool your coppers," he said in his mother's voice, and his father laid down his fork, narrowed his eyes, and said to her, "What did you say?"

"I didn't say anything," she told him. "It's that son of yours. He's tormenting me. He thinks he's a funny man. Ha ha, Jackie. Ha ha."

He didn't think he was a funny man, not in his heart of hearts. There he thought he was, to borrow something his father often said after coming in from his route, the saddest goddamn thing he had ever seen. "It's the saddest goddamn thing," his father said, and then he launched into a story of a customer down on his luck. It was 1976, and the high oil prices, in light of the drought, made it hard for the farmers to keep up with their fuel bills.

Jackie knew all the words for what he was: a cripple, a handicap, a gimp. Often, when he was alone in his room, he stared at himself in the mirror. He pressed his lips together and let his tongue form words in his own voice, speaking everything that was inside him that he couldn't bear for anyone to hear. He talked about how sad he was—"goddamn gimp"—how it wasn't his fault—"I didn't do anything"—about how angry it made him. "I'll mow 'em down," he said, using the old Charlie McCarthy line he had heard on a tape of the ventriloquist, Edgar Bergen. The line sounded paltry when Jackie said it. "I swear, I'll mow 'em down."

Their first stop was a farm off the Bethlehem Church Road, a family named Marks. The boy, Eugene, was in Jackie's class at school. He had silky blond hair, bleached white by the sun in summer. He had prominent cheekbones and brilliant blue eyes. Jackie would have thought him quite lovely if not for the fact that Eugene scared him. Eugene was too big for his age, much bigger than Jackie, and he was clumsy and also stupid with his lessons. But what terrified Jackie most was how sometimes he would glance over at Eugene and find him staring at him with his blue eyes, not with anger, but with hunger, taking in every bit of him, and it made Jackie nervous because he had no idea what Eugene wanted.

"Teach me how you do that thing," he said to Jackie one day on the playground. It was the last day of school that spring. "That thing with your voice," Eugene said. His own voice was raspy as if he were always hoarse from shouting, and he had a lisp that further distinguished him.

"It's hard," Jackie said.

Eugene's blue eyes narrowed. "And I'm just a dummy, right?"

"I didn't mean that."

"I know what you meant." He gave Jackie a half-hearted push.

"No, really. I just meant it takes a lot of practice."

Eugene grabbed Jackie by the front of his shirt and pulled him close. His lips, when he spoke, brushed against Jackie's chin. "You better never tell no one I asked you. You hear me? Not no one."

"I won't tell," Jackie said.

Eugene kissed him—a shy, soft kiss on his cheek—before shoving him away and running into the school.

Jackie didn't know what to do with that kiss. Later, as the teacher passed out their report cards, he said, in Eugene's raspy, lisping voice, "Sweet Jesus. All F's."

Their teacher took him out in the hall. She put her hand on top of his head and nudged it forward until his nose was touching the cold metal of a locker. "You just stand there," she said. "You think about what a tragedy it is when the only way someone can build himself up is by belittling someone else. You don't know the life Eugene has. You ought to leave him alone."

Later, as they were getting on the school bus, Eugene tripped Jackie and sent him sprawling across the asphalt. For weeks there were scabs on his knees. Now the new skin was bright and pink. He rubbed his finger over his right knee as his father turned the tank truck into the Markses' lane.

Mr. Marks was cutting wheat in the field along the lane. He was emptying the hopper of his combine. The wheat streamed out of the spout angled over the high sideboards of the grain truck. Jackie followed his father over the freshly cut field, the wheat stubble tickling his ankles.

Mr. Marks was cursing at Eugene, who stood in the bed of the truck with a scoop shovel. "Goddamn it. Shovel it to the back. Goddamn it. Keep up."

The grain rushed out onto the hump of wheat that had built up as other hoppers were unloaded, and it was Eugene's job to level the pile by shoveling it to the back. It was clear to Jackie that he couldn't keep up. The shovel was too heavy; the wheat was coming too fast. Eugene floundered around in the wheat, which was nearly up to his thighs, and Jackie could feel the stumbling motion in his own legs. Finally, Mr. Marks climbed over the sideboards and jerked the shovel from Eugene's hands. "Get out of here." He gave him a rough shove. "Go on. I'll do it myself."

Eugene crawled over the sideboards and jumped to the ground. Jackie's father was standing on the truck's running board now, shouting to make himself heard over the noise of the combine and the wheat showering out of the spout. "I need something on account."

"On account of what?" Mr. Marks bent and hefted a shovel full of wheat. He slung it toward the back of the truck's bed. His hands were big, the fingers short and thick. One thumbnail was split; the creases of his knuckles were black with grime.

"A few dollars." Jackie's father had his ticket book out. He licked the point of his pencil. "Just so I can feel good about carrying you a while."

"I'm cutting wheat. I don't have time for you now. You'll get your money."

"I'd like to be sure."

"I'd like to be rich," Mr. Marks said. "Shit in one hand and wish in the other and see which one fills up first."

Jackie was embarrassed for his father, embarrassed for himself. Eugene had wandered over behind the combine, where the belts were spinning on their flywheels and the screens were huffing out chaff. "Jackie," Eugene called to him. Jackie went to where Eugene was waiting, and the two of them stood face to face in the shadow cast by the combine. Eugene bit down on his lip the way Jackie had seen him do in school when he was trying to figure out an arithmetic problem.

Jackie heard his father and Mr. Marks shouting, but now their voices, swallowed up by the combine's noise, were merely drones, vibrations of sound that buzzed the way Jackie sometimes heard voices from other people's conversations bleeding over when he was talking on the telephone—voices that sounded small and frantic, coming from some far-off place he couldn't imagine.

Eugene unfastened his blue jeans and let them slide down his hips and knees until they settled in a pile at his feet. His legs were striped with welts—some old and fading, others fresh and pink—and Jackie understood that Mr. Marks had left them there with his belt. Eugene didn't say a word. He merely took Jackie's hand and laid his finger on one of the welts. It was hot and moist. Jackie was afraid to look at Eugene, but finally he did, and what he saw was a face of dread and expectation, a look similar to the one Jackie's teacher had when she was waiting for students to answer questions, to demonstrate how much she had taught them. Eugene bowed his head, and his fine hair lifted up in the wind around the combine's flywheels. Something fluttered inside Jackie. He thought of the way his hip sometimes ached in the night, and he longed for someone to make it stop. He couldn't keep himself from tipping his own head down until it touched Eugene's. Jackie felt Eugene's silky hair on his forehead, and he thought it the most delightful sensation, the soft tickle of that wispy hair.

"I'm sorry I pushed you down," Eugene said. "That last day of school."

"I shouldn't have done your voice," said Jackie. "That was mean."

They stood there in the shadow, their heads nuzzling the way Jackie had often seen newborn calves rubbing along their mothers' flanks. He worked up the courage to ask Eugene the question that had been puzzling him all summer. "How come you kissed me?"

"There's all kinds of mean." Eugene's voice was a hoarse whisper. "We know it, don't we? You and me."

"Yes," Jackie said. "We know it."

Then the tractor's throttle fell back, and the combine's flywheels stopped spinning. The quiet startled him. His father called his name.

He drew his hand away from Eugene's wound, and, calling, "Here I am," he ran out into the light.

That evening, after his mother had finished washing dishes, Jackie tried to tell her about the welts on Eugene's legs. But before he could speak, something about the way the light came into the house—a muted light just before dusk—and the way his mother moved about the kitchen, slow and dreamy, mesmerized him, and he couldn't speak.

She untied her apron and hung it on the hook inside the pantry door. She hadn't yet turned on a light. The white curtains at the kitchen window lifted with the breeze, and Jackie smelled the grapes in the arbor, the one his father had kept alive during the drought by hauling river water from Vincennes. The grapes' perfume was splendid, as was the cooing of the mourning doves gathered in the lane and the three-note call of the whippoorwill somewhere far back in the woods.

"Well, Mr. Jackie," his mother said, "another day."

"Another dollar," he told her, which was what his father sometimes said.

She polished the faucet until it gleamed. "Oh, dumpling," she said. "Let's not think of your father's nasty business just now."

A radio sat on the counter. She switched it on and the gentle strains of dance music drifted into the room.

"That's 'You Belong to Me.'" She closed her eyes and swayed her head. "'See the pyramids along the Nile.'" She sang along. "Come on, Jackie. Dance with me."

It was the most extraordinary thing—to be moving with his mother across the floor. He followed her lead, listened to her humming along with the song. For the first time ever, he felt graceful. "You're really very light on your feet," his mother told him. He could smell the lemony scent of the dish detergent still on her hands. "You're a regular Fred Astaire." Then the radio went dead. "We must have blown a fuse." She sighed. "Oh dear."

She tried to move away from Jackie, but he wouldn't let her. He kept the song playing by imitating a saxophone, muted and raspy. To its melody, he danced with his mother there in the twilight, and the moment with Eugene in the wheat field was so far away, it was as if it had never happened at all.

Later, after Jackie's father had replaced the blown fuse, the three of them sat on the front porch and listened to the faint grumble of thunder in the west. The sky flickered with lightning flashes along the horizon, and Jackie's father stepped out into the yard. The days had been so hot and dry. Cars moving along the gravel roads trailed plumes of dust. The dust settled over the milkweed and the foxtail in the fencerows.

"Heat lightning," Jackie's mother said. "Just a fizzle and a tease."

But then a few raindrops fell. Jackie could hear them hitting the leaves on the grapevines in the arbor. He held out his hand and felt one drop and then another.

"Maybe I was wrong." His mother clapped her hands. "Maybe we're going to get a shower. If it comes a soaker, I'll kick off my shoes and dance barefoot in the rain. I won't care how wet I get. What about that, Jackie? Wouldn't that be fun?"

Jackie imagined his mother dancing in the rain, stomping about their yard, mud splattering her bare legs. She would slip and stumble and laugh like an idiot. He rested his head against the porch post, closed his eyes, and listened to the slow patter of the raindrops. He remembered the radio playing "You Belong to Me" in the kitchen and how marvelous it had been to dance with her.

Soon the raindrops stopped. Jackie opened his eyes and saw his father still standing in the yard, his hands on his hips, his head tipped back, face to the sky. "Not enough to lay the dust." He looked down at his feet. He kicked at the hard ground. "This drought. I swear. It's got me in a tight spot."

"There are people worse off than us," Jackie's mother said.

His father laughed. "That's right." He came back to the porch and laid his hand on the post just above where Jackie was resting his head. "And they all owe me money." There was still the distant sound of thunder. "Hear that? That's God having a good chuckle over all us poor dogs down here, us saps."

Jackie knew that something had happened. The good-natured fun his mother and father had poked at the drought and the tease of rain had dried up, and now there was an edge to his father's voice. He slapped his hand against the porch post. Jackie felt the vibration in his head.

"And all we can do," his father said, "is take it."

Jackie started to speak, and what he told his mother and father was that Eugene Marks, that day in the wheat field, had let down his blue jeans and had shown Jackie the welts on his legs. Jackie described how hot the welts had been when he had touched them. "I think his dad did it," he said. "I think he whips him with his belt."

For a good while, neither Jackie's mother nor his father spoke. Jackie saw them glance at each other and then look away. His mother crossed her arms over her chest as if she had suddenly caught a chill. His father pressed his lips together, took a deep breath through his nose, and then let it out.

"You know we love you, don't you, Jackie?" he said. "No matter…"

His mother interrupted him. "He knows that. You do, don't you, sweetie?"

"But Eugene," Jackie said.

His mother opened her arms and held them out to him. "Come here and give me a hug," she said. "Don't you worry about such awful things."

The next afternoon, Mr. Marks came to call. Jackie was helping his mother pick grapes. The vines were lush and green, and the Concords hung in blue-black clusters. Wasps flitted about, drinking from the grapes that the birds had pecked.

"Well, it's cool here in the shade." Mr. Marks took off his feed cap, and, holding it by the bill, he fanned his face. He closed his eyes and tipped back his head. "This is the greenest goddamn place I've seen in a long time."

"My husband likes grape jelly," Jackie's mother said.

"Your husband." Mr. Marks lowered his head and opened his eyes. "He's a real go-getter, ain't he? He gets his nose down a hole, he don't say quit."

Jackie knew, then, that Mr. Marks's visit had something to do with his unpaid bill.

"Let me tell you how it is, missus." Mr. Marks put his cap back on his head and tugged on the brim. "This drought's about done me in." His voice was quiet, nearly a whisper, as if he could barely say the words. "I'll be lucky if I get enough from my crops to rub two pennies together. I don't much have a pot to piss in. You tell your husband to leave off with his pestering me for money. Can't get blood from a turnip." He tried to laugh, but it came out in a hoarse croak. "Ain't that what they say?"

"Yes, that's the old joke," Jackie's mother said.

"Ain't no joke," said Mr. Marks. "Not when it's you with your head in the ground."

Jackie opened his mouth, meaning to ask after Eugene, to say something like, "How's Eugene? Is he all right? Please tell him I said hello." But just then a wasp swooped down from the Concords. It flew into Jackie's mouth. He felt its papery wings brush the inside of his cheek. He tried to spit it out. Then he did the only thing he could think: he ran. He ran out of the arbor, his blocky shoes slowing him. He felt the wasp sting him on the tongue. He stumbled and fell face first to the ground. He lay there in the dust, his tongue throbbing, the wasp gone away from him.

"Jackie," his mother called. She was picking him up from the dust. "Jackie. My word."

"We all got our hardships, don't we, missus?" Mr. Marks said. "No money, crops burned up. Crippled boy. We're all just trying to get along."

"He's not crippled," Jackie's mother said.

Mr. Marks reached up and picked a grape from the vine. "No, and the sun don't set in the west," he said. Then he mashed the grape between his finger and thumb.

———

That night, when Jackie's father came home and heard the story of the wasp, he laughed. "Partner," he said to Jackie. "That's the saddest goddamn thing."

Jackie's mother was at the stove, cooking down the grape pulp. Steam rose from the kettle and left her hair limp and her face red.

"Don't talk about him like he's one of your sob stories," she said.

Jackie was sitting on a stool by the sink. His mother had made a paste from baking soda and water and spread it over the wasp sting on his tongue. He could still taste the cakey powder, and he held his mouth open and his tongue partway out as if he were an old dog panting.

"Oh, I'm just having fun," his father said. "You know that, don't you, partner? Just trying to take the sting out. You get it? The sting?"

Jackie wished that his father would turn away, go into the living room and read the evening newspaper. He wished his mother would go back to her canning. He loved to watch her pour the hot jelly into the glass jars and then cover it with melted paraffin. "Sealing in all the goodness," she always said.

But now she said to Jackie's father, "You should have heard Bob Marks. That horrible man. He called Jackie a cripple. Your son." She banged the stirring spoon against the kettle's rim. "Crippled boy," she said, imitating Mr. Marks.

Jackie could hear something boiling up inside her, something that had nothing to do with Mr. Marks at all. She had done him so well, she had revealed herself. Jackie had read in his ventriloquist's manual that people once thought that ventriloquists' sounds came from their stomachs—belly talk—as if they had swallowed words whole, as if everything they had kept inside was now speaking.

The rage was rising in his father as well. "He said that? Goddamn him. Goddamn him to hell. He's got his own boy to see to. What gives him the right to talk that way about mine? I ought to go over there. I ought to…"

"You're not going anywhere," Jackie's mother said. The grapes were boiling and hissing, spattering juice onto the stove. She turned down the flame. "Listen to yourself. You sound just like him. Ugly. I don't know what's got into us."

"Are you telling me what to do?"

"Yes, I'm telling you."

"You can't stop me. I'll go over there, and I'll take Jackie with me. I'll tell Bob Marks, 'Go on. Say it. Say my boy's a cripple. Goddamn it, say it and I'll knock your teeth down your throat.'"

The sun was low on the horizon when Jackie and his father got to the Markses' farm. It was a red sun, the kind that on any other evening might have prompted Jackie's father to say, "Red at night, sailor's delight." But he wasn't talking now. He hadn't said a word since his threat to knock Bob Marks's teeth down his throat. Jackie had followed him out of their house, knowing without having to ask that this was what his father expected. His mother said, "Jackie, you stay here," but he hadn't listened to her. Something about the way she had imitated Mr. Marks had wounded him—something about the way her mouth had twisted and her eyes had squinted and she had spit the words as if she truly felt disgust for Jackie. He hadn't wanted to be alone with her.

Mr. Marks and Eugene were in the wheat field, and Jackie could see that they were finishing their supper. There were chicken bones in the wheat stubble at their feet and Mason jars of sweet tea and the spiral of an orange peel. Mr. Marks had the orange in his lap. He pulled off a section and used the point of his pocketknife blade to pick out the seeds. Then he held the section out to Eugene, who tipped back his head and opened his mouth the way Jackie had seen baby birds do. Mr. Marks laid the orange section on Eugene's tongue and then went to work on another piece.

Eugene closed his eyes and held the orange section in his mouth, sucking at it, his cheeks folding in and out. Jackie knew he was letting the juice trickle down his throat, making the sweet taste last. The grain truck, and the tractor and combine behind it, cast long shadows over the wheat stubble, and the aroma of the orange put a pleasant tang into the evening air.

The scene was something Jackie hadn't expected: Mr. Marks feeding orange sections to Eugene there in the shadows, so cool after the day's hot sun. Jackie could tell his father was startled, too, because he stopped walking through the field as if he were suddenly ashamed of the sound his boots were making in the stubble.

Finally Mr. Marks spoke. "Boy don't like to feel the seeds in his mouth." He finished picking out the seeds in the last piece of orange and then wiped his pocketknife blade across his leg. "It don't cost me nothing to work 'em out." He put the last orange section in Eugene's mouth and then turned his attention to Jackie's father. "I told your missus for you to back off. Now here you are again."

Jackie followed his father into the shadow. The scent of the orange was stronger there, and Jackie thought about how sweet his own home had smelled—the grapes cooking down on his mother's stove—while she told the story of Mr. Marks and what he had said that afternoon in the arbor.

"I hear you said more than that when you were over to my place today," Jackie's father said. "You had no call to talk about my son the way you did."

"What was it I said?" Mr. Marks used his pocketknife to trim the top off a callus on his forefinger. "I don't hardly recollect."

Jackie understood immediately what had happened. Mr. Marks, with his question, had cornered his father. He would have to say what he had come to dare Mr. Marks to say—crippled boy—and when he did, there it would be, the saddest goddamn thing.

But his father hesitated, unable to bring up the words. He shifted his weight from one foot to the other as if the wheat stubble had suddenly poked through his shoe leather. Jackie thought how long a straw would have to be to penetrate the shoe on his own foot, the one with the built-up heel, the thick sole. He couldn't bear the way his father danced about and couldn't find his voice.

Finally, Jackie told Mr. Marks, "You said I'm a crippled boy. That's what you told my mother."

There was something about the fact that Jackie had said the words himself—said them simply and with no hint of judgment—that cooled the heat that had been building between his father and Mr. Marks. Jackie could see it right away. He saw it in the way Mr. Marks closed his pocketknife and wrapped his hand around it and made it disappear. He saw it in the way his father glanced back over his shoulder to their car, idling in the lane, as if he were now anxious to leave.

Eugene leaned over and spit an orange seed, one that Mr. Marks had missed, onto the ground. "You hadn't ought to have said that about Jackie," he told his father, and Jackie saw Mr. Marks's knuckles whiten on the hand closed around the pocketknife. Jackie wished, then, that he had kept quiet. Eugene had been sitting there in the cool shadows enjoying the sweetness of the orange, and then Jackie had said what he had, and everything had soured. "He can't help himself," Eugene said, and Mr. Marks told him to hush.

"I mean it, Eugene." Mr. Marks reached down with his free hand and snapped off a fistful of wheat stubble. "Don't be poking at me. Not tonight. I'm burning a short fuse."

Jackie's father took a step toward Mr. Marks, and Mr. Marks rose to meet him. "You pay me that money you owe," Jackie's father said. "You pay me by the end of the week, or I'll make it rough for you."

Mr. Marks poked the blunt tip of the pocketknife casing into Jackie's father's chest. "Mister," he said, "you don't know what rough is."

"End of the week," said Jackie's father, and then he turned, and Jackie followed him back to their car.

It was the scent of the orange that Jackie remembered the next day when his father came home with the news that Eugene was dead, that sometime in the night Bob Marks had beat him to death with his fists. Jackie was in his room, but he could hear his father and mother talking on the porch.

"Cracked his skull," his father said. "His own boy. I heard it in town."

Jackie's mother didn't answer right away, and when she did, it was in a whimper that chilled Jackie. He could imagine her at the moment when she first learned he was crippled, and he understood that everything he felt when he spoke to himself in front of his mirror—goddamn gimp—belonged to his parents, too.

"We knew all about it," his mother said. "We knew Bob Marks was whipping that boy."

"A lot of people knew. It wasn't just us."

"Yes, a lot of us, and not one of us said a word."

"Just Jackie."

"And I told him not to think of it. Doesn't he have enough to face? Don't we all? How ugly can the world be and any of us still be able to stand it?"

Jackie listened closely, not just to what his parents were saying but also to the silences around their words, to the shadows of breath. What he heard amazed him. He had no words for the feeling that came over him, but he recognized it from Eugene's kiss on the playground, from the quiver in his stomach when he had touched the welt on Eugene's leg, from the way his throat had filled when he had watched Mr. Marks feed Eugene that orange. It was theirs now, Jackie thought—his and his mother's and his father's. This trembling.

"Sweet Jesus," he whispered in Eugene's rasp and lisp.

He listened to the screen door creak open and then close with a faint tap against the jamb. He heard his parents' footsteps on the stairs—his mother's light scuff, his father's heavy tread. He waited for them to open his door.

"Sweet Jesus," he said again, this time in a voice so full it could be no one's but his own.

BAD FAMILY

EACH WEDNESDAY, MISS CHANG DRIVES DOWNTOWN TO THE YMCA where, for two hours, couples practice the waltz, the swing, the Texas Two-Step. Often, she stands at the fringe of the dancers because she comes alone and must wait until she has worked up enough nerve to say to another woman, "You must excuse, yes?" Usually, the other women relinquish their partners to her graciously, but from time to time someone will hesitate, obviously annoyed, obviously wishing Miss Chang would choose some other couple to disturb. "That Chinese woman," she hears someone say one night. "Why would a Chinese woman want to learn the Cotton-Eyed Joe?"

She wants to learn because she has never been graceful. When she was a girl, Mao sent people to the countryside to learn the meaning of work from the peasants. Miss Chang traveled to Inner Mongolia. She was fifteen, and for eight years she dug ditches and water wells. She wore men's trousers, the legs rolled to her knees. She slogged through the muck, her steps heavy and thick. Even now, her feet on solid ground, she carries the hobbled motion in her legs. All day at the Mane Attraction Beauty Salon, she moves in halting steps as she shampoos, cuts, and perms. Only her hands, small and delicate, are agile and quick. She rarely drops a comb. Her fingers massage other women's scalps. Sometimes she remembers how Mao's Red Guard, because her parents were intellectuals who had gone to the university, cut her mother's hair and shaved one half of her head so, when she went out on the street, everyone would know she came from a "bad" family. Now Miss Chang's customers tilt their heads back into the cupped groove of the shampooing sink. They close their eyes. "Mmmmm," they say, and Miss Chang closes her eyes too, and tries to feel the same luxurious motion they must feel when her fingers dance across their heads.

She has tried T'ai Chi, but she lacked discipline and balance; yoga, but she tired of tying and untying the knot of herself. She likes to watch *Club Dance* on The Nashville Network. She marvels over how women who have no natural claim to grace—who are too old, too heavy—can become so radiant, so lithe, in their cowboy boots and sequined shirts, bright scarves tied around their necks. The women spin and step, all of them smiling, never once looking down at their feet, as if this is a snap, this dancing, this beautiful liquid motion they have become.

"Some are water, some are stone," her mother told her when Miss Chang came back from Mongolia, her body bulky and hard with muscle, a slim, delicate girl no more. "You, Li, you shouldn't wait for a husband. You should go to the university instead."

By this time, the American president, Nixon, had come to China—Mao had opened his arms to the West—and now there were even Americans teaching English at the university. Miss Chang fell in love with one of them, a slim, gentle man named Don. No one could understand how she could love an American, but she did, and when Don promised to uphold China's socialist principles, the government gave him permission to marry her. Then they managed to leave China, a feat that thrilled both of them, particularly Don, who boasted to friends in America that he had smuggled a China doll out of the country.

And now she is Lily, a name she has chosen for herself. Lily Chang because she has taken back her father's name. Lily because she wants to think of herself as a water flower, pretty and delicate. Here in Nebraska, she sees the plains stretch out for miles to the distant horizon, looks up at the vast sky, open and blue above her, and believes all things are possible, even at her age, even now.

———

Since their divorce, Don has been eager to do whatever Miss Chang asks, even agreeing to allow her to attend the dance class he teaches with his new wife, Polly. Miss Chang knows he can't forgive himself for taking her from her family and her country only to divorce her. "You should come after me with a butcher knife," he said to her once. "I wouldn't blame you." She told him, "Life's too short to drag around a bitter heart. What's done is done."

She lets him take care of odd jobs around her townhouse. He changes her furnace filters, mows her lawn, tends to her landscaping. Polly never complains. The joke among the three of them is, all it takes is a divorce to make a marriage work. "Why can't people be kind to each other?" Polly says.

Miss Chang has never been able to dislike her, because before the divorce, the three of them were friends. Saturday nights, they would go to the Pla Mor Ballroom to listen to music, and sometimes Don and Polly danced. Miss Chang was always too shy, and besides, she liked to watch Don dance. His steps, precise and fluent, seemed to carry him back to some ancient form of himself—the patient, humble teacher she had fallen in love with in China. He had given her, his student, words and grammar, a language with which to speak her heart, but in America, his land, he became boastful and pedantic. "You don't know what it's like here," he told her. "It's a different world. Everyone's out for himself. You'll have to get an edge to you if you want to get along. I'll teach you."

He lectured her on customs and conduct. If a car cut in front of her on the street, she was to honk her horn and drive as close to the other car's bumper as she could. "Make the asshole sweat," Don told her. "He'll think twice before he cuts someone off again." When someone called on the telephone wanting money for this cause or that, she was to hang up. "We'll pick our charities," he said. "We won't have them forced upon us." And she wasn't to pay any attention to express line limits in the supermarket. "Groceries are groceries. It's all highway robbery. Who's counting?"

It was his constant watch and guard that eventually drove them apart. "You won't listen to me," he told her. "Why won't you listen?"

She wouldn't listen because she found the vulgar behavior he prescribed unsavory. She could never imagine Polly doing any of the things Don suggested. Polly was too kind, too polite. "Milk and honey," Don said once. "A real lady."

With Miss Chang, it was a different story. With Miss Chang, it was always, "You've got to toughen up. You can't let people run over you." Don harped and harped at her. But on Saturdays, when they went with Polly to the Pla Mor Ballroom, he was a gentleman. He held doors open for Polly and Miss Chang, pulled out their chairs, stood each time one of them left the table. He became the charming guardian who had first won her.

Even now, under Polly's spell, he is eager and quick to serve. When Miss Chang thinks of the three of them and the common affection they have been able to manage despite the divorce, she feels a spark kindle inside her, and she knows it is her heart, and she knows it fires with longing and with rage.

Wednesday nights, at the YMCA, it embarrasses Miss Chang to have to bow to the American women, to ask for their husbands. She understands what an intrusion she is, and deep down, though she knows it is mean-spirited of her, she imagines Don could see all this coming when he agreed to let her attend the class without a partner.

One night, he takes her by the hand and says, "Come on. Show me what you've learned."

Polly is strolling around the gymnasium, weaving in and out through the couples, stopping to watch this one or that. Miss Chang admires her small feet, her narrow waist, the way she steps across the waxed floor when she and Don demonstrate a dance.

But now Miss Chang is dancing with Don. Her left hand is on his shoulder; her right palm, meeting his left, is held out into the air at their side. They are doing the waltz, and she has no trouble following Don's step-close-step. But she is on guard, waiting for the moment when he will push against her left hand, the slightest pressure, and begin to promenade her backward. "Walk your lady across the floor, gents," he said the first night of class. "Don't bore her with the easy stuff. She deserves a chance to put on a show."

Don is chewing gum, and Miss Chang can smell his sweet candy breath. His gray hair is parted neatly on the side, and the soft knit weave of his polo shirt is pleasant to touch. She is dancing with him, and she knows people are watching. He has chosen her, Lily Chang, and she is in step with him, in time with the music, and soon he will press her backward, and she won't miss a beat. Her feet will glide back as his own come forward, and she won't stumble or hesitate. She'll escape the thick weight of herself, and even if, as her mother suggested all those years ago, she be stone, she will be, for a short time, a small stone, flat and smooth, skipping lightly across the surface of a pond.

But Don never presses against her hand. He keeps her moving in the simple one-two-three box, and soon she starts to feel the insult of it all. He doesn't think her capable of anything beyond tracing that box over and over, and once she knows that, she feels a great rage and shame rise up in her.

"Good," he says. "Good."

Miss Chang has already begun to despise him. So smug he is, with his neatly combed hair and his fresh breath and his soft, soft shirt. She intentionally botches a step, and another, and another, until their dancing is chaos, all helter-skelter, and he, for the first time, looks clumsy and inept.

"All right," he says, squeezing her hand to make her stop. "That's enough."

"Yes," she tells him. "It's quite enough. Thank you."

She sees Polly across the gymnasium, watching them, her hands on her hips as if to say, "What in the world was that?"

D-I-E

Miss Chang cuts the letters from newspaper headlines and glues them to a sheet of paper. The cliché—this stunt she's picked up from some detective show on television—irritates her, but still she uses her old

Underwood typewriter to address the envelope: "Mr. and Mrs. Donald Brawner, 811 South Waltz Road." The irony of the address only deepens her anger. She imagines Don and Polly falling in love with the fortunate coincidence—two dancers living on Waltz Road—and for a moment she wishes she had someone, anyone, to whom she could announce, "It's me. It's Lily Chang. I'm the one sending this note."

Miss Chang's townhouse is in a new subdivision called Sherwood Forest, but there are few trees there, only the ornamental Bradford pears planted along the driveways and some Japanese maples in front yards. Don cares for her carpet juniper and her evergreen shrubs and the chrysanthemums that bloom yellow and red each fall. In China, Miss Chang's father had been the director of a botanical garden, but when Mao's revolution came, the Red Guard destroyed the greenhouses, torched azaleas and dwarf cedars and rhododendrons because they were bourgeois. Here, behind her townhouse, there is only a large open space of lawn that stretches, without tree or hedge, from neighbor to neighbor. The lone exception is the house directly behind Miss Chang's, the house of Miss Shabazz Shabazz, whose backyard is shaded by the only oak tree the developers must have spared and a white pine that carpets the ground with its fragrant needles. And there is a willow tree, its feathery branches sweeping down like the hair of the beautiful young girls who come to Miss Chang at the salon.

Miss Shabazz Shabazz's daughter is also named Shabazz, but to avoid confusion she is known as Buzzy. Buzzy Shabazz is thirteen, and she has skin the color of caramel, a shade closer to Miss Chang's own than to the deep ebony of Miss Shabazz Shabazz. The day Miss Chang went to their house to welcome them to the neighborhood, Miss Shabazz Shabazz explained how she had recently divorced her husband. "A white man," she said. "I'm sure I don't have to tell you anything more."

From the beginning, there was this implicit bond between them. "Women of color," Miss Shabazz Shabazz seemed to be saying. "Women warriors. We'll look out for each other." It pleased Miss Chang to think of herself and Miss Shabazz Shabazz united, but at the same time, she had no desire to poison herself with distrust. Of course, she knew there were people in the world who thought her dirty and vile. Sometimes, when new customers came to the shop and Miss Chang told them she was ready, they made up flimsy excuses—they had forgotten to put money in their parking meters, they had left their ovens on at home— and they would hurry away, never to return, and Miss Chang would know. She tried to let her anger wash over her like a wave rolling to a crest and then falling away.

But the first time she met Miss Shabazz Shabazz, she felt the woman's rage seep into her. Miss Chang saw it in the glint of the heavy gold rings Miss Shabazz Shabazz wore, rings shaped like spear points, and in her high, sharp cheekbones, and the hair cut close to her skull and nubbed with patches of gray. "I gave my daughter my last name," Miss Shabazz Shabazz told Miss Chang. "My African name, just as my father did for me. 'That way,' he told me, 'no man will ever be able to take it from you.'"

This year, Buzzy Shabazz and her friends play a game called Marco Polo. It is a game Miss Chang has heard her customers talk about, a swimming pool game carried over now from summer to autumn, from water to dry land. Each evening after school, a large number of children gather in the open lawn behind Miss Chang's, most of them, like Buzzy Shabazz, almost at an age when such games will be lost to them. There is a desperate urgency to their play, as if they know they are leaving childhood forever and must celebrate its wild, rollicking joy as often as they can.

The game, as far as Miss Chang can tell, is a frenetic, almost maniacal combination of blind man's bluff and tag. One person wears a blindfold and runs about trying to tag someone else. The rule is this: the person who is "it" calls out "Marco," the others must answer "Polo." By repeating the call again and again and again, the person who is "it" tries to zero in on someone else. As soon as another person is tagged, that person becomes it, and the game goes on. It goes on and on until the light fades and Miss Chang can barely see the children, can only hear their feet thundering across the ground as they run and the incessant chant of "Marco," "Polo," until darkness finally takes the game from them, and in the sudden calm the call rattles around in Miss Chang's head.

One night, she closes her eyes and tries to imagine the children, blind to any limits of range or motion, racing across the grass. When they run, they come dangerously close to houses.

Sometimes they lose their balance and fall. They frighten away the birds that come to feed at Miss Chang's patio. She misses the birds, but she loves to watch the children run, especially Buzzy Shabazz, who is sleek and fast. When Miss Chang watches her, she thinks of the marvelous bodies of athletes she sees on television. While Buzzy and the other children run, their shouts disturbing the usual neighborhood calm, Miss Shabazz Shabazz strolls about her yard, off limits to the children because of its trees. She is regal and leonine, as if this wild abandon is somehow beneath her concern, and Miss Chang starts to resent her and her oak tree and her willow and her pine.

One night at dance class, a door slams shut, and Polly screams. "Not to worry," Miss Chang says. "It's just the wind."

B-A-N-G-! Y-O-U-'-R-E D-E-A-D

Polly comes in each Friday for a wash-and-set. She has fine hair, thinning on the top, and Miss Chang has to use a mild shampoo and conditioner and a pick to gently fluff the hair when she is done. Still, when she has finished, she can see Polly's white, white scalp shining through the airy puff of hair. Miss Chang imagines birds plucking away the strands one by one until Polly is bald.

Goldfinches, cardinals, chickadees, doves: these are the birds that used to come to Miss Chang's patio. But now, instead of their songs, she hears the raucous shouts of the children—"Marco Polo"—as if they are searching for him, calling to him over the barren plains of Mongolia where Miss Chang used to watch herds of running-free horses race to drink from the rock wells she had dug, all for the good of the Party, all for Daddy Mao.

Sometimes in Nebraska, the wind's howl unhinges her. The peasants in Mongolia believed a weasel could become a spirit and come into a person and make that person do crazy things. It must be the same with the wind, Miss Chang thinks, a wind like the one that swept Genghis Khan across Asia, a wind that makes her think she can do whatever she wants, can send note after note to Polly and Don, and no one will ever know.

I-'-V-E G-O-T Y-O-U-R N-U-M-B-E-R

One night, after dance class, Miss Chang walks into the ladies' room at the YMCA and finds Polly standing at the sink, sobbing. The delicate wings of her shoulder blades flutter.

"Please excuse," Miss Chang says, and turns to leave.

Polly grabs her by the hand. "Stay with me," she says. "Stay just a while. I don't want to go home."

"Something is wrong?" Miss Chang says. "Something at your house?"

"There are people in the world," Polly says. "Horrid people. We've been getting threatening notes in the mail."

Miss Chang feels, in the tight grip of Polly's hand, her tremendous fear, and she wants to tell her there is no need to be afraid; the notes have been a hoax. But of course she can't admit her guilt, and, too, Polly's confidence flatters her. Out of all the people she might have told, she's chosen her, Lily Chang.

"It's probably nothing," Miss Chang says. "Probably just some crank. Some cuckoo bird. Who would want to hurt you?"

"It's Don," says Polly. "He's the one they're after. He said this would happen, and now it has."

Toward the end of summer, Polly says, Don received a call from a man named Eddie Ball, the same Eddie Ball who had been a key figure a few years before in the trial of a Lincoln woman who had hired a hit man to kill her husband. Eddie Ball, the prosecutors contended, had been the one to put the woman in touch with the killer. Eddie

Ball, everyone said—though the trial had never proved it—had mob connections.

"He wanted someone to write his story," Polly says, "and someone at the university had suggested Don. Well, you can imagine Don's reaction. 'I won't do that,' he told Eddie Ball. 'Not for a lowlife like you.' You know how Don is. And Eddie Ball said to him, 'You should be careful what you say to a man. You should be able to live with whatever happens now. I've got your number. I know where you live.'"

"Those notes," Miss Chang says. "Have you told the police?"

Polly nods. "They drive by our house a couple of times each night. They've told us to be careful. That's about it. Lily, I'm scared. I think it's true about Eddie Ball. I think he knows people."

Miss Chang knows practically no one besides Polly and Don. She has acquaintances, neighbors mostly like Miss Shabazz Shabazz, and there are the other hair stylists at the Mane Attraction, and her customers, but no one she would really call a friend. Other than Wednesdays, when she goes to the YMCA for her dance class, she spends her evenings alone. She watches Buzzy Shabazz and her friends race across her lawn; then she turns on her television to catch *Club Dance*. Before she started sending Don and Polly the notes, her quiet life pleased her with its plainness and its modesty. Still, when she saw the flit and bob of a goldfinch in flight, its bright yellow could stun her, and when she watched the women dancing on television, their steps could make her heart ache for love. And now she has become a thug, a shady character like this Eddie Ball. Suddenly, it saddens her to think of all the people in the world and the ways they can find to hurt one another when all along what they want—what everyone must surely want—is to feel that they are safe and cared for, a part of some circle larger than any shape they could manage on their own.

In the middle of summer, not long after she had welcomed Miss Shabazz Shabazz to the neighborhood, a policeman came to Miss Chang's door. Someone, he explained, had stolen a birdbath from Miss Shabazz Shabazz's yard. And someone had dug up a crepe myrtle and had thrown it onto Miss Shabazz Shabazz's porch. Had Miss Chang heard anything, the policeman wanted to know. Had she noticed anything suspicious? No, nothing, Miss Chang told him. "Well," the policeman said, "your neighbor is plenty hot about this. She's afraid it's because she's black. I wouldn't want to be in her way if she got started."

After that, Miss Chang stayed away from Miss Shabazz Shabazz. She wanted no part of trouble. If someone had stolen the birdbath and dug up the crepe myrtle because they didn't like the idea of blacks living in the neighborhood, how easy it would be for them to feel the same way about Miss Chang, especially if they saw her keeping company with Miss Shabazz Shabazz.

One evening, Don comes to put in Miss Chang's storm windows. "So," he says to her, "Polly told you about Eddie Ball."

"Yes," Miss Chang says, "she told me."

They are upstairs in the spare bedroom, and Don has just opened a window. She can hear the squeals and shouts of Buzzy Shabazz and her friends.

"I've always had a big mouth, haven't I, Lily?"

"You tried to tell me too much."

"I thought I had to take care of you. You seemed so frightened when we first came here."

"I'm not frightened now," she says. "You are."

"You're right," he says. "And so is Polly. And we don't know what to do."

He bows his head, and Miss Chang, from habit, does the same. So many times, in China, they sat beside each other, arms touching, as he watched her write out verb conjugations. Now she notices that one of his shoes is untied. She remembers one day downtown, after she had come to America, a strange man asked her to tie his shoes. "I can't believe you did that," Don said when she told him the story. "His shoes were untied," she said. "He wanted someone to help him."

Don stoops to tie his own shoe; his fingers fumble with the laces. And suddenly something comes undone in Miss Chang, the knotted fist of her bitter heart, and she says to him, "You'll come here. That's what you'll do. You and Polly. You'll live with me until this is all over and it's safe for you to go home."

"Here?" Don lifts his head. Sunlight slants across his face. "Polly and I? We can't."

"You will," Miss Chang says.

"The three of us? Here?"

Miss Chang nods. "We will."

Her invitation startles her. She knows if she were telling a story, this would be the place where her listeners would frown and shake their heads and call her a liar. "You didn't," someone might say. "Well, I can't believe it." She thinks of her customers, and how they tell her things they wouldn't dare tell the people they love the most. She lets them talk until they know they've said too much and they're embarrassed by what they've shown of themselves. "You never would have guessed that about me, would you?" someone might say. "Oh, I shouldn't have told you any of that." Some stories, she knows, are too true to be told, but she can't escape this fact: she has asked Don and Polly, her ex-husband and his wife, to stay with her, and because they are frightened, they have said yes.

It is the first time since her divorce that Miss Chang has someone in the house each evening to take meals with her, to sit with her and chat, to make her feel safer in the night when she sleeps, pleased to know she isn't alone. And they are such good company. Relaxed now that they are away from their own home, they are cheerful and eager to please Miss Chang. The first night, Don plays records on his phonograph and takes turns dancing with her and Polly. Later, they watch *Club Dance* and Don shows Miss Chang the steps to the Achy-Breaky. When it is time to say goodnight, Polly kisses her on the cheek.

"I can't tell you how much this means to us," Polly says. "I'm glad we can still be friends, considering the circumstances."

"Ancient history," Miss Chang says with a wave of her hand. "Sleep well."

They sleep in the spare bedroom. They use the guest bathroom. Miss Chang lays out fresh towels and washcloths. Each morning, she rises early to prepare breakfast and sees a dove or two at the patio feeder. When she leaves the house for work, she starts to miss Don and Polly, not with the raw yearning she felt when she left her parents for Mongolia, but with a sweet, lovely anticipation that she will come home and there Don and Polly will be to welcome her.

"Lily," Polly says to her one evening. "My sweet, sweet Lily."

"Thank you," Don says. "Thank you for having us here."

Then one night Polly complains about Buzzy Shabazz and her friends and their game of Marco Polo. Polly and Miss Chang and Don are eating dinner, and through the patio doors they can see Buzzy Shabazz with a white handkerchief tied around her eyes. She is running wildly, her arms outstretched. She calls and her friends answer until the air is filled with their din, and it's impossible to distinguish their words. Their sound is a shriek, a siren, the wind's howl.

"That noise," Polly says. "That dreadful noise. I don't know how you live with it. I really don't. Whose children are they?"

"Neighborhood children," Miss Chang says. "The girl with the blindfold is Buzzy Shabazz. She lives with her mother in that house. There. The one with the beautiful yard."

Don leans forward to get a better look at Miss Shabazz Shabazz's yard. "Her white pine needs to be pruned," he says. "You should tell her that."

"Miss Shabazz Shabazz?" says Miss Chang. "You don't know Miss Shabazz Shabazz."

"I know those children are horrid," says Polly.

"They're trespassing," says Don. "This is your property. Don't they realize that? They have no right to be here."

After dinner, Miss Chang pays a visit to Miss Shabazz Shabazz. "Your trees are lovely," Miss Chang says. "But your pine. It needs pruning."

Miss Shabazz Shabazz is gathering firewood from the stack behind her utility shed, and when Miss Chang mentions the pine tree, Miss Shabazz Shabazz drops the canvas tote sling she has filled with logs and they clatter about on the ground. "Not a word for months," she says, "and now you come to stick your nose in my business? Speak up. Are you a mouse? Are you a little mouse who's crawled out of my firewood?"

Miss Chang remembers how, when the schools in China finally reopened after the revolution began, she and the other students recited from Mao's Red Book. "Chairman Mao says this" and "Chairman Mao says that," over and over until the slogans stuck in their heads. The one that comes to her now is, "Chairman Mao says, 'A revolution is not a dinner party.'" So she says to Miss Shabazz Shabazz, "It's your daughter. Your Buzzy. I don't want her and her friends playing their game in my yard."

Miss Shabazz Shabazz laughs. Her lips are the color of cranberries. Her teeth are white, white, white. The power of her laugh startles Miss Chang.

"Don't be silly," Miss Shabazz Shabazz says. "Look at your yard." She points behind Miss Chang to the open space. "There's nothing there. Let children be children. What harm can they do?"

Each evening, after work, Miss Chang stops by Don and Polly's house to collect their mail. She brings it to them, and they sort through the envelopes. When they find nothing out of the ordinary, they give each other a hug and Miss Chang knows she is one day closer to losing them. "It looks like this is all going to blow over," Don says. "Then we can go home, Lily, and get out of your hair."

I K-N-O-W W-H-E-R-E Y-O-U L-I-V-E

When Don reads the note, he runs a hand over his head, mussing his hair. "That's it," he says to Polly. "I won't be bullied."

Polly reads the note and folds it very neatly along the creases Miss Chang's own fingers have traced in the paper. "It's your fault," Polly says, and her voice is very low and even. "You had to open your mouth. You couldn't keep quiet. I've always hated that about you."

And suddenly, Don is shouting. "You put up with too much." He is waving his arms about. "Damn it, Polly. You always have."

"I just expect the best from people," Polly says, still in that calm voice. "That's all."

"Well, I'm going to put an end to this," Don says. "I'm going to stop it tonight."

Miss Chang remembers the last night Don spent with her. He was cutting a coupon from the back of a cracker box, and he was having trouble keeping the scissors moving in a straight line through the cardboard. Finally, he slammed the scissors down on the counter, and he told her he thought he should leave. "For how long?" she asked him. "A few hours?" "For good," he said. "Not come back?" "No, Li. I won't come back."

And now, again, he is moving toward the door.

"Lily, you talk to him." Polly turns to her, and Miss Chang thinks of how Polly comes to her at the Mane Attraction and begs her to do something with her thin hair, trusts her to do what she can to hide her baldness. "You tell him, Lily. You tell him he can't go."

Miss Chang knows she should stop him. She knows she should say, "Wait. Let me tell you. You won't believe this. It's the craziest thing." But all she can think of is Mao's Red Guard and how they tore silk clothes from people on the street, how they destroyed Ming Dynasty vases, burned books, bulldozed the graveyards because burial was an old custom and took up valuable land. No more old ideas, no more old culture, no more old customs, no more old habits. She remembers the times when Don told her how to behave in America. "Toughen up," he told her. "Get mean." If she confesses to sending the notes, she imagines his smug grin and how he might say, "You see. I was right all along." When what he can never know—what he never even suspected those days at the university, when she so meekly recited her verb conjugations—is the cold, cold heart she could never leave behind her in China.

So she says nothing. And then, Don is gone.

"Lily," Polly says. "You've been so good to us. And now look at what we've brought into your house."

After Don has left for Eddie Ball's, Miss Chang steps out onto her patio, and there is Buzzy Shabazz only a few feet away. She hoists her green schoolbag up on her shoulder. She is wearing high-top leather basketball shoes, the laces undone.

"Buzzy. Buzzy Shabazz," Miss Chang says. "I want to ask you something."

"My mother told me not to listen to you," says Buzzy Shabazz.

One night last summer before the episode with the birdbath and the crepe myrtle, Buzzy Shabazz came to Miss Chang's house and asked Miss Chang to please tell her about the pretty yellow birds she saw flying onto Miss Chang's patio. "Goldfinches," said Miss Chang. How, Buzzy Shabazz wanted to know, could she and her mother get such beautiful birds to come into their yard. Miss Chang remembered how long it had taken her to entice the goldfinches, how she had hung the feeding tube filled with niger seed and had waited and waited for her little goldies to find it. And now that they had, she hated to risk losing even one of them to her new neighbors. Of course, she knew it was selfish of her, but in China there had been so few birds (once Mao had even ordered all the sparrows killed), she delighted now to the brilliant yellow birds with their black caps and wings and the playful way they grasped the rungs of the feeding tube with their claws and then flipped upside down to peck at niger seed through the slots below them. "I'm sorry," she told Buzzy Shabazz. "This is something I cannot tell."

Now Miss Chang says to the girl, "Every night you and your friends run through my yard." Miss Chang points toward Buzzy Shabazz's house. "How would you like it if I came into your yard? If I was an intruder come there uninvited?"

Buzzy Shabazz's eyes open wide. "It was you," she says. "You're the one."

"I'm not saying I've ever done it," Miss Chang says. "I'd never even dream of it."

"You stole our birdbath, and you dug up our bush."

"No."

"You, you, you."

Buzzy Shabazz's voice is rising, the way it does when she plays Marco Polo. It echoes across the empty expanse of Miss Chang's yard, and all she wants is to make Buzzy Shabazz be quiet. She tries to clamp her hand over the girl's mouth, but Buzzy Shabazz grabs her arm, and somehow Miss Chang's hand ends up caught between Buzzy Shabazz's shoulder and the strap of her schoolbag. Miss Chang is trying to let go, but she can't. And Buzzy Shabazz is trying to yank herself away from Miss Chang. The two of them are dancing about the yard, and finally, the only way Miss Chang can free herself is to put her other hand against Buzzy Shabazz's sternum and push. When she does, Buzzy Shabazz falls backward, striking her head, with a loud thud, on the ground.

Miss Chang tries to apologize. "I didn't mean to hurt you," she says. "This is all a mistake."

But Buzzy Shabazz is on her feet and running to her yard, where Miss Shabazz Shabazz has come out to her white pine, pruning shears in hand.

Miss Chang goes into her own house, and there is Polly sitting on the loveseat, staring out the window. After the divorce, Polly came to Miss Chang, and she asked her if she would mind if she started dating Don. "If it bothers you, Lily, I won't do it."

"Do you love him?" Miss Chang wanted to know.

She remembers how Polly ducked her head like a starstruck girl. "Yes, Lily. I think I do."

"Then why ask my permission?"

"I don't want to hurt you, Lily. You've been so good to me. Dear Lily. I love you, too."

Now Miss Chang is crying. She is thinking about Don on his way to Eddie Ball's, and how Polly, staring out the window, must be so frightened for him. Miss Chang is imagining Buzzy Shabazz telling her mother that their neighbor, that crazy Chinese woman, has attacked her.

"I didn't mean to do it," Miss Chang says.

Polly turns and rises so effortlessly from the loveseat. She comes to Miss Chang and takes her in her arms. "Do what, Lily? Poor dear. Tell me."

There is a sharp knock at the patio door, the sound of metal on glass. Polly looks at Miss Chang, and Miss Chang sees the same terror she saw in her mother's eyes the day the Red Guard knocked down their door and dragged her mother out into the street.

Miss Chang feels Polly's shoulders tremble, and she remembers one day last summer when a goldfinch, convinced it saw clear passage through the glass, flew into the patio door and fell to the step. When Miss Chang picked it up, she could feel the wings trying to open—the slightest shudder—and she wished for something she could do, some miracle, to give the bird's life back to it. She remembers the letters she cut from the newspapers, the dancing turns and dips of her scissors, her gentle, flowing rill. She sees the letters in her mind, scrambled, swirling into words she hadn't thought to form: "LOVE," "ME," "NOW." They startle her. All along, she imagines, this plea has been rising—this sweet yearning—and now here it is, flaring up with such an overwhelming majesty and force, she can't help but confess it.

"It's me," she says, and her voice is barely a whisper. "I'm the one who's been sending you and Don those notes."

When the Red Guard took her mother, Miss Chang ran. She was just a girl, still light and fast. She ran and ran until she stopped in the botanical garden where the greenhouses were jagged with broken glass, where the azaleas and the dwarf cedars and the rhododendrons were charred and smoldering. She was so far from home. She was alone and ashamed. But she would never be able to forget the splendid motion of her swift and graceful flight. She recalls it now as Polly steps back and slips from her embrace, and all Miss Chang can do is turn, her feet clumsy and slow, to the patio door where Miss Shabazz Shabazz waits.

WHITE DWARFS

ONE SATURDAY IN JUNE, FRANK'S WIFE DISAPPEARED. THE POLICE found her car along Route 71, the hood up as if there had been some sort of mechanical breakdown, but a detective told Frank there wasn't "jack-stump" wrong with the car. It ran like a dream.

The detective wanted to know whether there had been any difficulty between Frank and his wife. Had she been depressed or upset in recent days? Would Frank mind if he had a look around the house? Sorry, but sometimes it happens, the detective told him. One day someone decides she's had enough—Frank's wife, maybe—and bingo, she walks away.

The detective's insinuations embarrassed Frank, because indeed he had been considering, just before his wife's disappearance, how different his life might be without her. From time to time, he would catch sight of some woman. A stylish hairdo, a bold shade of eye shadow, a daring skirt or blouse would attract his attention, and he might even strike up a conversation, harmless chit-chat. Later, he might allow himself to wonder what it would be like to be married to someone else. He had never felt guilty about his speculations, considered them par for the course after a couple had been together as many years as he and his wife—just a natural curiosity he suspected she herself indulged from time to time. The theory that she had run from him, perhaps escaped with a lover, would make good gossip, he knew, but seriously, he doubted she had been planning such a move. She had even asked him to go with her that morning, he told the detective, pleased that he could offer up this small piece of evidence that he and his wife had enjoyed each other's company.

"But you didn't," the detective said. "Go with her, that is."

"No, I didn't," Frank told him, ashamed.

He knew his wife's invitation to accompany her out into the country to pick strawberries had been an offer of reconciliation. A few days before, they had argued. He had taken her to a boutique downtown, one of those trendy shops, The Ozone, and he had encouraged her to buy something, anything she wanted—"Just pick it out, kiddo, something with a little pizzazz, and it's yours." She hadn't been able to find anything to suit her. She had been shy around the sales clerk, a girl with a gold loop pierced through her eyebrow, and refused to take anything into the fitting room. She preferred corduroy trousers in winter and twill skirts in summer, and blouses made from broadcloth that Frank thought made her look too severe.

On Sunday, one of his wife's credit cards showed up in Rocco, found there in the parking lot of the Free Methodist Church. That afternoon, a farmer came upon one of her shoes at the end of his lane. It was the shoe, a Keds tennis shoe, that undid Frank, the streak of mud across the white canvas, and he grieved, a deep, honest grief that left him raw with weeping.

For weeks, the police had nothing more to go on. No clues, they kept telling him. No leads. No further developments. They were "intensifying their search," they said, something they always said, Frank knew, when they didn't have "jack-stump."

With the help of friends, he organized a candlelight vigil, a prayer service. He helped distribute leaflets with his wife's picture on them. He had used a photograph of the two of them taken that winter for their silver anniversary. Someone had cropped the picture so it appeared it was only a shot of her, but if anyone looked closely they would see a hand, his hand, resting on her shoulder. That small detail made him feel that wherever she was, he was with her. He liked pointing that out to the news reporters who came to interview him, but after hearing it said back to him on their broadcasts, he decided it sounded delusional and terribly sentimental.

Then one night while he was sleeping, the telephone rang, and when he answered it, a woman's voice spoke his name. "Frank?" she said. The silken voice charmed him, and for a moment he felt something close to hope. "Frank Cain?"

"Yes," he said. He was beginning to understand that it wasn't his wife speaking to him, as he had first believed, but perhaps, he thought, someone who knew something about where she was.

The woman's voice shrank, nearly vanished, but still he could hear it, barely a whisper. "I want you to know something."

"Yes," Frank said again, impatient. "What is it? Tell me."

"It's like this," the woman said. "I'm HIV."

For a moment, he was amused. How absurd, he thought. The very idea that this woman had confused him with another man who happened to share his name. No matter what he had thought from time to time about his wife, Frank had always been faithful and aboveboard. He imagined this other man, asleep somewhere in the city, ignorant to what might be in store for him, and though Frank knew he should feel sorry for him, he couldn't manage it. In fact, he felt a flash of anger fire inside him. He hadn't asked for this woman's call or for the ugly news she was confessing. He had enough of his own misery.

"Why are you telling this to me?" he said. He lowered his voice, and it occurred to him that it might sound as if he and the woman, at one time, had been in cahoots, that he might actually be guilty of something.

"You think I wouldn't?" the woman said. "You think I'd let you slide? Baby, that'd be cold."

"But you're wrong."

"I'm not wrong, Frank. I've been tested twice. Trust me. You better get yourself checked."

And before he could tell her, straight out, she had the wrong number, the wrong Frank Cain, the woman with the voice like silk hung up.

"Just like that," Frank told his friend, Big Boy, the next evening when the two of them were outside on Frank's deck. "'I'm HIV,' she says. Can you imagine what that did to me?"

It was September, the tail end of warm nights, and Big Boy had his telescope and was trying to get Frank to recognize various constellations. Frank could manage a few, Capricornus and Cygnus, but others—Pavo, Delphinus—escaped him, seemed only skeins of lights strung through the night sky. Big Boy had studied astronomy at the university for a while before dropping out, and when he spoke about the stars, his voice was reverential and soothing.

"You're the estimator, Frank," he said. The backs of his hands were fat and dimpled like sponges, but his fingers, for a man his size, were surprisingly long and slim. "Give me an idea."

By this time, Frank had gone back to work. It was his job, at A-1 Metro Movers, to walk through a house, to open cabinets and closets, estimate cartons and weights, and then give the homeowner a figure. To do it right, he had to be nosy. He had to poke around and ask questions—"Does this go? How about this?"—and sometimes he saw things he knew people would rather he didn't: ratty bathrobes, pornographic magazines, enema bags. He always acted as if he didn't notice. He was there to do business, not to intrude, and over the years, he had developed a brisk, friendly manner that made everything go easily. He had a way of assuring people that their belongings would get to their new homes in tip-top shape. "We treat everything like we own it ourselves," he would say, when the truth was he couldn't guarantee a thing. The men who loaded the vans were men humping too much weight for too little pay, and who could blame them if they dropped a carton of dishes or banged the edge of an armoire, maybe even on purpose, just to remind someone they were all people, and, hey, sometimes people screwed up. Still, Frank had to pretend that everything was, and would always be, "A-1 a-okay." He had to keep himself in the perfect world of the brochures and moving tips booklets the company gave its customers, the ones where the workers wore clean, crisp uniforms and smiled as they wrapped dishes and loaded cartons onto two-wheeled dollies. Nothing ever went wrong in the pictures, and he had to live there in that world of protection and safety; otherwise, he wouldn't be able to offer the glib assurances that people expected.

"I'll tell you how it made me feel," he said to Big Boy. "Put-upon. That's the only way I can describe it. Like that woman was telling me something I didn't want to know. I don't need any of it, not on top of what I'm going through."

"Of course you don't, Frank." Big Boy put his hands on his hips. He was wearing a cream-colored jumpsuit, and his beard was neatly trimmed. Frank could tell he was meticulous about his appearance, and for a moment he could imagine Big Boy in a laboratory coat, the knot of a necktie barely visible, as he leaned over a lectern at the local planetarium. He was that smart about astronomy, a fact that amazed Frank. "So you felt put-upon," Big Boy said. "Who wouldn't? It's only natural. The question is, what are you going to do now?"

Big Boy was a packer. He wrapped people's glassware, their lamps and mirrors and knickknacks. It was up to him to make sure everything was snug. Nothing went anywhere, he always said, until he had it squared away.

"I tell you what I'd like to do," Frank said. "I'd like to tell him what I know. That schmuck."

"Have you looked in the phone book?"

"You think that should be my next move? Wouldn't that throw him for a loop? Knock the air right out of him. Jesus, can you see it?"

"No, Frank," said Big Boy, his voice flat with disappointment. "You've got it wrong. That's not the way it is at all."

There were stories around the warehouse about Big Boy, and more than one customer had complained. He had a habit, Frank knew, of telling people exactly what he thought. "That lamp's a piece of shit," he might say to someone. "And that couch? I can't believe you're spending good money to move it." He had a trick he liked to pull when he first went into a house to start packing. He brought in a box of broken glass, careful not to let it rattle. Then, when he was packing china and the homeowner was out of the room, he would drop the box of broken glass and say, "Oops." When the homeowner would come running to investigate, Big Boy would confess his gag, and the homeowner would be relieved. "Don't you feel lucky?" Big Boy would say. "Whatever happens from here on, remember how you feel right now."

It was the nerve of Big Boy, the balls-to-the-wind way he had of moving through the world, that first drew Frank to him. When Frank finally went back to work, too many people at the warehouse, after extending their sympathies, became cautious and shy in his presence. Their silence, their meek glances, surrounded him like the quilted pads they used to cover furniture. That was when he found himself gravitating toward Big Boy, the one person at the warehouse who treated him as if nothing out of the ordinary had happened. Often they would spend the evenings together. Sometimes they would just sit out on the deck and gab. Big Boy liked to talk about himself, and though Frank always felt guilty after an entire evening had passed and he hadn't said a word about his wife, he was thankful for Big Boy's stories and the way they distracted him from his own trouble.

The one story Big Boy told over and over was a story about his father. It was an account that disturbed Frank the first time he heard it, but after he had heard it enough times, he didn't mind it as much. He even started to look forward to it, because it was the kind of story that made him feel fortunate, lucky not to have been there when Big Boy, fifteen years old, found his father in a closet, his legs out straight in front of him, the toes of his oxfords knocking against the door jamb as he turned back and forth at the end of the cord burning into his neck. He had tied a curtain cord to the rod in his clothes closet. He had gone about it very scientifically, Big Boy said. It was clear his father had figured distance and space to come up with the exact length of cord he would need to do the trick. "The rest was simple," Big Boy said. "All he had to do was sit down."

Usually, that was where the story stopped, but one night Big Boy told Frank something new, how his father, a professor at the university, had left a box of letters he had written to one of his students, a boy named Larry Kiel, letters he'd never sent. Most of them were brief lessons in physics, pedantic discussions of matter and energy, motion and force. One of them explained the closed paths described by the lines of force in a magnetic field. Another talked about thermodynamics and the diathermic wall that was necessary to conduct heat between two systems.

But one of the letters, the last one Big Boy's father would write, had turned personal, and he had expressed his admiration for Larry Kiel. The line from the letter that Big Boy remembered was one that under any other circumstances would have seemed an embarrassing attempt at conceit, a farfetched metaphor from a man whose only language was science: "Perhaps in some other universe—some other creation—you and I might have been a thermoelectric couple." But when Big Boy repeated it, his voice full of forgiveness, the words seemed all the more urgent and heartfelt, a declaration of love from a man inadequate for the task. And when Frank heard them, he imagined all the times he had disappointed his wife, and he wished he had managed, in their time together, to have been more considerate.

So that night on the deck, when Frank was trying to find the constellations, and Big Boy told him it was cruel, now that he knew what he did, to keep this other Frank Cain in the dark, Frank listened.

"The way I see it," Big Boy was bent over the telescope, his face pressed to the eyepiece, "with news like this, you've got to give it to him straight. You've got to say, 'Look, pal. Here's the story.'"

"Right," Frank said. "Look, pal."

The way it was, Big Boy explained—"And believe me, Frank. I've done some thinking about this"—was that people were always moving through one another's lives, and there were reasons for them coming together, opportunities to be grabbed. "Never turn a blind eye to anything, Frank. It's all there for a purpose. That woman told you something meant for someone else. You're the messenger now. You know something you have to deliver."

"That call was a wrong number," Frank said. "And she didn't even know it. She had sex with this guy and she didn't even know him well enough to know she had the wrong number."

"There's a lot we don't know." Big Boy straightened and looked at Frank. "Did you know that only four percent of the universe is stuff we can see, stars and galaxies and stuff? The rest of it, the missing mass, is invisible. Go ahead, Frank. Take your best guess. What do you think makes up the other ninety-six percent?"

"I couldn't begin," Frank said.

"Dead stars. That's what it is, Frank. Lightless bodies we can't see because they've burned themselves out. White dwarfs, astronomers call them. That's what you're carrying, a white dwarf. You've got the missing mass. That's your payload. All you have to do is pass through this other Frank Cain's life for an instant. Just a few moments of your time."

In the house, Frank laid the telephone book on the kitchen counter. Lincoln was a good-sized city, the state capitol, and it took him a while to locate the page where the "Cains" were listed. There were fifteen, not counting his own entry, but there were no other Frank Cains, nothing even close—no Cain, Francis, or Cain, Francisco, or Cain, F., or even "F" as a middle initial, which might have been a clue.

One of Big Boy's long fingers traced over a line on the page. "'See Also Cane-Kane,'" he read.

Under C-A-N-E, there were two entries, Camille and Roger.

"Check 'K,'" Big Boy said.

And there it was: KANE, FRANK, 131 N. 26TH.

Frank knew the neighborhood only from driving through it on his way to somewhere else. It was the north central part of the city, near the university, a pocket of homes that had seen better days, occupied now by people who couldn't afford more or students looking for cheap rent and a short walk to school. People, in other words, who had no money for professional movers when it came time to leave for somewhere else. Frank recalled a few landmarks from the area that had stayed with him from his trips down North Twenty-Sixth: Captain Zig's Guns and Ammo, Fast Bucks Check Cashing, King Dollar Jewelry and Loan, Rocky's Hungry Eye Tattoo.

"So we'll call," Frank said to Big Boy. "That's the way to do it, right? We'll say, 'Look, pal.'"

Big Boy tapped his finger on Kane, Frank's address. "I wish it could be that easy," he said, "but is this the kind of news you'd want to get over the phone?"

Kane, Frank's house was a one-story home with a screened-in front porch edged with Christmas lights—red, blue, green, and orange twinkle lights that kept flashing on and off.

"Now that's smug," said Big Boy. He eased himself out of his utility truck and slammed the door. "Christmas lights still on in September. Like this guy's got something to celebrate and the rest of us are just mutts. I'm going in there and tell him what's what."

Frank followed Big Boy up the narrow walk to the house, recalling with a sudden pain that Saturday in June when his wife told him, "I wish you'd come with me, but don't worry, I won't be long." He had spent the morning noodling around with some lawn work, thinking how pleased his wife would be to see the freshly cut grass, the trimmed hedges. He would help her carry in the flats of strawberries, and the house would be fragrant with their scent.

Big Boy threw open the screen door and stepped up onto the porch. Frank could hear music inside the house, some sort of polka tune all bouncy with tubas and accordions. An orange extension cord poked through a crack in the window frame and snaked across the arm of an old brown sofa. Big Boy traced the cord and found the connection for the Christmas lights. He grabbed the plug and yanked it free. The porch went dark. "That's smug," he said again. "This joker's got to know what Christmas lights in September can do to people."

Inside the house, footsteps thundered across the floorboards, then a porch light came on, and a glaring white shaft fell over Big Boy and Frank.

The front door opened and a man stepped out. He was wearing a sleeveless undershirt, and his skin was a babyish pink. He had a strand of barbed wire tattooed around his arm, just above the bicep, and for a moment Frank wondered how he had hooked up with the woman who had called, a one-night stand most likely. It probably hadn't meant jack-stump to Kane, Frank. A quick pop with a woman who later wouldn't even know how he spelled his name. He was wearing glasses with small, round gold rims, and he tipped back his head and squinted to better see exactly what the fuss was on his front porch.

"Fellas," he said. "What's the story?"

"Are you Frank Kane?" Big Boy said.

"Hey," the man said with a laugh. "Don't tell me I'm in trouble."

Big Boy stepped up to him, up close, and he said, "We've got something to tell you. My buddy and me."

Frank understood he was to say nothing. He understood this had somehow become Big Boy's show.

And then Big Boy said it, just the way he promised he would, straight out. "Look, pal. The other night my buddy got a call from a woman. She said she was HIV."

"I'd say that's tough luck for your buddy," the man said.

"My buddy's name is your name," said Big Boy. He even had the nerve to reach out and poke his finger into the bare, pink flesh above the neckline of the man's undershirt. "That call was a wrong number. Think again, pal. Tough luck for you."

The man looked at Frank the way so many homeowners had, their faces anxious and pleading. They were trusting everything they owned to A-1 Metro Movers, and they wanted him to tell them it would all be safe.

"Hey, that's a good joke," the man said. He tried to laugh again, but it didn't come out with much force. "You must have sat around all night thinking up that one."

"It's no joke," Frank said, knowing something in his voice would convince him.

Kane, Frank took a step back and sat down on the brown sofa. He took off his glasses and rubbed his eyes. His shoulders were quivering, as if all of a sudden he was freezing.

"That's a good piece of music," he said. The polka music was still blaring. "That's Moostash Joe. You ever catch his band?"

"You won't be dancing the polka when the AIDS hits," Big Boy said, and Frank realized that when Big Boy had told him the story of his father and Larry Kiel, it hadn't been forgiveness Frank had heard in his voice, but a fierce, burning hate. "We're talking lesions, blindness. You'll lose your hair and your skin will come off in flakes. And then there's the pneumonia. They'll try to scrape your lungs, but it won't work. All because you stuck your prong in a strange socket." Big Boy poked Kane, Frank in the chest again. "Happy holidays, pal."

And just like that, it was over. Frank got back into Big Boy's truck and sat there staring at the house. The Christmas lights didn't come back on. "Did you see that asshole go white?" Big Boy said. "All the pink just went right out of him." Big Boy gave his horn a long blast. "He won't sleep tonight. Christmas lights in September. Did you see that tattoo? Tough guy. Who does he think he is?"

Frank felt the anger that had flared inside him when the woman had called burn out and go cold. He thought of his wife. When the first panic hit, when she knew she was in trouble, did she call out for him? Or for an instant, and maybe beyond, did she despise him, because she had asked him to come with her and he had said no?

"Wasn't that a kick in the pants, Frank?" Big Boy said. "Who's put-upon now? Wasn't that a hoot?"

Frank didn't answer. He was trying to imagine Kane, Frank's trembling shoulders and how they would feel if he were to step back onto the porch, reach out, and touch them.

"I want to go home now," he said, and he could hear his wife saying that to whoever had taken her, because he was convinced now this is what had happened. "Please," he said to Big Boy. "Take me home."

That night, for the first time since his wife had vanished, he opened her closet, and when he did, the memory of her overwhelmed him. She wasn't like other women who bought on impulse—he had seen plenty of those women's closets—but she had trouble getting rid of clothing, so he had let her have the walk-in while he used the closet in the guest bedroom.

He pressed his face into the collar of a broadcloth shirt and unashamedly breathed in the faint scent of her cologne. It was the same cologne she had worn since they had met in college, a clean, light smell of fresh flowers and baby powder. She hadn't changed it once in all the years they had been married; the bolder, more alluring fragrances had never appealed to her. Frank realized he had married her because of her predictability. She had seemed such a safe, stable woman, someone who would never break his heart or abandon him. He ran his hand over the skirt of a long denim jumper and thought of how he would sometimes come home and find his wife ironing, the air warmed with steam and pleasant with the healthy scent of fresh laundry. "We'll have to be quick," she would say to him. "My husband will be home any minute." He would make his voice go hard with menace. "Then maybe we should take a ride," he would say. "How about it, toots? Maybe you should come with me." Her eyes would go wide with feigned terror, and she would beg him not to hurt her. "Please," she would say. "Please." Their playfulness seemed so arrogant now, so certain that they would stay outside harm's reach. They wouldn't go dead, she had promised, like so many other couples they knew who had never had children. "It won't be so bad growing old together," she had told him. "You'll see."

The decision not to have children had been hers—the idea of giving birth terrified her—and though he sensed they were both missing some vital experience, he had no choice but to accept her will. Now he wished for some child—a daughter, he thought—who would look like his wife and would be there to remind him what love was so he wouldn't fall in with someone like Big Boy and the bitter disdain he had let poison him.

The closet was in order: summer clothes hanging toward the front, his wife's winter wardrobe stored away toward the rear. She had snugged her sweaters into boxes on the shelves and aligned her shoes along the floor. Frank sorted through the hangers, wanting as much of his wife as he could get; he wanted the feel of denim and twill and chambray and linen. He let his fingers linger over pleats, buttons, hems.

And then, in the middle of the closet, sheathed in plastic, he found something that astounded him. It was a marbled silk jacket, royal blue, with handspun mohair sleeves. He had spotted it at The Ozone when he had taken his wife there to pick out something jazzy. It was an original, he had pointed out to her, reading from a card that explained how the designer, a local woman, "marbled" the silk. The process, as he remembered it, involved mixing powdered seaweed with water until it thickened, then pouring inks on top of the gel where they floated. The designer then created patterns in the inks and laid the silk on the surface to absorb them. "How about this?" he said to his wife. "It's chic." She laughed. "Oh, Frank. You can't be serious. Those fuzzy sleeves. They look prehistoric, and I bet they itch like crazy." Then a sad look had come into her eyes, and she had said to him, "This isn't me. Really, Frank. I'd think you'd know that."

She had obviously gone back to the boutique and bought the jacket and then hung it in her closet, and she had never said a word about it. Frank ran his hand up under the plastic. He stroked one of the mohair sleeves, which wasn't scratchy at all, but soft, the way his wife's hair had been when, in bed, it would sweep across his face. And the silk of the jacket, so thin, reminded him of the translucent skin, blue-veined, along the inside of her thighs.

She had wanted to please him; he saw that now. She had always so desperately wanted to please him. Standing in her closet, the evidence at his fingertips, he saw how truly terrified she had been that one day she might lose him. That knowledge filled him with a guilt deeper than any he had ever known. Suddenly, he felt like an intruder in her closet, someone come there uninvited. All these years, his very presence had threatened some basic part of her, the modest and sensible woman she was. Without him, that woman would have always seemed familiar to her and safe.

It was then that he decided to call Big Boy.

"What have we done?" he said when Big Boy answered his phone.

"We did what you wanted," Big Boy said. "We gave the schmuck the news. I wouldn't want to be Kane, Frank, would you?"

"No, but still…"

"Count your lucky stars, Frank."

Frank didn't feel lucky. He felt all used up, tired, as if there were nothing left of him, and he sensed that he was beginning to come to the end of his grief, or maybe, he would think later, he was only falling into a darker grief, indelible, one that would never leave him. He was standing in the dark at his bedroom window looking up at the sky, and suddenly a thought came to him. "This missing mass," he said. "How do we know they're there—dead stars and the like—if we can't see them?"

"It's all gravity." Big Boy's voice hushed, the way it did whenever he tried to guide Frank through the constellations. "An invisible object—a dead star, say—passes directly in front of another star, one we can see, and that star, the bright one, gets brighter. The gravitational field of the dead star bends the light rays of the visible star and makes it more brilliant."

"That's all very complicated, isn't it?" Frank said.

He was having a hard time following Big Boy because he was working through a new thought, one about him and his wife and how somehow she had sensed that they had been moving in different directions, that the force of unspoken desires had brought some unidentified presence into her life on Route 71 on a Saturday in June when she had been thinking of strawberries and perhaps the silk jacket she had bought, not knowing in a few moments she would be gone, not knowing that Frank would find the jacket in her closet and would understand that from then on he would always be ashamed in the company of women.

"Think of it this way," said Big Boy. "We can see what's not there by its effect on what is. That's all you need to know."

It would be a few months more—months of no leads, no clues—before Frank would start to pack his wife's clothes into boxes and cart them away to the Salvation Army Thrift Store. For a while, in public, he would find himself trying to catch a glimpse of someone wearing one of his wife's broadcloth shirts, one of her denim jumpers, but that would never happen.

He liked to imagine the marbled jacket with the handspun mohair sleeves and the woman who would buy it. She would be his wife's size, he knew, and because it pleased him, he decided she would have his wife's hair, her skin, her eyes. He liked to think that he and this woman might pass someday on the street, and he would stand there, amazed, unable to tell her how thankful he was that out of all the possible junctions in the universe they had ended up there, the two of them, moving for just that instant, at last, through the same space.

REAL TIME

THE TROUBLE STARTED FOR DEL AND LIZ WHEN HE INVESTED MONEY in an oil well that pumped nothing but saltwater. After that, it was a cattle breeding operation that produced diseased calves, a Florida orange grove that disappeared into a sinkhole. Finally, he lost so much money she had to sell the jewelry she had inherited from her mother—the brooches, necklaces, and rings Liz liked to call her "pretties."

"Ah, my pretty," she said the last time she wore any of her jewelry. She sat at her vanity table and lifted a strand of pearls from its velvet-lined case. She held the strand to her throat and asked Del to fasten it. He kneeled behind her and worked the delicate clasp with his clumsy fingers. Then he kissed her neck, and she drew away in mock annoyance. "Cool it, buster," she said. "Dinner first and then dessert."

Each Saturday, for years, they had gone to the Top Hat Supper Club and maybe later to Peg's Piano Bar before driving home, Liz sliding over to sit close to Del, letting her hand come up to stroke the back of his neck.

"Imagine," she had said one night. "I'm the age my mother was when she died, fifty-one. I've outlived my looks. Oh, don't try to tell me it isn't so. I need all the help I can get to make myself attractive. Thank God I've got my pretties."

There were diamonds and sapphires and emeralds and amethysts. When she finally had to sell them, she told Del not to worry. Just a string of rotten luck, that was all. Couldn't be helped. Chin up. But from time to time, he caught her staring at him, and he saw the heat in her eyes, and he had to look away.

One night, he left a window open. It was a window on the front porch near the door, and sometime in the night he woke and remembered the window and went downstairs to close it. When he reached the bottom of the stairs, the front door opened, and a man stepped inside.

Del's first move was toward him, and the man stumbled backward, turned, and fled. "Get out," Del thought he was shouting at the man, but later, with a laugh, Liz told him the only sound from his mouth had been a goofy, guttural lowing—one of the funniest things she had ever heard. "Like a demented cow," she said. "I didn't know what was going on. I thought, what in the world."

She hadn't heard the sound of the door unsticking from its rubber seal, or smelled the reek of cigar smoke clinging to the intruder, or seen his shadowy form fill the doorframe as suddenly as a nightmare. Del wanted to share all of those details with her, but the two of them were able to manage such a pleasant, what-the-hell mood as they waited for the police, he didn't dare disturb it.

So he went along with her kidding that he had left himself "open" to criminals because of all those letters he wrote to prisoners in New York, Alabama, California, even there in Illinois to Vandalia and Marion and Menard. He got the convicts' names from pen pal ads in a magazine called *Real Time*, a tabloid he had discovered when he still worked at the post office. Now he carried on regular correspondence with men named Clifford, Michael, Donald, even though Liz told him it was nutso to think anything he had to say to those jailbirds could possibly matter. She liked to give the convicts nicknames: "Dago," "Honey-Boy," "Chop." She decided to call the man who had broken into their house "Sneaky Pete."

"That's not very intimidating," Del said. "He deserves a scarier name than that."

"You were the scary one," she said. "You should have heard yourself. Mooing your head off. What a scream."

She told the story again and again, to their friends, even to strangers in restaurants and grocery stores. And when she reached the part about the noise Del had made, she put her hand on his shoulder or his wrist, and she said in a coaxing voice he loved, "Go on, sweetie. Show them how you did it."

He threw himself into it, thankful that Liz was being good-humored about the fact that he had left the window open. He made the garbled noise deep in his throat, revised it each time, and turned it into the bellow that would bring the most laughs from those who heard it.

"That's it," Liz would say, hugging him. "Oh, sweetie. That's rich."

Late one afternoon, on the steps outside the post office, he found a set of keys. His first thought was to pass on by. He was carrying a stack of envelopes he had to mail before the post office closed, and since the break-in and his own complicity in it, he could barely imagine becoming a witness now to someone else's careless mistake.

Then he noticed a tarnished whistle on the key ring, the kind a woman might carry for safety, and he got the picture of this woman, frantic, afraid that some lunatic might find her keys and somehow, though the chances were nearly impossible, figure out where she lived.

There were no women inside the post office. In fact, there were no customers at all, only the postmaster—"The Ogre," Liz called him, because after Del had hurt his knee, the postmaster had taken him off his route and put him on the night shift, where he sorted mail under the watchful eye of a supervisor.

Del had missed being out on his route, where he could make his own decisions. If he wanted to duck into the Uptown Café for a cold drink, he could, and if someone on his route wanted to make small talk, he was glad to oblige. Sometimes the elderly residents asked him to help them with some chore, and he would go inside their houses and change furnace filters, open jars, raise storm windows. But then one day he stepped off a curb, landed on a pebble, and twisted his knee. He tried to explain to Liz what the night work did to him. He told her about the frenetic pace of the sorting machines, their loud clackety-clack, and the odd feeling of working under the fluorescent lights, the windows dark all around him. It made him feel like he had left the living and would never return.

"No one talks," he told her. "Everything's happening so fast, and there's all that noise. We walk around like zombies."

"Give it a chance," she said. "Don't jump the gun."

But soon he decided to opt for early retirement, and then, too much time on his hands, he started risking cash on dicey business schemes.

The postmaster was counting money. He had a handful of fives, and he gave each bill a tug that made it pop before he slapped it down on the counter.

"These keys," Del said, but then the postmaster held up his hand and furrowed his brow, making it clear he was engaged in important business and that Del should wait.

The postmaster wore mutton-chop sideburns and a thick-banded Masonic ring that clanked against the counter every time his hand came down. He smelled too strongly of cologne, an alpine scent Del supposed would be described as "rugged." He watched the postmaster wrap the stack of fives with thick rubber bands, stretching each one back and snapping it to make sure it could be trusted.

"So, Del," the postmaster finally said. "Liz says you had some excitement over at your place the other night." He snugged the stack of fives away in a cash bag. "You should have closed the window. I check all my windows and doors every night before I turn in. Regular as clockwork."

Del closed his hand around the keys he had found, and thought how small he would feel now if he had to turn them over to the postmaster. So he put the keys in his pants pocket and asked for a roll of stamps.

"Plenty of time for letter writing now, hey Del?" the postmaster said. "You're living the life of Riley."

Before he left the post office, Del took a spiral notepad from his shirt pocket, and with the Cross ballpoint he had always carried with him on his route, he printed, in his neat script, FOUND. KEYS. TO CLAIM: CALL 595-0819. He tacked the note to the bulletin board in the entryway, knowing it wasn't the best way of handling the situation, but the only one that suited him at the time.

There were two keys on the ring, and Del could see from the pattern of the teeth that they were identical though one of them was newer, a duplicate of shiny gold. The other, its nickel plating dull and scratched, had a slight bend in its shaft, and Del imagined someone had been careless with it. He ran his finger along the crooked shaft and found himself suddenly undone with regret, overcome with remorse for all the times he had disappointed Liz. He meant to go home that instant and tell her how sorry he was that he had become the kind of man, unwise and ineffectual, she could turn into a piece of gossip, the boob in an anecdote told to someone like the postmaster.

But when he got there, she was gone, and standing alone in the quiet house, he thought again of the woman who had lost the keys and how upset she must be. He wished he'd had the courage to leave them with the postmaster in case the owner returned—perhaps even that afternoon, though the post office had been open only a few minutes more. Now it was too late.

Del hated being alone in the house. He hated the beeps and codes of the alarm system they had had installed after the break-in. He hated the wrought-iron grates over the windows and the way they darkened the rooms. He had insisted on the alarm and the grates and an answering machine so they could screen their calls, anything he could think of to make him feel safe. But still the slightest noise could spook him: a knock at the door, the phone ringing, a tree branch scraping across the roof.

Liz had told him to relax, but he believed she secretly enjoyed his anxiety, contributed to it, even, by opening windows and setting off the security alarm, or picking up the phone on the first ring, or answering the door without first looking through the peephole to see who was on the other side. He imagined she was glad, after he had squandered so much money on foolhardy investments, that he was finally being cautious, finally afraid to take a chance.

It was late when she came home, long past the hour when they would have normally eaten their dinner. She was carrying a cardboard pizza box from Caesar's, and the security alarm was beeping, the signal that they had thirty seconds to punch in their code and disarm it.

"Beep, beep, beep," Liz called out on her way to the kitchen with the pizza. "Beep, beep, beep."

"The code," Del said, but she was already opening cabinets and drawers, rattling dishes and silverware, and trying to tell him something about a trip she had made to a Super 8 motel.

He punched in their code, 1964, the year they had gotten married, but his fingers were too fast, and it didn't take. He had to start again, and all the while he imagined time was almost out, and the alarm, its blaring siren, was about to sound. But it didn't. Finally, the system accepted the cancellation code. The beeping stopped in time for him to hear Liz say, "Oh, it might have been risky, but I did it anyway."

"Did what?" Del walked up to the breakfast counter and sat down on one of the rattan stools.

Liz tossed two saucers onto the counter. "You haven't been listening to me," she said. "Not a word."

She raised her head to look at him, and he noticed, then, the flames of rouge scoring her cheekbones, and the scarlet lipstick, and the lavender eye shadow. Her hair had been fixed in some way that made it look like the wild hair he saw on young girls, a tangled mop of ropy strands, shiny with gel.

"For Pete's sake," he said, thinking that if he had met her in a foreign land where he wouldn't have been expecting to see anyone he knew, he might have walked right by her, just for an instant, before he realized who she was.

"Like it?" She gave her head a shake.

She looked, he hesitated to say—and he knew, too late, he had made this clear to her with his silence—sluttish. She looked like the women on his route, the ones past their primes, who tried too hard to look young and provocative. "Desperate women," Liz had always called them. One of them, a home economics teacher, ended up strangled by an ex-boyfriend, and Liz had dubbed the incident "Betty Crocker Croaked."

She put a slice of pizza on a saucer. "Willum said it would float your boat."

"William?"

"Will-um," she said. "He's the photographer who did my shoot."

She had gone to the Super 8, where a company called Private Pics had been offering boudoir photos. She told Del how she had gone into a room where a girl had styled her hair and "done her face," and into another room where she had chosen an outfit. There had been silky peignoirs and feather boas and, for the especially daring, g-strings and garter belts.

"What do you think I wore?" she asked Del. "Go ahead. Guess."

"I don't know," he said.

She licked tomato sauce from her finger. "You'll see," she told him, "when the photos come."

After she had chosen the outfit, she had gone into yet another room, where Willum, the photographer, had been waiting with his cameras, and his cloth-draped platforms, and his backdrops of lace and velvet and mirrors.

"Just the two of you?" Del said.

"That's right."

"Were you afraid?"

Liz put her hands on her hips and stared at him. "I say live a little, sweetie."

The phone on the breakfast counter rang, and Liz started to answer it.

"No," Del put his hand over hers. "Let the machine get it."

They listened to the caller's voice. It was raspy and severe, but nervous, too, clearly a young boy who was trying to be menacing but wasn't quite succeeding. With great deliberation, a pause between each word, he said, "This…is…a…prank…call."

"What kind of joke is that?" Del said.

Liz was laughing. "He said it's a prank call. What a hoot. He's trying so hard to be mean, but all he can do is tell us it's a prank."

"I don't think there's anything funny about it." Del pressed the delete button and erased the message. "That takes nerve."

Liz slapped her hand down on the counter. "Don't tell me you're spooked by that."

"I didn't say I was spooked."

"Del, it's just a kid."

They were eating their pizza when the phone rang once, and then went still. A few minutes later, it happened again.

"It's that kid," Del said. "He's one-ringing us."

"So, what's it hurt? Sooner or later, he'll get tired of it."

"I wish I knew who that kid was. If I knew where he lived, I'd do something."

"What?" Liz said, her voice steeled with challenge. "What would you do?"

Del realized that whatever he said, he would appear foolish, a coward picking on a kid.

The phone rang again, and Liz reached across the breakfast counter and unplugged the line from the jack. "If it bothers you so much, that's all you have to do." She got up and went into the living room to unplug the phone there, and then moved upstairs, where Del knew she was doing the same to the one in their bedroom. When she returned, she was smiling. She sat down on her stool and spread her napkin over her lap. "There," she said. "He can't bother you now. Happy?"

Del was thinking about Liz, scantily dressed, posing for a strange man in a motel room.

He imagined her telling him, this Willum, about the night of the break-in and how her lamebrain husband had left a window open so the burglar could waltz right in.

"I suppose you told him the story," Del said. "That photographer. He probably got a kick out of your idiot husband."

Del could imagine Willum's smirk, his bemused chuckle. What a shame, he had probably been thinking as he studied Liz through the camera's lens, a woman with such spunk stuck with a dolt like Del.

"No," Liz said. "I didn't tell him."

"You didn't tell him?"

Now it all seemed even sadder to Del, the fact that Liz had been unable to speak of him. He wanted to tell her what the convicts had taught him in their letters, how easy it was to lose the lives they once thought they would have forever. "Some nights, I dream I'm a boy again." He could recall bits and pieces from the letters he had read. "I slept on ironed sheets." "My mother made French toast for breakfast." "I had a collie dog named Scout."

Early on, he had tried to read parts of the letters to Liz, but she had pooh-poohed them. "Please," she said. "What a snow job. They're yanking your chain."

Deep down, he imagined that was the case, and though it shamed him to be the convicts' patsy, he couldn't resist the small, clear truth in all their stories: once they had been different people, perhaps no more loved or hopeful than they were now, but, at the least, innocent. They hadn't stolen yet, or assaulted, or killed. There had been this time when they had the chance to live regular, decent lives, and that was the time Del tried to remind them of in his letters. He wrote of ordinary things—the scent of a wood fire, the sound of rain dripping from leaves, the white blossoms of pear trees in the spring—all the things he missed from his days on the mail route.

And when the convicts asked, he sometimes sent money so they could know some small pleasure: candy, cigarettes, perhaps a fresh apple bought in the prison commissary.

Then there were the ones like the Korean boy, Kim Ye, who claimed he'd been convicted of a murder he hadn't committed and waited now on death row at the state penitentiary in Nebraska. If he could raise enough money to secure competent representation, he would prove his innocence in the appeal case. "Mr. Del," he had written, "I could not do this thing they say. Won't you help to save me?"

Del was sitting at the desk in the living room writing Kim Ye a check for five hundred dollars when Liz came in to plug in the phone. She put her hands on Del's shoulders and gave them a sharp squeeze. He heard her sigh. "Oh, Del," she said, her voice weary with disappointment, and he knew it was useless to try to explain.

Then the phone rang. Liz took her hands from Del's shoulders. The phone rang again and again.

"All right," Del finally said. "I'll answer it."

The man on the other end of the line sounded like one of those late-night talk radio hosts, his voice low-pitched and soothing. "Chief," he said, "I've been trying to get you. Two hours I've been trying."

"There's been a problem here," Del said. "A screw-up with our phones."

"You get a problem, chief, you fix it."

"Things are all right now. We're back in the pink."

"All right for you," the man said. "But me? I'm in Dutch."

"Who are you?" Del asked. "What's this got to do with me?"

"Everything, chief. You've got my keys."

For a moment, Del was disappointed that the owner of the keys wasn't a woman, as he had first imagined, an anxious woman he had planned to reassure by returning her keys. But then he heard something new in the man's voice, a hint of desperation—"tell me where you live"—and he knew the man was in something up to his ears and that Del was the one between him and whatever it was.

"You're lucky I'm the one who found them," Del said.

"All right. Yes, I'm lucky. Now tell me. Please. Where do you live?"

After he hung up the phone, Del told Liz about the keys and the man who was coming to claim them.

"Coming here?" Liz said.

"That's right." Del took the keys from his pocket, tossed them into the air and caught them. He shook his fist as if he were rattling dice. "We've got what he needs."

"A visitor," said Liz. "Goodness, there's been no one but us in this house since the night Sneaky Pete broke in."

"We don't need to talk about that anymore," said Del. "That's ancient history."

But it was the first thing she told the man, and she told it all, the part about the window Del had left open, the goofy noise he had made when Sneaky Pete stepped into their house. They were standing just inside the doorway, and Del said to her, "He doesn't want to hear that. God, Liz. Don't be a pain. He's just here to pick up his keys."

"Come on, sweetie," she said. "Let's do it together." She lifted her head, stretched out her neck, and bellowed. "Was it like that, Del?"

"All right," he said. "That's enough."

She clapped her hands together and laughed. She shook those ropy strands of hair that didn't seem to Del like her hair at all. Then she said to the man, "Isn't that a scream?"

The man was thin with a shaved head just starting to ash over with stubble. There was a bruise on one of his cheekbones, and above it, a streak of blood muddied the white of his eye. He winked that eye at Liz. "Sis, that's fine. I need a good laugh. I tell you, I've been on the skinny side of paradise quite a good little bit."

"Trouble?" Liz said.

"Sis, like you don't know."

It was his wife, he said. One morning, she bumped her head on a cabinet door. "Just a tap," he said. "She didn't give it another thought. A few weeks later? She's telling me she can hardly see out of her left eye. 'Sonny,' she tells me, 'it's like someone pulled a curtain over half of my eye.' Now she's having surgery tomorrow. Detached retina."

"All because of a little bump?" Liz said.

Sonny nodded. "Like I told you. Just a tap."

"That was enough," Del said. He knew how little it took to throw everything out of whack. He remembered stepping from the curb that day on his mail route and feeling the small lump of the pebble beneath his foot. For a moment, he balanced on it—then it rolled, and his ankle turned, and his knee twisted, and he heard the tendon break with a pop.

Sonny reached up to the security alarm's control panel on the wall beside him and traced his finger lightly over the keys. Then he turned back to Del and winked again. "Life can get strange. Can't it, chief?

You think you're just rolling along, and then out of nowhere there's something you didn't expect. Like this joker who broke into your house. He saw that open window and thought he'd take a chance. Now you're all closed in here."

"Yes," said Liz. She put her hand on Sonny's arm and gave it a squeeze. "Closed in. That's exactly how I feel."

Del handed the keys to Sonny, then, just so Sonny's arm would move and Liz's hand would slip away from it.

"I was on my way to the hospital." Sonny curled his fingers around the keys. "I stopped by the post office to pick up a package. Then I was going to make a stop at the storage unit I keep out on University Drive."

"ELF Storage," Liz said.

"That's right," said Sonny. "The 'S' is missing on the sign."

Del cleared his throat. "Why do you need a storage unit?"

"Business," said Sonny. "I'm a businessman."

"Del knows all about business," Liz said. "Don't you, Del? Del's an investor."

"A man with money," Sonny said.

"Money?" said Liz. "Del's thrown it away by the fistfuls."

Sonny put the keys in his pocket and then reached out his hand to Del. "Put her there," he said. "Chief, this is your lucky night."

His business, as Sonny explained it, involved wrapping people with bandages. "Head to foot," he said. "Even your face. Just like a mummy. It's all done with these plastic bandages soaked in a special mineral solution. Forgive me for not revealing the ingredients, but I can't give away my secret." The objective of the wrap was to reduce fat cells and the toxins and fluid around them. "Squeezing out the poison. When my wife had it done in California, she lost fourteen inches all around. I'm going to call my salon Suddenly Slender."

Del could remember as a kid standing in a doorway, stretching his arms out to the sides, and pressing against the jamb until his muscles gave out and started to tingle. When he stepped back, his arms, which he could no longer feel, lifted into the air as if they were filled with helium. Now he could imagine the body wrap Sonny had described—the tight bandages and the incredible lightness customers would feel once they were released.

"This can be a real moneymaker," Del said.

"You've got that right," said Sonny. "This is going to be killer. That is, if my wife doesn't kill me first." Since yesterday, she had lain in a hospital bed, only on her right side, so the corner of the retina in her left eye could fold back into place before her surgery. "She's been waiting for me, and now I'm afraid she's never going to believe why I'm late."

"Why wouldn't she believe you?" Del said.

"Long story. Let's just say I've been late before. The thing about this detached retina is, it's my chance to finally prove I can be dependable."

"We could help you," Liz said. "We could go to the hospital with you, and Del could tell your wife how he found your keys."

"Would you do that, chief?"

"Sure," Liz moved over to Del and slipped her arm around his waist. She stood on her tiptoes and kissed him on the forehead. "Won't you, Del?"

He thought of Kim Ye and how he claimed on the night of the murder he had just happened to pass by the alley where later the woman's body was found, and someone driving past had seen him. "Wrong place, wrong time, Mr. Del," he had written. "A minute early, a minute late—no problem."

Even if Kim Ye was lying, Del couldn't help but marvel over the mesh of movement and time, and how only one second, given the proper witness, could mean salvation or doom.

He kissed Liz on the cheek and tasted the oil of her makeup. "Glad to," he said. "Sure thing. Whatever I can do to help."

Sonny's panel truck, an old Ford Econoline, was parked in front of Del and Liz's house. The streetlight was shining through the windshield, and Del could see a pair of panties—baby blue lace—hanging from the rearview mirror. The top of the dashboard was littered with tools: screwdrivers, pliers, a carpet knife.

Liz was chattering away, talking too loudly, the way she had to the police officer the night of the break-in. "Del can tell your wife about the keys," she said. "And then I'll explain how we unplugged our phones and you couldn't get through."

Del could see she had concocted this plan, both of them working together to help smooth things out between Sonny and his wife.

But Sonny didn't look pleased. He ran his hand over his shaved head. "You told me there was a problem with the phone," he said to Del.

"It was this kid," Del tried to explain. "He was one-ringing us. You know. Being a pest."

"So you were being a snob."

"No," Del said. "We just wanted some quiet."

"Now I'm in Dutch." Sonny slapped the side of the panel truck. "All because you were a stuck-up SOB. Goddamn it, chief. You've put me in a bind."

"Don't worry," Liz told him. "Calm down. We're going to help you. We're going to get in our car right now, Del and me, and we're going to follow you to the hospital, and we're going to take care of everything."

"Okay," said Sonny. "Right. You're going to follow me."

That's what they did. Out Bonnie Brae, then right on University. Del kept his eyes on Sonny's panel truck—the dull chrome of its bumper, the two squares of glass in its back doors. "Well, I'm glad we can do this," Liz said.

"Yes," said Del. "It's the least we can do."

"His poor wife." Liz tilted her head to the side and held it there. "Imagine having to lie on one side so long. I'd go nuts."

"Healing takes a lot of patience," Del told her.

"I don't know if I could do it."

"You'd do it because you'd want to be you again."

He was about to try to explain to her why he had shouted at the burglar the way he had, but then Sonny's panel truck slowed and his turn signal started to blink, and Del, who had gotten too close, had to slam on his brakes.

Liz pitched forward and caught herself by grabbing onto the dash. "Del," she said, "be careful."

Sonny turned his panel truck into the lot of ELF Storage, and Del followed because it was what he had promised to do, and from here on, he had decided he was going to be the kind of man people could count on. He remembered all the times he and Liz had driven by and joked about the missing S in the sign, and how one day—he couldn't recall when—they had stopped joking, the sign just as familiar as any other they expected to see.

So now it didn't seem unusual to be driving through the gravel lot, turning down an aisle flanked by rows of storage sheds with red sectioned fronts that could be raised like garage doors.

Sonny stopped his panel truck at the end of the aisle, got out, and came back to the car. He motioned for Del to roll down his window. "Sorry for the detour." Sonny rested his arms on the car door and leaned in toward Del. "I just happened to think I needed to load up some cartons of that mineral solution. Heavy suckers, chief. Can you give me a hand?"

"But your wife," Del said.

"We'll just be a minute. Besides, she's not going anywhere."

Liz put her hand on the back of Del's neck and stroked him the way she had always done when they drove home on Saturday nights after dinner and dancing and maybe a nightcap at Peg's Piano Bar. Sometimes he would take the long way home—down Riverside and out Bellemeade until it curved into Bonnie Brae—just so he could have her there beside him a few minutes longer, so he could feel her hand on his neck, breathe in the scent of her perfume, and catch from time to time the exciting glint of gold from a necklace or pendant or earring as the car slipped through the soft glow of the streetlights.

"Go ahead, Del," she said. "Take a look at Sonny's operation. It might be just the winner you've been looking for."

Del noticed she had picked up Sonny's soothing way of talking, and it filled him with a great hope. "All right," he said. "Sure. Let's see what you've got."

At the storage unit, Sonny took the keys from his pocket and put the shiny gold one into the padlock. He yanked it open and then lifted the door. The sections clacked over the rollers as they folded and disappeared overhead.

"Step on in, chief." Sonny smacked his hands together. "Make yourself at home."

Del walked into the storage unit and let his eyes adjust to the dark. A dim glow from the vapor lights outside washed over the walls and the floor, and he could see that the unit was empty except for an Army footlocker at the rear against the wall. Because it comforted him to think it, he imagined Liz had felt a similar uncertainty when she first stepped into Willum's motel room for her boudoir shots—just a brief panic as she wondered what she was getting herself into.

"You told me there were cartons," Del said to Sonny.

Sonny chuckled. "You fell for that, didn't you? I'm not surprised. I could tell right away you were that kind of dope."

"No body wraps?" Del said.

"I read about it in the paper."

"And your wife?"

"Sorry, chief. No wife."

Del heard Sonny pulling down the overhead door. The light faded, and Del stood there in the dark. Then he felt a sharp blade against his throat, and he knew it was the carpet knife he had seen on Sonny's dashboard.

"I want you to get down on your knees," Sonny said, and his voice was so gentle and kind. Del felt a hand on his shoulder pushing him down to the floor. "I want you to stay here. Just like you're praying."

The knife blade came away from his throat, and he heard Sonny's footsteps on the cement floor.

For a moment, Del thought about trying to run—nothing seemed as sweet to him, then, as the idea of him and Liz alone in their car driving through the night—but then Sonny said, "It's a hell of a story for a man's wife to tell on him. What was that noise you made? Like a cow? She made you out to be a fool."

"Don't hurt her," Del said.

"Give me a break." The footlocker's lid slammed shut. "I watched you when she told that story. You wanted her to pay."

Del bowed his head. Suddenly he felt guilty, a criminal at heart. Since the night of the break-in, what he had wished more than anything was that Liz could know the same alarm that had overwhelmed him the moment he had seen the burglar come into their house. Then she would know why he had shouted. He had been afraid, yes, but more than that, he had loved the world too much to leave it. He had loved himself and Liz and the life, though imperfect, they had together. There had been no words for all this, only a fierce and strangled bawl.

Now he heard Sonny moving toward him in the dark. "Put your hands behind your back," Sonny said, and Del did. He heard the ripping sound of duct tape unwinding from its roll, felt it sticking to the hairs on his arms as Sonny wrapped it around them where his wrists were crossed. "There are people," Sonny said. He whispered it in Del's ear. "People like me."

Del imagined Liz waiting in the car. Sooner or later she would hear the door to the storage unit open and see Sonny coming toward her. How long would it be before she would know she was in trouble? And once she did, would she call out? Would she say, "Del?"

"Del," he imagined her saying again and again until it wasn't "Del" at all, but a wail so high and thin it could barely hold the weight of such fear—at last, something private and intimate between them.

DRUNK GIRL IN STILETTOS

WE CAME UPON HER SOUTH OF TOWN ON THE BLACKTOP, WINK AND me, this girl looking all whoop-de-doo in high heels, her hip jutted out, her thumb stuck in the air, begging a ride.

"Pull over," I said. We were running eighty in his Mustang GT, and it was going to take a while to shut it down. "Damn it, Wink. Now."

"Jesus, Benny." He pressed his lips together and squinted at me with his right eye. His left one—or the empty socket, I should say—had a black satin patch over it. He owned an artificial eye made from acrylic, but he wasn't wearing it that day. The patch gave him a tough look that I suspected he secretly liked. The thin strap slanted down across his forehead. "All of a sudden you're a Boy Scout?" He was busting my balls, but he'd already put his foot to the brake. "Thought you were in a hurry to get home."

"Just do it," I said, and he did.

He was in one of his pissy moods and more of a mind to keep heading up the blacktop, but I saw a girl who needed a ride, and I knew what that was like. Let me say it plain: I've not always been an upright man, and as a result, I've had to rely on the kindness of folks; some, like my mama, loved me, and some were strangers who didn't owe me the time of day.

We were maybe a hundred yards beyond the girl, and Wink was stubborn and wouldn't back up, so we waited while she came to us, teetering along on those spiked heels. I got out of the car and watched her come. In the sunlight, her bare legs looked whiter than they probably really were, but she was a fair-skinned girl anyway. I could see that. She was wearing a short denim skirt and a black T-shirt with writing in pink letters across her chest. I could finally read the words when she came up alongside the car: I'M SHY.

A little straw purse dangled from her wrist. It had a picture of that cartoon character, that Betty Boop, on it. Her red dress—Betty's, I mean—was lifting up over her hip, and I could see her white stocking and the garter with a red heart on it.

"Hey, know what Lady Godiva said toward the end of her ride?" I asked the girl. I waited just long enough for effect. With comedy, like with women, the trick is in the timing. "I'm nearing my clothes," I said, but I could tell she didn't get it. I opened the Mustang's door, folded back the passenger seat, and motioned for her to get in back. "Her clothes," I said again, taking one more shot at the punch line, but again I got no reaction.

"He thinks he's a funny man," Wink said.

I bowed to the girl. "I'm Benny. I'm a funny man."

She had on big round sunglasses with white frames. She pushed them up on her head and stuck her face up close to mine. "I know who you are." I could smell the liquor on her breath, and for an instant I wanted to kiss her just for the taste of it, even though I was too old to do that. She was just a girl, and I was a man on the downhill side of fifty. "You're Benny Moon."

"You've been drinking," I said.

"Yeppie." She pressed a fingernail into my chest. "But I know who you are."

"Everyone knows Benny," Wink said. "He's about as famous as they come round here. Aren't you, Speed Racer?"

Odds are you've heard of me. Back in the summer, I got arrested for DUI. No big news there, just that I happened to be driving a barstool at the time. That's right. A barstool. Welded to a frame and powered by a five-horsepower Craftsman lawn mower engine. Topped out at thirty-eight miles per hour. Slick as can be. For a couple of weeks there, I drove it around. Didn't have much choice. I'd lost my license, and the only way to get from here to there was to hoof it or to ride that barstool. We live in a dry town, and it's five miles to the nearest tavern. A man gets thirsty? Doesn't have the legal right to drive a car? You do the math.

Anyway, I'd been to Bridgeport to the Hilltop Tavern one day, a Saturday, and I made sure to start back to Sumner while there was plenty of daylight left. Then I remembered that I'd left my billfold on the bar after I settled my tab. I tried to do a U-turn right there on Route 250. Guess I didn't cut my speed enough. Next thing I knew, I was down, scraped all to hell from the pavement, a knot on my head. Then I made my mistake. Called 911 on my cell. Said I'd had a wreck. Said I was out on 250 just before King's Hill. The dispatcher wanted to know how bad I was hurt. "Bad enough to call you," I told him.

Then the ambulance showed up, and a county sheriff's deputy, and, well, one thing led to another, and before I could say snap, I was all over the Internet and on CNN and in newspapers coast to coast. Even Letterman and Leno and Conan and the other late-night funny boys were telling jokes about me. I was that guy, the drunk who wrecked his barstool.

You'd think it'd make me feel foolish, but I can't quite manage it. Truth is, that's what stopped me—took me off the booze for good, near as I can tell anyway—and what's a little ribbing compared to the grace of that? I'll be Speed Racer. I'll be that guy. I'll be an idiot forever as long as I can say I'm a sober man.

We drove on up the blacktop, Wink and me and the girl. It was a nice fall day—Indian summer—warm enough to have the windows down, sun filling the Mustang, shining bright on the hood, the fields flashing by, bare now except for corn and soybean stubble, a few red and orange and yellow leaves still holding onto the maples and oaks and sweetgums in the woodlands. We were at that time of the year when things were letting go, giving up, hunkering down—soon there'd be snow and ice and the long freeze until spring—but for a while yet, there was sun and enough warm air to make me want to believe it could last forever. Wink had a CD in, Drive-By Truckers' *Gangstabilly*, and we were just heading up the blacktop, almost to Sumner, the water tower already in sight and the silos of the grain elevator, and we were listening to "Late for Church": *All this hollerin' makes me wonder. Does a whispered prayer get heard?*

Sweet autumn day, sweet music, and now this girl and those stilettos. She seemed like a gift, the sort of thing handed to you when you're not expecting a thing. I'd been out at Wink's shooting up bottles and cans with my rifle, a Ruger 10/22, just target shooting to pass the time, and now he was running me home.

We'd had a little tiff. He'd got off on a jag—just a lot of bullshit, really—about what it would take to get me drinking again. I told him not a thing. Ever. End of story. That was enough to make him set his jaw. "Must be something," he said. "How about if you won the Mega Millions? Hell, even the Little Lotto." No, I told him—not even hitting the state lottery, not even the Mega Millions, would make me backslide. "What if you knew you only had a month to live?" Ixnay. "Finding yourself on a desert island with Madonna and a fifth of Maker's Mark?" He was starting to tick me off, picking at me the way he was, determined to prove there'd be something to touch a weakness in me and send me back to the bottle. No, I told him. Then he said, "Okay. What about if some psychopath had a gun to my head, and the only way to stop him from pulling the trigger was if you took a drink. Surely you'd do it then?"

Well, of course there'd be a limit to how long I'd hold out. I wouldn't let a man die, but Wink was too sure of too many things. He thought he knew me. His little game was his way of saying he'd bet good money that before long I'd be that guy again. That drunk guy. So I said to him, "Nah, not even then."

"All right, just be an asshole," he said. I tossed the Ruger into the backseat of his Mustang—didn't even bother to take out the mag—and we started up the blacktop.

Drive-By Truckers were now singing "Panties in Your Purse," and that song about a woman called a whore and a tramp, her man catching her with her stockings in her hand and her panties in her pocketbook—a song I ordinarily never gave a second thought—now broke my heart to hear because I was listening to it in the presence of that girl in stilettos. I guessed she was up against something hard and didn't need to be hearing a song like that. I reached over and changed the track to "Steve McQueen," the coolest doggone motherscratcher on the silver screen. Wink always sang along with that one. We saw that movie, *Bullitt*, and the chase scene through the streets of San Francisco, when we were thirteen, and that was enough to sell us on Mustangs and speed. We didn't know, then, that I'd turn into a drunk. We didn't know that Wink would get beat in a bar fight and lose an eye. None of us can guess what life will do to us until it's done, but that doesn't excuse the misery in the world. Not by a long shot. I can say that now that I'm a sober man, and I intend to stay that way, no matter what Wink might believe.

He knocked my hand away from the CD player. "Who made you DJ? I was listening to that."

Wink's a big man with a shaved head and rolls of fat on the back of his neck. When he wears that eye patch, he looks dangerous. I used to tell him jokes. What did the brave pirate tell the fraidy-cat pirate right before the big battle? "Nothing to be scared of, matey. I'll keep an eye out for you." "Ha ha," Wink said when I told him that one. "Ha-frickin'-ha." He told me to can the crap. Said he'd had enough of my jokes. Said his eye was gone-baby-gone, and every morning when he looked at his face in the mirror, there wasn't a damn thing, far as he could tell, to laugh about. I thought I was just lightening things up for him, just playing the fool to give him a chuckle. It wasn't that way, though. He made that plain. He said in a hurt voice I'd never heard from him, "Damn it, Benny. No matter what slips and shakes you've had, you're still a whole man. I'll never be that. Never again."

So I backed off. Stopped telling those jokes. Even resisted the one about the man having dinner in a restaurant and noticing the beautiful woman eating alone at the table across from his. All of a sudden she sneezes, and her glass eye comes flying out. The man calmly reaches up, catches it, and returns it to her. She's embarrassed. She puts the eye back in and insists that the man allow her to buy his dinner. He agrees.

They dine together and hit it off. They go out for drinks and end up back at her place. In the morning, she makes him a grand breakfast. "I bet you do this for all the guys," he says. "Nah," she tells him. "You just happened to catch my eye."

Even a joke like that—one that makes me happy to know there's still something to laugh about in this world—I stopped telling Wink because he was my friend and had been for years. If he wanted me to stop, I'd stop, and if he wanted to switch that Drive-By Truckers CD back to "Panties in Your Purse," I'd let him do that, too, despite what I thought about that girl and what she didn't need to hear.

It left me disappointed in myself—I'll admit that—on account there was that girl and I should have done right about her. A drunk girl. Trust me, I know what it's like to be loose from right thinking, to be hard on the end of a bad shake, to reach for that bottle and not give a fiddler's fart about anything else. I could tell she needed something good and happy in her life, something that'd last, and not that song reminding her exactly how grim things were. But like I said, Wink, no matter the little spat we'd had—no matter how bad he wanted to make me feel like it was only a matter of time before I went back to being a drunk—was my friend. He'd stuck by me through all my drinking days, stuck by me when I'd been an embarrassment and everyone else had given up on me, everyone except my mama who got down on her knees by her bed each night and sent a prayer to heaven for my redemption. I'm not sure what it was that kept Wink at my side. Maybe he needed me in order to feel better about himself. As long as I was drinking, and as long as he stayed true to me, he could be the long-suffering friend who, though he might be maimed, wasn't—praise Jesus—a drunk man. I guess there are reasons people are friends even if we don't know as much at the time. I guess it takes something like what happened that day with the girl to make it clear.

She tapped Wink's neck with the barrel of that 10/22. "Hey," she said. "What happened to your eye?"

Jeezy Pete. She had that Ruger, her finger on the trigger. As luck would have it, the safety was still on.

Wink tucked his head toward his right shoulder to see what was poking him in the neck. "Shit fire." He jerked away from that 10/22, and the Mustang swerved over into the other lane for just a few ticks before he could bring it back. "Drunk girl with a loaded rifle." He narrowed his eyes at me and gave me that what-the-fuck-you-thinking look I knew so well from my drinking days. "Now that's just exactly what I need."

"I'm just a little bit drunk." The girl put the barrel right up to Wink's temple. "But that doesn't mean you've got a right to treat me mean."

"Darlin'." I used my gentle voice, the one I'd heard so many women use on me when I was falling-down drunk and they were trying to coax me into bed so I'd sleep it off. "Sugar." I reached around and took hold of that 10/22 by the stock. "Sweetie, you don't need to be playing with that."

I gave a gentle tug, and she let the Ruger slide out of her hands. I laid it across my lap, but that put the barrel in Wink's crotch. He gave me that look again, and I swung the rifle up and over and propped it between me and my door.

A loaded rifle uncased in a moving automobile in Illinois? Well, sure it was illegal, but I'd been in a hurry when Wink and I were done shooting. He'd given me that interrogation about what it would take for me to start drinking again, and I just wanted to hit the road and get back to my place as quick as I could. I've gotten good at being alone. I put on my white noise machine, close my eyes, and listen to rain or ocean surf or a babbling brook. I hear grace in the water; I hear forgiveness.

The girl was crying a little now. She opened up that Betty Boop purse and took out a wad of Kleenex, the kind that'd been in that purse forever and were now one big crumbling tissue biscuit. Little white flakes fell off onto her shirt. I reached into my hip pocket and pulled out my handkerchief—white and freshly pressed that morning and folded into a neat square.

"Don't cry, darlin'." I gave her the handkerchief. "Where is it you're on your way to?"

By this time, Wink had the Mustang pulled off onto the shoulder. We were just out of the last curve before the straight shot into town.

I could see the population sign—1,200—just up ahead, and beyond that the city cemetery with its tall cedar trees and its monuments and mausoleum and the lake with the statue of Jesus rising out of it, his arms outstretched to gather you in if you were of a mind to let him, as I'd been more than once when I'd walked through that cemetery in the twilight just for the peace of it.

"Get out." Wink was shouting. He had his door open, and he folded down his seat so he could reach the girl. He took her by her skinny arm and pulled so hard her sunglasses got all cockeyed on her face. "Hold a gun on me, goddamn it." I heard her knees hit the floor. Then Wink jerked her out of the car and she fell into the weeds and her sunglasses went flying. He got down there with her, lifted his patch, and said, "There. You want to know about my eye so bad? Just take a good look." His socket was all scar tissue and an empty place where an eye should be.

The girl was crying. "I didn't mean anything."

"I don't care what you meant." Wink let her go. "Now you can just walk."

"Not in these heels." She stood up, took off one of the stilettos, and showed him the back of her heel. "I've already rubbed a blister."

It broke my heart to see her broke down like that in the turkey-foot grass and the milkweed and foxtail. I got out of the Mustang and walked around the front until I could lay my hand on Wink's shoulder. I had the 10/22 in my hands. "How come you want to go and make a scene? We're almost to town." I clicked off the safety. "Don't you hurt her." I asked her again, "Darlin', where is it you're going?"

To the funeral home, she said, for Jackie Frutag's laying out.

"Jackie Frutag?" Wink got to his feet. "You know Jackie Frutag?"

The girl nodded. "He's my daddy."

I put the Ruger's safety back on. Then I found her sunglasses in the grass. I studied her face, and it all came clear to me. "You're Lily, aren't you?"

That sobered her up. She gave me a shy grin. "How'd you know my name?"

I handed her the glasses and she put them on top of her head, the stems stuck through her thick brown hair. "Your daddy used to be a friend to us. I haven't seen you in a good long while."

There was a time when Jackie ran with me and Wink. This was back in the day when we were too young to know a damn thing even though we thought we knew it all. Jackie Frutag—a scrawny mutt with long stringy hair and a knobby chin. We called him Pygmo because he couldn't have been more than five foot two and that was in his Dingo boots. We all worked pipe for Marathon Oil for a few years and spent most of our nights helling around. Then Jackie married a Bridgeport girl, Cathy Catt, and got religion. He started lay preaching for the Church of Christ, where my mama went, and she made sure she let me know what a miracle it was that he'd turned his life around and had a little girl now, Lily, and wasn't she just the most darling thing. I got tired of it in a hurry.

Jackie Frutag stuck in my face as an example of what a man could do with himself if he took a notion. I'd see him uptown on a Sunday, coming out of Piper's Sundries with his *Evansville Courier*. He had his hair cut, of course, and most generally he'd have on a pair of dress pants, a short-sleeve white shirt, and a necktie. Cathy and Lily would be waiting for him in the car, and they'd head off to church. Sometimes he gave me a nod. Once he tried to talk me into coming along with them. I told him I didn't want his religion. I told him I was just fine with living the way I was. If I could, I'd let him know now that he was right—there was a peace to be found—but I couldn't on account he was laying corpse up there at Sivert's Funeral Home, dead in an unremarkable way ("He just went to sleep one Sunday after service," my mama told me, "and never woke up."), and his girl, liquor on her breath, was on her way there.

"Jesus," Wink said. "Jackie Frutag. I bet he'd turn over if he could see you drunk and dressed like that."

Lily stood up and smoothed her denim skirt over her legs. She tugged at the hem of her T-shirt. She slipped her blistered foot back into that stiletto. "I don't have to stand here and listen to you talk to me like that."

She was a tender-hearted girl. I could tell that. In spite of the liquor and the Betty Boop purse and those stilettos and all her tough talk, she was a girl who'd lost her daddy.

"Where in the hell you been to be drinking the day of your daddy's wake?" Wink shook his head at her. "And you a preacher's kid."

She'd been to a party in the country. "Just a party," she said, like she knew there was no way to explain the logic of a girl going out on a drunk with her daddy just dead, and here she was still a little lit the day of his laying out.

Wink was disgusted. No matter what he thought of Jackie Frutag and his Bible shaking, he couldn't get cozy with Lily's disregard. "You ought to think more of your daddy than that." He snapped his eye patch back into place. "You ought to have more respect."

But it wasn't like that, I wanted to tell him, and would have only I didn't want to say it in front of her. She was just at a loss. That's the story I told myself. She didn't know how to face the fact that her daddy was dead, so she tried to go on like the world was running its regular course, like there was nothing she had to accept. Trust me, I wanted to say. I know the extremes we'll go to so we don't have to face the truth, particularly when that truth is the ugliness of our own living. Eventually, though, we come to the facts. Jackie Frutag was dead. She was his daughter. Drunk or not. Stilettos or not. Short skirt and T-shirt or not. Betty Boop or not. She had a place she needed to be.

Then she said, "Mama told me if I came to the funeral home, she'd have me arrested."

"Now, darlin'," I said. "Why in the world would she do that?"

It was a stupid question. I knew it as soon as the words were out of my mouth. How many times had my own mama threatened to call the cops when I was drunk and out of hand? "Benny, I don't want to do it," she said one night, when I was in a craze. I'd already ripped the curtains down from their rods, all because I couldn't stand to be in my own skin and didn't know any way to say that but by tearing something all to hell. "But I will," she told me, "if I have to. Believe me, Benny. I surely will."

A family is a family up to a point, and I'm lucky that my mama, turning toward her last days now, believes in forgiveness. Since I got sober, I'd heard about Lily's troubles: the meth, the scrapes with the law for writing bad checks, the shack-up boyfriend in Lawrenceville, the rumor of an abortion. "Such a shame," my mama said. "And Jackie and Cathy just the best people you could know."

It was plain that the Frutag family had their rough spots, and now here we were—Wink and me—in the midst of their drama.

"I've not been the best daughter." Lily flipped her sunglasses down. "I guess you know that. I'm sorry you're mixed up in it now."

Wink gave me one of those looks again, and I knew he was thinking that if I hadn't insisted on stopping to give the girl a ride, we'd be long up the road—smooth sailing—with nothing at all like this to deal with. What could we do now? Leave Lily there along the blacktop to walk the last half mile into town? Carry her on to the funeral home and wish her well? Put her back in the Mustang and drive her somewhere, far away from the mess of her life? Whatever we did, we'd be thinking about it later. I knew that for sure.

A car was coming from the south, and we watched it come. A shiny new Cadillac Escalade—white—one of those 70K-plus SUVs. It slowed down just enough so the people inside—a man and woman I didn't know—could give us the once-over. The woman, an older lady with her gray hair swept up on her head, actually pointed at us. The man—he was wearing a black beret—turned to follow her pointing finger, and there we were, two men in Carhartt bibs and thermal undershirts. Two redneck men, one of them wearing an eye patch and one of them holding a rifle. Two scruffy-assed, potentially psychopathic men, and a girl in a short skirt and stilettos.

The Escalade went on past, toward town. The brake lights came on once, as if the man was trying to decide whether to stop. Then he sped up and was gone.

"Come on," I said, ashamed now on account of those looks from that man and woman, but determined, too, not to let them tell us who we were. "Wink, this lady needs an escort."

There comes a time when you have to own up to your life. That's what I was thinking as we all got back in the Mustang and Wink drove nice as could be into Sumner. We drove past the cemetery and that statue of Jesus with his open arms. We drove past the first houses. They had pumpkins on their front porches, cornstalks gathered up into shocks, bales of straw, scarecrows posed this way and that. The Borla X-pipes on the Mustang guttered along, making that rumble that would wake you from your bed with your heart fluttering if you heard it in the middle of the night. Wink didn't have any music playing now, so I listened to the somber rumble of those pipes, and I heard Lily draw a deep breath and then let it out as the funeral home came into view.

Cars were parked up and down the street. The sidewalk was full of people—women taking men's arms and walking with ginger steps over the uneven concrete and the leaves that had fallen there, children holding parents' hands and skipping along because they were too young to understand where they were going.

I knew the feeling. My first day without a drink was a snap. I thought I had clear sailing ahead of me. I thought I could just walk through a door, easy as pie, into a brand new life. The next day taught me I was wrong, and the next one after that, on and on. Then finally I reached a place where the life of a sober man seemed right to me, and little by little I moved away from the drunk man I used to be.

Then this day came, and Lily flagged us down on the blacktop, and because of her, I called back what it felt like to be about to walk into a group of people and have everyone stare because you were who you were and they were who they were, and the difference was something they'd never let you forget.

"I can't go in," Lily said. She put her face in her hands and started to cry. "I just can't."

Wink pulled the Mustang in behind the Cadillac Escalade that had gone past us on the blacktop. It was empty now, and the man and woman, obviously folks who somehow knew Jackie Frutag, were inside the funeral home paying their respects.

"This is your daddy's laying out," I told Lily. "This is a day that won't ever come again. You need to be present." I reached back and snapped my fingers next to her ear. "You need to pay attention."

She took her hands away from her face. She dug around in her Betty Boop purse and found the handkerchief I'd given her. She dabbed at her eyes. She leaned across the console, looking for her reflection in the rearview. Wink turned it so she could see. She patted her hair. "All right," she said, "but I don't know that I can do this alone."

Wink said he wasn't going in there. He said he hadn't signed on for anything like that. He bristled for a tick, and then he turned a little shy. He ducked his head and touched a finger to his eye patch, tugging down on the corner, resetting it, and for an instant I felt the kind of life he had. "I'm not dressed proper," he said.

"Me either." I slapped at the legs of my Carhartts. "But you know what, Wink? It doesn't matter a flip as long as our hearts are in the right place. Even Jackie would tell you that."

"Please," said Lily.

That's how we ended up at Jackie Frutag's laying out, Wink and Lily and me. We walked in big as day. I didn't care how we looked. I didn't care what people would say. "Wink," I'd say later. "It was what we had to do. It was the right thing. I'll never have doubts about that."

They had Jackie in the main visitation room, the long center room with rows of folding chairs and the comfortable armchairs and sofas along the side. The double doors were open, and we stood in the vestibule, looking in at the people who'd come. They stood in little groups or sat on the folding chairs. A few folks were gathered at the casket. I looked for my mama, who I figured would be stopping by, but she wasn't anywhere I could see.

Cathy was sitting on a sofa near the casket, her hands in her lap, fiddling with a handkerchief. She had on a dark dress and black stockings. She'd always been a pretty woman, and she'd come to middle age in a fine way. Just a sprinkle of salt in her brown hair, just a few lines around her eyes. Jackie lay in the casket, his eyes closed, his folded hands resting on his stomach.

There's nothing quite like the smell of all those fresh flowers carried in for a funeral—all the gladiolus and mums and carnations and roses. There's that smell of flowers and the murmur of voices and the feel of the carpet under your feet to make you understand that this is a special place, a place where things come to an end.

"There's your mama," I said to Lily, and I nodded my head. "You ought to go up and let her know you're here."

"I'm afraid," Lily stuffed her sunglasses into her purse. "I won't know what to say."

"That's easy." I cupped her elbow and gave her a little nudge forward. I knew from my own missteps that it was best in times like this to come clean. "Just tell her you're sorry for the hurt you've brought her. Go on, darlin'. Just start there."

The woman from the white Escalade was signing the guest register. The man, still wearing his beret, stood a few feet away from her, waiting. He wore a black suit and one of those white shirts without a collar, the sort that buttons right at your Adam's apple. He had on a pair of black loafers with tassels, and he seemed fascinated by them on account he kept tapping first one foot and then the other, staring down at his feet to watch those tassels jounce.

The woman turned and saw us. She had on dressy black pants and a black wool poncho that tapered down in a vee. Half-frame reading glasses perched on her nose, and she squinted at us over the tops of them.

"We saw you on the highway," she said.

Her husband looked up from his loafers. "Were you having trouble? I wasn't sure whether to stop." I knew he was thinking about that Ruger. I knew he was trying to determine whether he should be afraid of us. "No, wait a minute. I know you." He chuckled. "You're that man. The one who drove the barstool." He shook his head. "Lord a mercy. What a fool thing. What in the world were you thinking?"

Wink took a step toward him. "That's ancient history, mister." He poked him in the chest with his finger. "Leave it alone."

The man—he was ballsy for his age, I'll give him that—knocked Wink's hand away. "Are you some kind of goon?" he said. "Is that why you wear that eye patch? Are you this fellow's henchman?" He laughed, tickled, I guess, on account he thought he was being a funny man. "I bet you don't even have a reason to wear that patch. I bet it's just for show."

Wink said, "That's right. I'm his henchman."

He said it in a low, even voice, like that was a word he was used to saying every day of his life. He said it like he was stating a fact and there wasn't anything funny about it.

But the man laughed again. A little chuckle. "Henchman," he said with a smirk, like it was a word that people like him owned and it didn't belong on the tongues of people like Wink and me.

Something went through me, then, the feeling I used to get when I'd stagger out of a bar, maybe puke on my shoes or piss myself, or fall over on the street and end up scraped and sore, and I'd hear people laughing, or worse yet, they wouldn't say a thing—they'd just stare, and when I caught them, they'd look away like I wasn't right there in front of them. Standing there in that funeral home, I got that old sick feeling of hating myself and the life I had. I let that man do that to me even though I thought I'd squared things and was moving on.

I took Wink by the arm and pulled him back so I could get up between him and the man. I reached up and tore that beret from the man's head—he was all-over bald—and shoved it into his hands. "Take off your lid, brother. This is a funeral home."

That's what did it, set off a chain of events that went too fast for anyone to stop. If I had to do it over again, maybe I wouldn't have— maybe I'd have just told that man, no, there'd been no trouble out there on the blacktop, thanks for asking—but there's no use wondering about it now. What's done is done, and all I can do is tell it, plain as I can, the last part of this story, the part that'll haunt me forever.

The bald man slapped that beret back on his head, and I said, "Maybe you didn't hear me." I snatched the beret again, and this time I stuffed it into the bib of my Carhartts. "Do you need a lesson about respect? And another thing, I don't like the way you talked to my friend."

I looked around for Wink, but he was gone. I felt alone, then, hung out to dry, but I didn't have time to feel sorry for myself on account the man was giving me what for.

"Respect," he said with a snort. He looked me up and down. "A man like you is lecturing me about respect?" He gave me one of those exaggerated laughs—ha, ha. "Look at you," he said. "Ridiculous."

That's when I took him by the throat. I'm ashamed of it now. He was an old man who happened to be in the way of everything that ailed me. I took him by the throat, right above the top button of that ridiculous shirt, and I told him to shut up. I told him he didn't know anything about the sort of man I was.

Maybe I didn't either. Maybe that's what I was about to find out.

The man's wife screamed. The people in the visitation room turned to see what was happening in the vestibule.

Cathy rose from the sofa and saw Lily. The white handkerchief fell from Cathy's hand, and it was like she was frozen, like she was afraid to move one way or the other for fear that what she was seeing might disappear.

That's the last thing I saw before the funeral director put his face in mine. He was a blond-haired man with one of those tanning parlor bake jobs. He tried to loosen my hands from the man's throat, but I hung on. Then he got me in a headlock. He wrestled me away from the man, and we sort of scrabbled across the vestibule until we knocked into the guest register stand and we both went down.

Everything was a flurry of feet to me, then, and the rise of people's voices. The funeral director still had me in that headlock, twisting me around, and every once in a while I caught a glimpse of someone's shoes. The carpet smelled of some sort of floral cleaner, and the funeral director had on too much pine-scented aftershave, something from Avon, I'd wager. Probably some of that Wild Country that my father always wore. I heard a man say, "What in the world?" A woman said, "He's a drunk, you know."

I felt a stir of air around me. A woman screamed. Everything went quiet, then, like all the air had gone out of the place, and that's when I heard it, the sound I knew so well, the gentle click of the safety going off on my Ruger. I knew, without having to look, that Wink had been so pissed over what the man with the beret said that he'd gotten the rifle from his Mustang and had it shouldered up now and ready to use.

"Let loose of him," he said to the funeral director, and then I was free. I rubbed at my neck. "All right, then," Wink said, and he swung that Ruger around, pointing it into the viewing room, where people scrambled to crouch down behind the sofas and chairs.

That's when I saw the most wonderful thing. Lily, still wobbly on those stilettos, was very patiently making her way up the center aisle. She stepped around folding chairs knocked cockeyed, waited patiently for those who were still trying to get somewhere safe. She made her way to her daddy's casket, and, once she was there, she reached her hand out and put it on top of his. She stood up straight, her back to all the ugliness we'd wrought behind her, and she had that moment, one she might not have had without me, without Wink.

"Put down the gun," I told him. I nodded toward the front of the visitation room.

He took the Ruger down from his shoulder. He rubbed at his good eye. He was seeing what I was, the grace that'd come to someone we'd thought, only minutes before, was a drunk girl in stilettos looking for a ride up the blacktop. Now she was Lily. Now she had the chance her mama said she'd deny her. "Mercy," Wink said.

It was a no-good prayer on account, at least in one sense, it was over for him and me. Of course you can't cause a disturbance and point a loaded rifle at folks in a public place and not pay the price for it, particularly after all the times I'd been arrested when I was drunk. Aggravated assault. What would you expect, folks would say, from the likes of them?

Lily, though, was at the start of something. I felt it in my heart. This was the day she'd start to turn everything around. Or maybe that was only my hope talking. I really don't know a thing about what happened to her after the county sheriff carted Wink and me off to jail. I just remember seeing her mama easing up beside her at the casket.

She put her arms out and gathered her in, her little girl—the one she'd sworn she'd disown—and they held onto each other.

I'll carry the picture of that to my grave, and though I'm sorry for all the fright we brought folks that day, I can't say I regret it. I can only hope they finally saw the good that lay on the other side of what we did. I hope my own mama knows it, too.

She was outside the funeral home, just arriving, when the sheriff brought me out in cuffs.

"I'd do it now," I said to Wink.

He was in front of me in the company of a deputy. "Do what?" he wanted to know.

"Have a drink."

A million drinks. I'd have drunk myself to death to keep my mama from seeing me in trouble, the way she'd seen me so many times.

"Oh, Benny," she said. She lifted her arms a little like she might try to touch me, but, of course, she couldn't. The law had me, and when that's the case, you don't have many choices; you just go. "Benny," she said, "is that you?"

Like she'd been waiting. Maybe I'd been gone on a long trip somewhere—I closed my eyes an instant and made it true—and now here she was, glad in the heart.

I'd tell her to take me home, and we'd have a good laugh over how at first she hadn't seemed to know me. "Oh, I did, too," she'd tell me. She'd lean over and whisper in my ear, "You didn't have me fooled. I knew it was you all along."

A MAN LOOKING
FOR TROUBLE

MY UNCLE WAS A MAN NAMED BILL JORDAN, AND IN 1972, WHEN I WAS sixteen, he came home from Vietnam, rented a small box house on the corner of South and Christy, and went to work on a section gang with the B & O Railroad. If not for my mother and her romance with our neighbor, Harold Timms, perhaps my uncle would have lived a quiet and unremarkable life, but of course, that's something we'll never know.

"He'll do all right," my father said one night at supper. He looked out the window and nodded his head. It was the first warm day of spring, and the window was open. I smelled the damp ground, heard the robins singing. "I'm glad he's back," my father said, and I believe now, for just an instant, my mother and I let ourselves get caught up in his optimism, a gift we desperately needed, although we were the sort of family that never would have admitted as much.

"How's your pork chop?" my mother asked.

"Bill's going to be aces," my father said.

Then we all sat there, chewing, not saying much of anything else at all. Bill was home, safe, and for the time that's the only thing that mattered.

By summer, though, he was fed up with Harold Timms, who happened to be his foreman on the section gang. It was generally known throughout Goldengate that Mr. Timms was keeping time with my mother, a fact that rankled Bill day in and day out because on the job he was tired of acting like he didn't know better. My father, a withdrawn man who kept his troubles to himself, had apparently decided to ignore my mother's adultery.

"I have to do what Harold Timms tells me every day," Bill said to my father one Sunday afternoon. They were in the shade of the big maple alongside our house, changing the points and plugs on our Ford Galaxie. "And all the while everyone in town knows he's getting it steady from your Annie."

I lay on my bed, listening. Out my window, I could see Bill leaning over the fender of the Galaxie. The hood was open above him, and he was going to town with a spark plug wrench. He had on a black bowling shirt with a print of a teetering pin wearing a crown and the words KING PINS across the back. He'd rolled the short sleeves tight on his biceps. From my position, all I could see of my father, who stood on the other side of the Galaxie, was his long, narrow hand on top of that fender. The face of his Timex watch seemed enormous on his slender wrist. A brown leather band wrapped around that wrist with plenty of length to spare. I knew he'd had to punch an extra hole in it.

"Damn it, R.T." Bill banged the spark plug wrench against a motor mount. "You need to put a stop to that monkey business. For Roger's sake, if for no other reason."

My name came to me through the window and caught me by surprise, as if my father and Bill knew I was eavesdropping even though I was sure they didn't. My father's hand pulled away from the fender, and I imagined him, outside my view, fuming.

The leaves on the maple rattled together. It was August, the start of the dog days, and we were grateful for every stir of air. Next door, at the Timmses' house, a radio was playing. The curtain at the window lifted and fell back with the breeze. I could hear the faint strains of "Too Late to Turn Back Now," and the chorus—*I believe, I believe, I believe I'm fallin' in love*—annoyed me because I knew it was Connie Timms listening to it, and I was fretting about her because she'd told me after church that she and I were through.

"I can't do this anymore," she said. We were outside on the sidewalk, and people were coming out of the church and down the steps. "I want a boyfriend I can tell the world about. I don't want some…" Here, she struggled to find the words she wanted, the ones that would describe what she and I had been up to that summer. "I don't want an affair," she finally said.

Now I can almost laugh at the way that word sounded coming from a girl her age. At the time, though, my heart was breaking.

She wanted a boyfriend she could show off, parade around with on Friday and Saturday nights, maybe go to a movie at the Avalon Theater in Phillipsport and later drive out to the Dairy Queen to see who was sitting around on the hoods of their cars before heading to the state park or the gravel pits for that alone time in the car, that baby-oh-baby time, secretly hoping that some of the other kids would happen by, so come Monday there would be talk all over school. That was the sort of gossip she wanted to be part of—the kind that said you were part of the cool crowd—not the kind I could give her, the kind filled with shame.

I watched her run down the sidewalk to her father's Oldsmobile 98, fling the door open, and get inside. I knew she didn't mean for me to come after her. I wanted to, but I didn't have the nerve.

If not for my mother and Mr. Timms, everything between Connie and me might have been fine. My mother and Mr. Timms. Like my father, I tried to ignore what was going on between them, but it was impossible.

Earlier that summer, Connie and I began to take note of each other, and as we got cozy, we agreed to keep our hey-baby-hey a secret. What would people think? Apples didn't fall far from the tree. Why did that concern me? I suppose there was a part of me that believed I was betraying my father, who lived with the pain my mother caused him every day, and who surely wouldn't be happy if he knew I'd thrown in with Connie. How could she and I make our affections known when her father and my mother were the subjects of so much gossip? I'd like to say we wanted to be better than that gossip, but I suspect we were just embarrassed. We were afraid the town was watching us, and every time we were together on the sly, I felt guilty. I wanted to think that we'd found each other solely from our two hearts syncing up, but as long as I had to worry about my mother and her father, I wasn't sure. Maybe we were just following their lead.

We couldn't have said any of this at the time. At least I couldn't have. I won't presume to speak for Connie. I only know this: No matter what we could say then, or what we knew by instinct, one fact was plain—whatever was happening between the two of us could never be separated from the fact that her father and my mother were lovers.

"We can't let anyone find out," I told Connie early on. "We can't be trashy like them."

"My father's not trashy." She had a pageboy haircut and her bangs were in need of a trim. We were talking over the wire fence that ran between my backyard and hers. She had on Levi's and white Keds sneakers and a T-shirt that advertised Boone's Farm, a soda pop wine popular in those days. She brushed her bangs out of her eyes and stared at me. "He's lonely. He's a very lonely man."

I loved her brown hair and her blue eyes. I loved the smell of her perfume—something called Straw Hat that was sweet and woodsy and made me want to press her to me and breathe in that scent. She could have said anything to me at that moment and I would have taken it as gospel. So I let that statement about Mr. Timms's loneliness absolve him, and with my silence—much to my shame—I allowed my mother to become the wicked one in the story of their affair.

Mr. Timms was a widower. His wife, a nervous, fretful woman, took sick one winter night when a heavy snow was falling. It started around dusk, and before long the streets were covered. The snow kept coming down as night crept in. My father and I went into our living room to watch it out the window. By that time, the snow was up to the top of the drainage ditches that ran alongside the street.

"It's like a picture out there," my father said. I was thirteen then. We stood in the dark room and watched the snow coming down past the streetlights. No cars passed by. We could see lights on in the houses around us. Everyone was hunkering down to wait this one out. Over twenty inches by morning, WAKO radio out of the county seat,

Phillipsport, said. The wind was up, and already the snow was starting to drift against the side of our shed. My father's Galaxie, parked in our driveway, was barely holding its shape under the snow. "Roger, I swear." He put his hand on my shoulder and gave me a squeeze. "It's like we're in a picture," he said, and I've always remembered that because it was one of the first times he ever said anything that I sensed came from some private place inside him that he generally kept to himself.

My mother was in the family room with the television playing. It was a Saturday night. I'm sure of that because I remember that *The Jackie Gleason Show* was on. My mother laughed at something, and I could hear the television audience laughing, too. My father and I turned at the same time, looking back through the French doors that separated the living room from the family room. We saw the lamplight there. He squeezed my shoulder again, and at his touch we headed toward those French doors. Once we opened them, we stepped back into the life that was ours.

"Baby, you should've seen," my mother said to my father. She was kicked back in her Barcalounger, her arm bent at the elbow so it went up at a right angle. She held a Virginia Slims cigarette between her fingers and the smoke curled up into the lamplight. "It was the funniest thing. I was afraid I was going to wet my pants."

She was wearing a pair of black slacks and a black turtleneck sweater. She'd just had her hair done the day before, and her loose blond curls came down over her shoulders. I'd always known she was a pretty woman—prettier than most of my friends' mothers—but she looked particularly glamorous in the lamplight. Big gold hoop earrings dangled against the sides of her turtleneck.

"We were watching it snow," my father said.

I believe now he must have been uncomfortable with my mother's beauty. He wasn't the kind of man who could enjoy knowing that wherever he went with his wife, other men would be looking at her. Thoughtful and shy, he preferred to live a private life. If there were pleasures to be had, he'd rather the world not know about them. He was the county tax assessor and he knew that it was a man looking for trouble who chose to parade his riches and not expect someone to take notice and wish himself into a share of that wealth.

"Everyone has to pay for what he has," he told me once. "That's what I know, Roger. No one gets off scot-free."

He wasn't a looker. Not that he was an unattractive man, but next to my mother, he paled. He had sloped shoulders and a long face and a nose that was too big. I expect he spent most of his married life shaking his head over his dumb luck in landing a woman as beautiful as Annie Griggs.

One night, at the Uptown Café, we walked away from our table, and just before we got to the door, I heard a low wolf whistle. I know my father heard it, too, because just for an instant his back stiffened, and he gave a quick glance behind him. My mother took his arm, and that claiming gesture must have soothed him because he opened the door and we stepped out onto the sidewalk. Later, when I was supposed to be sleeping, I heard them talking about what had happened. "Dang it, Annie," my father said, and after a while my mother answered in a quiet voice, "It's not like I ask for it."

What she was asking that winter night, when she told my father about the comedy sketch she'd seen on TV, was for us to sit down with her and be a family—to give her, I imagine now, a reason to be happy with her home and the people in it. But before any of that could happen, someone knocked on our front door.

"My word," my father said. "Who could that be on a night like this?"

He went into the living room to open the door, and after a while, I heard Mr. Timms's voice. It was a loud voice, full of dread and fear. "It's Jean," he said. "She's sick and I don't know what to do about it."

"Sick?" my father said in a way that told me he didn't know what to do about it either.

"She went to bed for a rest after supper, and now I can't get her to wake up."

My mother had already put the footrest down on her Barcalounger. I could feel the cold air around my legs, and I knew my father was holding the front door open as he talked to Mr. Timms.

"Tell him to come in," my mother called to my father. "Harold, come inside," she said.

The ceiling light snapped on in the living room. The front door closed, and I heard Mr. Timms stomping snow from his boots on the rug just inside the door.

I followed my mother into the living room, and there he was, bareheaded, the collar of his black wool coat turned up to his ears. He'd stuffed his trouser legs into the tops of a pair of green rubber boots from which snow was melting. He wore a pair of glasses in black, plastic frames, and those glasses were steamed over now that he'd come in from the cold.

"Annie?" he said, and he sounded so helpless.

"Don't worry, Harold." My mother walked right up to him. She reached up and took his glasses off his face. She used the hem of her sweater to wipe the steam from the lenses. "I'm going to get my coat and boots on," she said. "Then I'm going to come see to her. Everything will be fine."

Mr. Timms reached out and touched my mother lightly on her arm. "Thank you, Annie," he said, and I believe it may have been then, though he surely couldn't have known this, that he started to fall in love with her.

It must have been a feeling that simmered those three years after Mrs. Timms died. She died that night, was dead already, in fact, when Mr. Timms stood in our living room, putting his glasses back on and waiting for my mother.

"There wasn't a thing I could do," she said later, after the ambulance had finally made its way through the snow and taken Mrs. Timms away. "Poor Jean. She was gone when I got there."

My father and I had eventually put on our own coats and boots and made our way next door. My mother called for the ambulance, which was something, my father said later, that Mr. Timms should have done instead of coming to our house. "He didn't know what to do," my mother said with a sharp bite to her voice. "That poor man. He was lost."

Connie wasn't crying. That would all come later. She sat on the couch in the living room and stared straight ahead, not saying a word.

My mother finally sat down beside her and took her up in her arms. "You sweet girl," my mother kept saying, rocking Connie back and forth. "You sweet, sweet girl."

Mr. Timms was in the bedroom with Mrs. Timms, and from time to time I heard a thud and I imagined that he was banging his fist into the wall. "Go see about him," my mother said to my father. After a while, I heard his and Mr. Timms's voices coming from the bedroom. "Oh, Jesus," Mr. Timms said, and I heard my father say, "We're right here, Harold."

Then finally my father came out of the room, and without a word he went outside. Soon I heard the scrape of a shovel, and, when I looked out the Timmses' front window, I saw my father clearing the sidewalk and the steps up onto the porch. He kept at it, digging out the driveway. "The ambulance was coming," he told me once we were back in our own house. "I didn't know what else to do but to clear a path."

In the weather, it took a good while, but finally the ambulance was there, its swirling red lights flashing over the house. The paramedics took Mrs. Timms out on a gurney, and later we learned that she'd died because of a bad heart. "Who'd have thought?" my mother said. She told us that it made it plain how quickly we could go. "If you want something, you better grab it," she said. "You never know if you'll have another chance."

After Bill and my father finished with the Galaxie that Sunday in August, they decided to go squirrel hunting. Bill called for me, and I got up from the bed and went outside to see what he wanted.

"Grab your .410," he told me. "We're going after bushytails."

I looked toward my father. He was putting down the hood of the Galaxie, and he said, "How 'bout that, Roger? It's just the three of us here, anyway. Just the three bulls. What say we get out and roam around a little? Shoot a few squirrels, have a little boy time."

That summer, he'd been trying extra hard with me, imagining, perhaps, that he and my mother were close to being finished, and once they were, he'd want to have me on his side. The problem was he'd never been the kind of har-de-har-har man that Bill was, and any attempt on my father's part to be friendly with me came across as forced and left me feeling uncomfortable.

We should have been talking about my mother and the fact that our family was on the verge of coming apart. We should have considered what was causing that to happen and what we might be able to do to stop it. Instead, my father was puffing himself up, getting all wink-wink, palsy-wowsy, pretending there wasn't a thing wrong. It was just a summer Sunday and we were going hunting. Men out with their shotguns. A part of me thought that if my father were truly a man, this thing between my mother and Mr. Timms wouldn't be going on and Connie and I would still be sweet on each other. I wouldn't be living in the shadow of my mother's indiscretion and my father's inability to do anything about it. As wrong as it was, I found myself giving him the blame, thinking there was something about him—a lack of heart, or courage, or by-God-you-won't—that made my mother do what she did.

So when he made that big show about the three bulls going off to have some boy time, I got a little fed up with the way we kept acting like we were charmed when, really, we weren't at all. We were gossip. We were the family folks could feel sorry for or judge. Either way, our lives weren't ours anymore. We belonged to the town and its prying eyes and clucking tongues. I was tired of that. I wanted my father to finally acknowledge it.

So I said, "Where'd Mom go?"

She'd slipped out of the house after dinner. We'd gone to services at the First Christian as usual and then come home to the meal she'd prepared. Bill came by and had coconut cream pie and coffee with us. Then he and my father went out to work on the Galaxie. I lay on my bed and heard Mr. Timms fire up his Olds. He honked his horn as he went up the street, and Bill said to my father, "There he goes."

From my bedroom, I could hear my mother singing along with the radio next door. She had a pretty singing voice, and as I listened to her, I couldn't help but think how happy she sounded. Soon I heard our screen door creak open and then slap against the jamb. I sat up and leaned over to look out the window. She had on a red summer dress with a halter top and a pleated skirt. Her bare shoulders were shiny in the sunlight. She carried a box purse made from woven straw. It had strawberries and white blooms on it, and she held the handle and swung it back and forth as she walked. Her shoes, a pair of strappy sandals, slapped over the sidewalk. Her curls bounced against her bare back.

She turned back once and waved at my father and Bill. "Going fishin', boys," she said, and then walked on up the street.

Now, as I waited for my father to answer my question, I saw the slightest grimace around his lips.

"She went visiting," he said.

I wouldn't let him off that easily. "Visiting who?"

Bill was wiping off his hands with a red shop rag. "Get your gun, hotshot." He threw the rag into my face and gave me a hard look that told me to shut up and fall into line. "Chop-chop, buddy boy. I mean it. Right now."

It was a quiet ride down into the country. Bill drove his El Camino, and the three of us crowded onto the bench seat. I was crammed in between Bill and my father. Our guns, my .410 and my father's and Bill's twelve-gauges, were cased and stowed behind us in the bed.

"Damned hot," Bill said.

We were on the blacktop south of town, and the fields were flashing by, the corn stunted along the fence rows, the ground cracked from lack of rain.

"No good for the crops," my father said, and it went like that for quite a while. Just a thing said here and there. The windows were down and the hot air was rushing in, and it was hard to carry on a conversation, but I knew, even if we'd been cruising along in air-conditioned quiet, no one would have felt much like talking.

That was unusual for Bill, because he generally had something to say and he wasn't afraid to say it. He was a different sort of man than my father. He was blustery and hot-tempered, but fun-loving, too. He was always pulling a prank on someone and then looking so doggone happy about it that everyone forgave him. He was a trackman on the section gang, and one day his trickster ways finally caught up with him. He pulled a joke on Mr. Timms, stuffed five cigarette loads into one of his cigars, and when Mr. Timms put a lighter to it, the cigar exploded and frayed at its end. Mr. Timms, startled, jumped back, slipped on the rail, and fell onto the slope of the gravel bed.

He was all right, just shaken and bruised, but he was pissed off, too. "I don't have to ask who did that," he said, staring right at Bill. "Some people are ignorant. That's all that needs to be said about that."

What Bill didn't know—or if he'd ever known, had no reason to recall—was that day was the anniversary of Jean Timms's death. "Now how was I to know that?" Bill asked my father later. "He's got it in for me now. You can by God know that for sure."

True enough, Bill had spent the rest of winter and on into spring and now summer suffering the brunt of Mr. Timms's anger. "Any shit job you can think of," Bill had said to my father while they were working on the Galaxie. "You can bet I'm the one who'll get it. I've just about had enough." Bill blamed this all on my father. "R.T., if you just told him you know what's what between him and Annie, maybe then he'd ease off. He likes to think he's a decent man. Let him know he's a phony, R.T., and he'll be more humble."

My father wasn't made for such a thing. As we went on down the blacktop in the El Camino, I took note again of that Timex he was wearing—the face so big on that delicate wrist—and I found myself thinking, he doesn't have the heart. I'm ashamed of that thought now, considering everything that was about to happen—things I still can't get straight enough to suit me.

Bill and my father owned eighty acres in Lukin Township just off the County Line Road. The farm had belonged to my grandparents, but my grandfather was dead and my grandmother was living in a nursing home. She'd deeded the place to Bill and my father, and they leased it out to a tenant farmer. Often, on Sunday afternoons, they came down to give the place a looksee. The home place, they always called it. Sometimes, like the day I'm recalling, they brought their shotguns.

We uncased our guns and started out. We skirted the old chicken house and the clump of horse weeds taller than the roof.

"Should've brought a hoe to cut those down," Bill said.

"Next time," said my father.

We walked single file along the edge of the field that came up to the chicken house and the patch of ground my grandparents had always used for their vegetable garden. The tenant farmer had plowed up the field and sowed it in soybeans once he'd cut the wheat. The bean plants were already reaching toward knee-high. We had to crowd up into the foxtail growing along the wire fence to keep from tromping the beans. The leaves on the plants in that outer row brushed against my legs.

"Sowing fencerow to fencerow, ain't he?" Bill said.

He was in the lead, and my father was right behind him. "Using all he can," he said. "Getting everything he can get."

A little air stirred the bean plants. A covey of quail got up from the fencerow, their wings a loud whirring and clacking that startled me. Bill got his twelve-gauge to his shoulder, but already the covey was banking over the tree line.

"Damn, I should have been ready," Bill said.

"Out of season," my father reminded him.

"Who would've known?" Bill lowered the twelve-gauge and cradled it. "Just you and me and Roger out here. Far as I can see, there's no one else around."

The sky didn't have a cloud in it, just the contrail from an invisible jet stretching out little by little. I thought about Connie—wondered what she was doing, wondered if she'd really meant it when she told me we were through. Some nights that summer, we'd driven down to the farm so we could be alone and out of sight. I had a '63 Impala I'd bought with the money I'd saved working hay crews since I was thirteen and the last two summers on a Christmas tree farm west of Goldengate. Connie sat close on the bench seat when she rode with me, her hand on my thigh.

Our routine was she'd go for a walk in the evening. I'd hear her screen door slap shut, and I'd see her going on up the sidewalk. She'd have on a pair of Levi's and one of the halter tops she favored that summer, her breasts loose beneath it, a blue or red or white bow tied under her hair at her neck and another sash tied at the small of her back, the tails of that bow trailing down over the waist of her jeans and bouncing with the roll of her hips. She'd walk out Locust Street to the City Park at the edge of town and wait for me in one of the dugouts at the baseball field. I always gave my horn a honk when I took the last curve out of town, and, when I pulled in behind the concession stand, she'd be there, ready to open the passenger door and slide across that bench seat and kiss me.

I had a blanket in the trunk of the Impala, and at the farm, we spread it out on the grass and lay next to each other and waited for the stars to come out. It got so dark out there in the country, and under all those stars we said the things that were most on our minds, the things we could barely stand to face when they were in front of us in the daylight.

Connie said she missed her mother, and sometimes she cried a little and I held her hand and didn't say a word.

One night she said, "Why doesn't your mother love your father?"

I told her I didn't know, which was the truth. I've had years to think about what the trouble between them might have been, but I've never been able to say it was this or that. Maybe it was my father's caution. Maybe my mother grew tired of the careful way he lived his life. One evening, when they were hosting a pinochle party for a few couples they knew from church, my father kept underbidding his hands. Finally, my mother said, "Oh, for Pete's sake, R.T. Live a little." Little things like that have come back to me as time has gone on, but I can't say for certain they mean anything.

One thing I remember keeps me up at night, and that's the event I told Connie about on the Saturday night before the Sunday when she told me she couldn't see me anymore and later Bill and my father and I were moving into the woods with our shotguns. It may have been the story that spooked her, that made her believe what we were doing was ill-fated and could never come to a good end.

I said to her, "Last night, I heard him beg her to stop."

My mother and father talking stirred me from sleep in the middle of the night. I don't know how long they'd been at it, trying to keep their voices low so I wouldn't hear, but by the time I was awake, they were beyond that point. They weren't thinking about anything except what had brought them to where they stood—in the midst of an ugliness they could no longer deny or ignore.

My father said, "Please, Annie. I've always tried my best to give you a good life, to give us a good life…" His voice trailed off and then I heard a noise I couldn't at first identify as anything that might come from a human being. A groan, a growl, a whimper at the end. In the silence that followed, I remember thinking, that's my father. "Annie," he finally said. "You've got to stop this. If you don't…"

His voice left him, then—swallowed up, I imagine, by the terror he felt over the prospect of a life without her.

"You want a divorce," my mother said after a time. "Is that it?"

My father was weeping now. I could hear that. "Annie," he said in a breathless, shaking voice. "I want you to love me."

For a good while, there was only the sound of him trying to choke down his sobs and get his breath.

Then my mother said, in a gentle voice I've always tried to remember for what it was, the voice of a woman who'd found her way to trouble and didn't know how to get out: "I'm here." She said, "R.T., shh. Listen to me." I like to think that she touched him, then—touched his face or his hand, maybe even put her arms around his neck and pressed him to her. "I'm right here," she said again. "That's the most you should wish."

Connie hadn't asked for this story. We'd only been lying on the blanket, looking up at the stars, not saying much of anything, just enjoying being close to each other in the dark, and I'd felt safe telling her what I'd overheard. I was sixteen. She was my first love. She was the only person I could tell.

What did I know, then, about the ties that bind one person to another? I had to live through what was waiting for me that Sunday to know anything about love at all.

"My father's the cause of that." Connie sat up on the blanket. She crossed her arms over her stomach and started rocking back and forth. "He should have left your mother alone."

"She made a choice," I said. "It wasn't just him."

For a good while, Connie didn't say anything. Then in a whisper she said, "Yes, they both made their choices."

Just then, a set of headlights came down the lane. They lit up the gravel roadbed and spread out over the fencerows. They came so far that they shined on the wire fencing around the farmhouse yard. I could hear the engine idling and the faint sound of the car radio. The tires crunched over the gravel as the car rolled forward an inch or two. Then it stopped.

I knew whoever was in that car was looking at the grille of my Impala. Those headlights had caught the chrome. Whoever was in that car knew now they weren't the only ones who'd come down that lane, and they were trying to decide what to do.

Connie was still sitting up on the blanket. We were on the grass to the left of the Impala, about even with the trunk, and just barely out of the glare of the headlights.

"Roger," she said, and I could tell she was scared.

I reached up and put my hand on the small of her back, felt the heat of her skin. "It's okay," I said. "Everything's okay."

It seemed like the car in the lane would sit there forever, the driver unable to decide whether to keep coming. A drop of sweat slid down Connie's back and onto my hand. Then somewhere nearby a screech owl started its trill, a call that seemed to come from the other side of the living, and I felt my heart pounding in my chest.

"Oh, God," said Connie.

Then the car in the lane started backing up. It backed all the way to the end, where it swung out and pointed itself north. I watched the red taillights, and what I didn't tell Connie, though maybe she knew this on her own, was that those long vertical rows of lights, set wide apart, were the taillights of an Olds 98 like her father's.

"Whoever that was, they're gone," I said.

I let my hand fall to the bow of her halter top. I started to untie it, but she slapped my hand away.

"That was spooky," she said. "That car. C'mon. Let's go."

In my mind now, the image of the two of us walking toward my Impala and driving back to town is forever tied up with the picture of me stepping into the woods that Sunday with Bill and my father.

We waited and waited around a stand of hickory trees where we'd seen husks on the ground, and though from time to time we heard a squirrel chattering in the tree mast high above us, we could never get a clear shot, and after too much time keeping quiet, Bill finally said, "Fuck it. I'm done."

He was all for heading back to town, but my father said, "Let's walk on over to the end of the next field and see if there's any better hunting in Kepper's Woods. We're here. We might as well."

Jean Timms had been a Kepper before she married Mr. Timms, and those woods had been in her family longer than I could imagine. I didn't know any of that on that Sunday; Kepper's Woods was just a name to me, like Higgins Corner or McVeigh Bottoms—places marked by the names of families, the history of whom I had no reason to know.

Surely my father knew about Jean Timms and Kepper's Woods. I wonder now whether he had any thought at all of what he might find there.

"Might as well," Bill said, and off we went.

Marathon Oil had a lease road running through those woods, and that's where we came upon the car—Mr. Timms's Olds 98—nosed deep into the shade of the hickories and oaks and ash trees and sweetgums.

A flash of my mother's red sundress caught my eye first—just a quick glimpse of red as she came around the front of the Olds—and then, just like that, the whole picture came into view: the dark green Olds with road dust coating the top of the rear bumper, the gold of Mr. Timms's Ban-Lon pullover shirt, the bright red of my mother's sundress. She walked a few steps behind the car, back down the oil lease road, before Mr. Timms caught up to her. He took her by her arm and turned her around to face him. He put his arms around her, and she put her arms around him, and they held each other there in the woods on that road where they thought no one could see.

"There's Mom," I said, and as soon as I said it, I wished I hadn't.

When I saw her with Mr. Timms, I found the sight so strange and yet somehow familiar, mixed up as it was with what I felt about Connie, that I couldn't help but say what I did.

I imagine my father would have eventually spotted them, and what took place next would still have happened, but even now I can't stop myself from believing that if I'd kept my mouth shut, perhaps we would have veered away from that oil lease road and Bill and my father never would have seen what I did. I can't keep myself from thinking that maybe there was that one chance that we would have gone on, maybe found some squirrels, maybe not, and then driven back into town, and our lives would have gone on the way they'd been moving all summer. Maybe there was that one possibility of grace that I cost us. There's Mom, I said, and Bill and my father stopped.

We were hidden in the woods, maybe fifty yards away, and my mother and Mr. Timms had no idea we were there.

My father said to me, in a very quiet, very calm voice, "Go back to the car, Roger."

But I didn't move. I was afraid that if I did, my mother and Mr. Timms would hear my footsteps over the twigs and hickory nut husks. The thought of my mother's face turning in my direction, her eyes meeting mine, was more than I could stand, because what Bill and my father didn't know was that one day that summer my mother said to me, "You like Connie, don't you?"

We were alone in the house. My father was at the courthouse in Phillipsport. It was a hot, still afternoon with storm clouds gathering in the west. Soon there'd be a little breeze kick up—enough to stir the wind chimes my mother had hanging outside the back door, the ones I'd brought her from my class trip to McCormick's Creek State Park. They're pinecones, she said when she saw the chimes. Little gold pinecones, she said, and even now, whenever I want to feel kindly toward her, all I have to do is call up the memory of how she held the chimes and blew on them to set those pinecones to tinkling.

I'd just come in from mowing the yard and, when my mother asked me that question about Connie, I was about to take a drink of grape Kool-Aid. I stopped with the glass halfway to my mouth, and then I set it down on the kitchen counter.

Soon the thunder would start, at first a low rumble in the distance, and eventually the lightning would come and the sky would open up, but for the time being it was as if there wasn't a breath of air. My mother was sitting at the kitchen table writing out a grocery list on one of my father's notepads that had his name stamped at the top—ROGER THOMAS JORDAN, PHILLIPS COUNTY TAX ASSESSOR. She hadn't made much progress. EGGS, she'd written. MILK. Then she'd stopped and the rest of the notepage was covered with her name, written in her beautiful hand again and again. ANNIE, ANNIE, ANNIE.

"I mean, you really like her," she said. "It's all right to like someone that way, Roger." She looked up at me, then, and there was such a sadness in her eyes. I've never been able to get the memory of that moment out of my head. "It's the way I felt about your father," she said, and then she ripped the sheet of paper from the pad and wadded it up in her hand.

Somehow I knew that what she was telling me, with all that talk about Connie, was that she and Mr. Timms didn't like each other in quite the same way, that what they had between them was very different from what had brought my father and her together. I think she was telling me that if she'd had her druthers she would have felt that way about Mr. Timms—she would have liked him, and he would have liked her—but this thing between them was something very different. It was something born out of loneliness and desperation. I want to believe she was trying to tell me that what Connie and I had was special and that she wished it would last.

"You know I'm an old woman, don't you?" she finally said to me.

She was forty-one that summer. If she were alive today, she'd be seventy-nine. I like to think she'd have become an elegant woman, well-suited to her age, happy with what she had left in life. That Sunday, when she clung to Mr. Timms in the woods, no one knew she'd only live ten more years, or that my father, who divorced her, would come to the hospital and sit by her bed and hold her hand as she was dying.

"You're not that old," I told her.

She looked at me, shaking her head, her lips turned up in a sad grin. "Oh, honey," she said. "You just wait."

So there we were that Sunday, Bill and my father and me, and my father said again, "Roger, go back to the car."

When I still wouldn't move, he said, "We should all go back. We should go home."

That's when Bill said, "Jesus Christ."

Then he was tromping through the woods toward that lease road, where my mother raised her head and pushed away from Mr. Timms and saw that they weren't alone.

"I don't know who you think you are," Bill said when he got to where they were standing. "How can you live with yourself? And you, Annie." Here Bill shook his head, took a long breath and let it out. "I thought you were better than this."

There comes a moment when all that's been denied rises up and leaves you raw and trembling. That's what I was learning that day as I stood there, listening to Bill's loud voice ringing through the trees.

Now, I find myself wishing again and again that it would have been possible for me to tell him something that would have made a difference. Something about how broken we were. Something about how a time comes when it's best to just walk away, even if it means leaving behind someone you swore you'd love the rest of your life. Maybe we thought we could save ourselves, but it was too late.

Although I felt all this inside me, I couldn't find anything to say that would matter. Even now I can't put it into words. I can only remember the way it felt in the woods in the moments after Bill shouldered his twelve-gauge, and I knew that all of us were about to move from this world into another one that would hold us the rest of our days.

Bill said to Mr. Timms, "Get into your car. Go home." He motioned to the Olds 98 with the barrel of his twelve-gauge. "You've got a daughter," he said. "Can't you try to be a decent man for her sake? Go on now. This is over. Annie's coming with us."

"Bill, calm down," my mother said. "You should take care."

"Don't tell me that," said Bill. "Not you. Not the way you've been whoring around. R.T. might not know how to handle you, but by God I think I do."

My father was moving, then, his long legs striding quickly through the woods. I remembered that winter night when he'd put his hand on my shoulder and we'd watched the snow come down. The beauty of it all amazed him. It's like we're in a picture, he said. I knew he wasn't made for such ugliness as was upon him now, and I couldn't bear to see him walking toward it. I didn't know anything to do but to follow him.

"Bill, let's go." He rested his hand on my uncle's shoulder just the way he had mine. "Put that shotgun down." He was talking in a quiet voice, but I could hear the fear in it. "I mean it, Bill. We need to go."

My mother looked at me then, and she was ashamed. "Oh, Roger," she said. "You hadn't ought to be here."

"Bill," my father said, "listen to me."

"Better do what he says, Bill." Mr. Timms had his hands in the pockets of his blue and red plaid golf pants, standing there in a way that told me he felt positive my uncle was bluffing. "I can make things plenty rough for you," he said. "I can see to it you lose your job."

"I've put up with enough shit from you, Harold." Bill shook free from my father's hand. "I'm not going to put up with any more of it."

That's when Mr. Timms said to my mother, "Annie, tell him. Tell R.T. what's what."

My mother couldn't speak. She looked at Mr. Timms, and then at my father. From where I stood beside him, I could see she was afraid. Her eyes were wet, and there was just the slightest tremor at the corner of her mouth.

"Annie?" my father said.

"Go on, Annie," said Mr. Timms. "Tell him what we've decided."

Bill stepped closer to him. He pressed the barrel of the twelve-gauge into the soft spot beneath Mr. Timms's chin, and Mr. Timms tilted his head, trying to get free from the nick of the bead sight.

"You're not deciding anything." Bill walked Mr. Timms backward, away from my mother along the driver's side of the Olds until they were out of the lease road and off in the woods. "If anyone's running this show, it's me."

I should tell you that Bill was a violent man, but I can't because the truth was, prior to that moment in the woods, he wasn't. He was my uncle, my father's younger brother, who had done his stint as a grunt in Vietnam and come home, seemingly no worse for the experience. He had his job with the railroad and that little box house on South Street not far from the Uptown Café, where he ate breakfast every morning before heading to work. He kept a pot of wave petunias on each side of the front steps of his house. Some evenings, I'd go driving by, and he'd be outside with his watering can. He'd have on a pair of khaki shorts and his old Army shirt with the sleeves cut out. He'd throw up his arm, his fingers in the vee of a peace sign, and I'd think, there he is, the happiest man alive. Whatever he carried inside him was a secret to me.

"I don't know what got into him," my father would say, time and time again over the years. "I guess it was like he said. He'd just had enough."

Enough of Harold Timms and the way he shoved him around on the job. Enough of the fact that Mr. Timms thought he could take another man's wife and not have to answer for it. Enough of his gold Ban-Lon shirt, and his flashy plaid golf pants, and that Olds 98. Enough of things we had no way of knowing about as he tried his best to live a regular life in the aftermath of whatever he'd gone through in Vietnam. Enough.

So when Mr. Timms said what he did—"I'm going to tell you something, Bill. And, R.T., I want you to listen to this, too."—Bill pulled back on the hammer of that twelve-gauge.

"Don't talk," he said to Mr. Timms. "Don't say another word."

The squirrels were chattering high up in the hickory trees. The sun was splintering through the branches. In the distance, a mourning dove was calling for rain. A little wind had come up, and it was cooler there in the woods. I thought for a moment that everything would be all right. Bill backed away from Mr. Timms, and he let his arms relax, the twelve-gauge now held crosswise at his waist. He came back to the lease road, walking backward until he cleared the Olds and was standing a couple of feet from its rear end.

Mr. Timms followed him, stopping finally about midway down the side of the car. I could see his head and shoulders above the roof. He said, "R.T., Annie doesn't love you. She loves me, and we aim to have a life together."

"I told you to shut up." Bill's voice was loud and shaking. "I gave you fair warning."

But Mr. Timms went on. "She hasn't loved you in a long time. She's just stayed with you for the sake of the boy." Here, he pointed at me. "And I know what you've been doing with my Connie. I saw you… we saw you, your mother and me, Saturday night, two lovebirds on a blanket over there at your grandparents' farm. I want you to leave Connie alone. She's told you, hasn't she? She's only fifteen, for Christ's sake. She's too young to be laying in the dark with a boy."

"I love her," I said, and though I said it in a quiet voice, I could tell right away I'd spoken with force.

I knew that because for a good while, no one said a thing. They were stunned—struck dumb because in the midst of all this ugliness, a boy had spoken his heart and reminded them all of what it was to be young and smitten with the first stirrings of something sweet and pure.

Then my mother said, "Oh, honey."

And my father said, "We should all just leave now before this gets out of hand."

"Hell," said Mr. Timms. He laughed, throwing back his head, his mouth open so wide I could see a single gold molar. "You love her?" he said. "You don't know what love is. You just love your pecker."

He took a few steps toward us, and Bill shouldered that twelve-gauge again and said, "You better stop. I swear, Harold. I won't let you drag Roger into this."

"Oh, he's in it, all right." Mr. Timms took two more steps—he was at the rear of the Olds now, about to step out into the open. He stopped walking and rested his hand on the trunk. "Well, at least there's one man in your family." He laughed again, only this time there was no joy in it. Then his eyes narrowed, and he said, "Son, you must have inherited your mother's hot blood."

The blast from the twelve-gauge was sudden and explosive. The back glass of the Olds shattered, blown backward onto the bench seat. For a moment, that's all I could take in—how there was a loud crack and then the glass came apart in more little pieces than anyone would ever be able to count.

Then my mother called Mr. Timms's name. "Harold." She was moving past me, toward the Olds. "Harold. Oh, God."

It all came into focus for me then—Mr. Timms on the ground, his torso hidden alongside the Olds. I could see his feet and the white loafers he wore, the ones with gold buckles, and I understood that Bill had shot him.

My father was running after my mother. He caught up to her just as she got to the rear of the Olds. She looked down at Mr. Timms and put her hands to her face. Her shoulders heaved. My father took her by those shoulders as if to hold them still.

He turned back toward me and his eyes were wild. "Don't come over here." He was shouting though I was only a few feet away. "Whatever you do, don't."

My mother twisted around and pressed her face into the collar of his shirt. She beat against his chest with her fists, and he let her do that until she was all wrung out. Then he wrapped her up in his arms, and as I watched him holding her, I understood that Mr. Timms was dead, that Bill had killed him, and now the world would be a different place for all of us.

———

My father wanted to pass it off as a hunting accident, but Bill said no, we'd call it exactly what it was.

"I'm not going to ask Roger to carry a lie," he said. "I may not be much, but I know what's right and what's not."

"You?" my mother said. "You don't know anything."

"At least I'll own up to what I've done."

A hickory nut dropped from a tree and hit the top of the Olds with a bang. Then everything was quiet. Just the mourning doves somewhere in the distance and a squirrel chattering and the leaves stirring in the wind.

My father said, "And what did you do, Bill? Do you intend to tell me that you meant to kill him?"

Said Bill, "I just wanted him to shut up."

My mother pushed away from my father and went running off into the woods, trying to get away, I imagine, from what we were all going to have to face. Bill had shot her lover and killed him, and all of this had happened while Connie was listening to the radio at her house, and soon she would have to know about it.

My mother stumbled over a fallen branch and went down on her hands and knees. She fell over onto her side and lay there in the dead leaves and the dirt, and she pulled her knees up toward her chest, as if she were going to sleep, as if she'd never get up from that spot.

"I used to know you," my father said to Bill.

Bill nodded. Then he set his jaw and looked off into the distance for an instant. He swallowed hard. "Well, I'm not that person now." There was a crack in his voice. "And I won't be ever again." He looked at my father again and his voice got steady. "It wasn't your fault, R.T. It wasn't anyone's fault. My life got taken to hell a long time ago."

After that, there was nothing left to do but to pick my mother up from the ground.

"My purse," she said.

It was still on the front seat of the Olds. Before my father had a chance to stop me, I went to the car and opened the passenger door. The purse, that woven straw box purse with the strawberries and the white blooms on it. I picked it up by its thin handle. I resisted the urge to peer out the driver's side window to see what a man who'd been shot with a twelve-gauge might look like. I didn't want that picture in my head. I was just a kid, but I knew enough to know I didn't need that. So I concentrated on the purse. I carried it to my mother, and then the four of us started back to town to call the sheriff. I rode in the bed of the El Camino, so whatever got said in the cab was outside my hearing. I wasn't concerned with it anyway. I was thinking about Connie, and how she was an orphan now, and how unfair it was for me to know that before she did.

My mother was the one who told her. While Bill was on the phone confessing to the sheriff exactly what had he'd done down that oil lease road, my mother went next door and pounded on the frame of the screen until the radio music stopped and Connie came to see what the fuss was all about.

I watched from the window of my bedroom. My father was sitting on our porch steps. Soon, Bill would come out and sit beside him, and after a while, I'd hear my father say, "I should have walked out on this a long time ago. Then it wouldn't have been yours to deal with."

Bill let a few seconds go by, and then he said in a flat worn-out voice, "R.T., I think I've been looking for something like this ever since I got out of the Army." In the months to come, he'd go on in letters that came first from the county jail and then Vandalia Prison about how he'd gotten out of Vietnam, but he hadn't been able to let loose of the rage that filled him. *If it hadn't been Harold Timms*, he wrote, *it would've been someone else. I was just pissed off, R.T. I wanted someone to have to pay for something. I guess that's the best I can put it.*

That Sunday, I watched my mother reach out her hand to Connie as if she were about to touch her face. The she said, "Honey, can I come inside?"

Connie had on cutoffs with frayed threads dangling down her legs and a white T-shirt. She had cotton balls between her toes. She'd been painting her toenails a bright red, and it made me wonder how she imagined her life being the next day and the next one after that—if she was thinking that she was glad to be rid of me so she could have a boyfriend she wouldn't have to sneak around to see. However she saw her life unfolding, it wasn't the life my mother was there to give her.

"It's about your daddy," my mother said, and then she stepped inside the house, and I couldn't hear anymore.

I couldn't watch that silent house and the little shaded porch with the wooden swing bolted to the ceiling. So many nights, I'd seen Connie in that swing and heard her singing to herself. All the love songs that were popular then: "Let's Stay Together," "Precious and Few," "Puppy Love." She was a girl without a mother, and I was a boy who felt abandoned, so it was easy for us to love each other.

Soon the sheriff's car pulled into my driveway, and I heard Bill say, "Well, I guess this is it."

I went to the other window of my bedroom, the one that looked out over the front yard, and I saw my father and Bill get up from where they were sitting and walk across the grass to meet the sheriff, a tall, lumbering man with a dark moustache.

"I'm going to have to take you in," I heard the sheriff say to Bill. "I've got deputies headed down to that oil lease road."

"I'm ready," said Bill.

And like that he got into the backseat of the sheriff's car, and then it was just my father and me and my mother and Connie, whom we'd watch over until her grandparents could arrive from Indianapolis.

"Go over and sit with Connie," my mother told me when she came back to our house. "I want to talk to your father."

What they said to each other when they were alone, I don't know. I only know that later that night he packed a bag and got into his Galaxie and drove off to find a motel in Phillipsport until he could locate a more satisfactory arrangement.

"It's going to just be the two of us," my mother said. She put her arm around my shoulders and squeezed. "Just you and me, Roger. Can you believe that?"

I couldn't believe anything then, and I knew she couldn't either. It was that sort of day, a day that felt like it should belong to someone else, the way so much of my life would seem from that point on. It would be a long, long time before I'd let myself trust anyone who said they loved me.

That night, I couldn't say I loved my mother, or Bill, or my father, who had gone without saying a word to me. I could only say that I felt sorry for them—sorry for all the trouble they'd found—and I felt sorry for Connie, who didn't deserve to be on the other side of that trouble. It would be a while before I'd be able to say that I didn't deserve it either.

"You've always been nice to me," Connie said to me that evening when we sat on her bed, waiting for her grandparents.

She wasn't crying. She was sitting with her legs crossed under her, rocking back and forth, and she let me put my arm around her waist, and then she laid her head over on my shoulder, and we sat there for the longest time, not saying a word.

The Philco radio sat on the table by her bed, but we didn't turn it on. She had a bulletin board on the wall above her desk, and from where we sat I could see it was covered with things I'd never known had meant that much to her—a wrapper from a Hershey bar I'd bought for her once when we were out and she was hungry, a book of matches we'd used to light a candle on our blanket at my grandparents' farm, the plastic rings from the candy pacifiers we liked. Just little things like that. Nothing that mattered at all, but they did to her, and now, given what was about to happen, they did to me, too.

"They won't let me live here anymore," she said.

I told her Indianapolis was only three hours away. "Not far at all," I said.

"Not too far," she said.

The sun was going down and the light in the room was fading. Through the window I could see lights coming on in the houses down the street. We sat there in the twilight, not saying a word. She let me hold her, and I smelled the strawberry shampoo in her hair and the fresh nail polish on her toes, and there was nothing really we could say because we were in a world now that wasn't ours. It was run by people like my parents and her grandparents and Bill, who sat in jail waiting for what would come to him.

"You'll come see me?" she finally said.

I told her I would.

"I won't forget you." She tilted her head and kissed my cheek. Then she settled her head back on my shoulder and I felt her eyelashes brush my neck. "And I won't blame you for any of this. Never. Not ever."

Then we sat there, and after a while, we lay down side by side. She turned her face to the wall, and I slipped my arm around her and fit my legs up against hers. She let herself cry a little then, and I told her everything would be all right. I'm not sure I believed it, but soon she stopped crying and then she said, "I wish we were the only people in the world right now."

"I wish that, too," I told her, and it was true. I did.

We stayed like that a good, long while. Maybe we even drifted off to sleep. Then headlights swept across the wall, and we heard a car door slam shut outside and frantic steps on the porch and her grandmother's voice calling, "Connie, oh Connie, oh my precious girl."

"Shh," Connie said. "Don't move."

And we had that instant longer—that instant alone—at the end of a story that was never meant to be ours.

She was in my arms and then she wasn't. Her grandmother was there, and I let her go. Connie Timms.

I walked out of her house and stood on the porch. I looked across the way to my own house, where a single light was on, and I saw my mother's shadow move across the closed drapes. I thought how strange it was that I lived in that house, how strange it was that my uncle had killed a man and my mother and father, as I would soon learn, were at an end.

Connie's grandfather, a short man with a big chest and blue sport coat, came up the steps.

"Who are you?" he said.

"No one," I told him.

"Young man, I asked you who you are."

I just shook my head, already moving down the steps. There was too much to say, and I didn't know how to say it.

"Come back here," he said. But I kept moving. I still think I should have had a choice, but I was sixteen. What else could I do? I went home.

THE DEAD IN PARADISE

IT STARTED WHEN THE TREE FELL. MAIZY SAID THAT WAS THE FIRST sign: that big old linden tree, that heart tree she claimed was the reminder of steadfast love, just toppling over, stretching out across our backyard like it'd had enough of standing there, nearly ninety feet tall, and wanted nothing more than a good long rest.

Then the Mister Peanut Barbeque on East Main burned down— the very place we'd first met and tossed our hearts into a tangle, and Maizy worried there'd be a sign following—a third omen—and that we should be on the lookout.

"Maybe someone's not living right," she said, and she lifted her eyebrows, making it plain that she thought I was suspect.

I won't deny she had call. It'd been a winter of snow and ice and frost on the heartstrings. We'd been married over thirty years—there we were, on the other side of mystery and surprise—and back in December I'd made the mistake of saying one night to Maizy, "You know, hon. You could have done better than me," and she'd said, "Nah, Baby. I did the best I could."

I woke up the next morning stewing about what she'd meant, and I aimed to ask her straight out, but before I could, she stuck her finger up in my face, and she said, "You're guilty of something. That's why you said what you did last night. I don't know what it is, but I suspect sooner or later I'll find out."

Had I been untrue? I most certainly had not, and, another thing, I had nothing to do with that linden tree falling. I want that in the record. The trunk just hollowed out and couldn't stand the weight of all those limbs.

Anyway, when I said that bit about Maizy being able to do better than me, I meant it, and if I was guilty of anything it was only lack— or greed, depending on how you choose to study my situation. The fact was, on those long winter nights when the sun went down by five and there wasn't much to do but prowl the house and get all rotten and wheezy inside my skin, I got to thinking of everything Maizy deserved that I'd never been able to give her. Let's get this out in the open: I've always been a man willing to piss away my last dollar on a chance. Said plain: I've done things I'd be ashamed to admit, made bonehead moves that my sweet Maizy suffered, all for the sake of some memory of love.

"I remember that first night you walked into the Mister Peanut," she said one day. "I took one look and thought, good god, help me. I'm going to marry that man."

Sometimes that winter, when she was gone to her mama's or just out at the IGA to do the groceries, I'd get down the wedding album and look at the pictures and I'd try my best to remember who we were back then: Maizy still in high school and working nights at the Mister Peanut, and me—gap-toothed, goofy-grinning me—scrawny as shit but drawing a steady wage hauling anhydrous ammonia for United Prairie Farm Supply. Like most people setting out, we were blind to what was ahead of us; we couldn't have seen that winter coming even if we'd tried. So I'd get all soft in the heart looking at those wedding pictures: Maizy in that dress her mama sewed, the one with the empire waist and the double-layered sleeves, so the wedding announcement clipped from the *Daily Mail* said, and me in a cream-colored polyester suit my daddy gave me the money to buy. "Don't let yourself go to fat," he told me, "and maybe Maizy can use that suit when she has to put you in the ground." That was my daddy, ignorant to the ways of romance. If he'd still been breathing, I'm sure he would've been ashamed to know I sat there those winter nights, tears coming to my eyes, because that boy and girl in those pictures seemed familiar to me, but so far away I couldn't touch them or know them to call them by name.

Then I fell in with Doogie Roy.

"Oh, Baby," Maizy said. "I wish you wouldn't."

"Business, hon," I told her. "That's all it is."

"Keep it to yourself. Whatever it is you're scheming. I don't want to hear a word about it. Your daddy was right. You're going to end up in prison or dead, one of the two."

Here's the truth: when you spend your life short on cash, you keep looking for any chance at all to get on the long end of prosperity. I'd already fallen sucker to a pyramid scheme, tossed away money on lottery tickets, invested unwisely in oil wells—not to mention, as eventually I know I'll have to, my most grievous sin, the one I can't yet bring myself to say.

One night at the Mister Peanut, Doogie Roy said, "Baby James. I've got a proposition."

Folks like Doogie started calling me Baby James a long way back in high school when I looked like a young James Taylor, the Sweet Baby James of "Fire and Rain" and "You've Got a Friend," and even now, when my hair's thinning, I still carry the resemblance. "How about it?" Doogie said. He turned a chair around backward and straddled it. "My man, let's talk."

He had a tattoo on his forearm: a neatly printed list that said 3 QTS. MILK, YOGURT, LESTOIL.

It was the last part that got me—Lestoil. Less toil, I thought, and though it seems funny to say it now, I believe that was the first sign, and not that linden tree like Maizy supposed. Less toil. I felt it rise up in me like a plea, and I realized, then, the truth that Maizy and I had been spending the winter trying to avoid: our time together had started to feel like work.

"What's on your mind?" I said to Doogie.

He crossed his arms on top of the chair back and nestled his chin down on his hands. He had gray eyes, clear with just a tinge of blue. Icy eyes, I suppose some might have said, but to me, at that moment, they were the color of everything I'd ever come close to, everything I'd never had. They were almost pretty, those eyes. He winked at me. "Ammonia," he said.

In high school, he was an all-conference quarterback—Lord, he could heave that ball—but since then? He was almost fifty years old, and here he was washing dishes at the Mister Peanut. Let's just say he'd had his troubles. A few stints up at the penitentiary in Vandalia—nickel and dime stuff, stealing cars, assault and battery—but now he was into the dope.

"Ammonia?" I said to him.

He grinned. "Anhydrous, my man." Then he broke it down into syllables, his voice a whisper. "An-hy-drous. You know what I'm talking about, Baby. Don't let on like you don't. That's what all the crank heads need to make the go-juice. Crystal meth, Baby. You know the score."

Our part of the country is filthy with methamphetamine. Word had it that Doogie had gone mobile. Sometimes he cooked meth in a rental unit out at the U-Store, sometimes on a john boat on Borah Lake, sometimes after hours in the kitchen at the Mister Peanut. He'd never said as much to me, but that was the story around town. He knew I hauled anhydrous, so I always figured it would only be a matter of time before he came asking. Once he did, I felt that old itch: money to be had, a door to open, a new and marvelous life.

I could have said no. I'm aware of that. It could have been that easy. But you don't know the whole story yet. You don't know about Doogie Roy and a certain night in 1982 and a talking bird named Coco Joe and the words we say to the dead in paradise.

"All right," I said to Doogie. "How much?"

It's amazing, the turns a life can take. You might see me and Maizy now in the IGA, the Walmart, or the Toot-n-Totem, and never have a clue that once upon a time we were Daddy and Mama to a sweetheart little girl. April Renee, that was her name. We had her six years, and then she left us. Tumors in her brain. Medulloblastoma. That's the fact of it, but the whole story? How in God's name does anyone ever tell it all? How do I tell you about the trips to St. Jude's in Memphis and the checks that came in the mail—money from people who knew us and sometimes from total strangers who'd heard about our trouble and wanted to do what they could to help? How do I say, without risking that you'll turn a stone ear to me forever, that I cashed those checks and gambled the money—threw it away at riverboat casinos all along the Mississippi—all while April was dying?

That's the hardest part for me to say, that I did that, and here's the truth, ugly as it is: sometimes it tears me up more to remember that part than to call to mind the day April died.

On that day—February 14, 1982—we were, for just a few minutes, blessed, and it was all the doing of Doogie Roy.

Doogie had this mynah bird, Coco Joe, and he'd taught it to hop up on April's shoulder and say, "Are you my little buddy?" That was enough to make April think Doogie hung the moon—that bird and the way it'd lean over and take a peanut out of her hand. "Little buddy," Coco Joe would say. "My little buddy." Then he'd fly up and sit right on top of April's head. That was Coco Joe.

On the last day April was with us, Doogie came into her room at St. Jude's—he'd driven six hours to get there, the first half of it through an ice storm—and slung over his shoulder was an old gym bag. You guessed it. He'd used that bag to smuggle in Coco Joe.

I like to think it mattered, somehow it made a difference, even though by this time April was barely with us. She was there in the bed, covered over with the tubes and whatnot, her little bald head—all her pretty blond hair gone to fuzz—too small for the pillow. You wouldn't have known to look at her that not more than a year ago she'd been mascot for the high school cheerleading team, cute and feisty with her hair pulled back in a ponytail and her skirt and sweater that Maizy had sewn and those little red and white pom-poms we'd special-ordered just for her. After a basketball game, she'd yabber about how she wanted to go see Doogie and her little buddy, Coco Joe, and I'd drop by his trailer in Goosenibble, no matter that it was getting late and time for April to be in bed. "Just this once," I'd always say, convincing Maizy it was all right. That was the way life was for us then. We thought we owned it.

That day at St. Jude's, Doogie's hands were shaking. Imagine it: this big old red-headed boy, mitts like potatoes, trembling as he reached into that gym bag and brought out Coco Joe. They looked at us—I swear the bird did, too—waiting for the go-ahead.

We let him. What was the harm? He set that bird down on April's pillow, and Coco Joe bowed his head. He rubbed against her face. For what seemed like the longest time, he kept nuzzling her. Then he said, "I'm cuckoo for Cocoa Puffs," just like April had taught him one Saturday morning when she was watching cartoons, and if that was the last thing she heard before she slipped off to heaven, I'm not ashamed to say I take comfort from it, or that to me Doogie Roy will always be a good-hearted man, no matter the wrong turns he's taken—a better man than me more than likely, even though Maizy said she couldn't look at him after that day without feeling her heart tear. The night the linden tree fell she dreamed about April, who was up in the tree with Coco Joe— the two of them sitting on a limb, all those heart-shaped leaves around them and those white flowers that always filled our yard with their sweet perfume—and what April said to Maizy was, Are you my little buddy?

"That Doogie Roy," Maizy told me. "That SOB. I don't know whether to love him or cuss him to his grave."

It was easy, handing over the anhydrous. All I had to do was meet Doogie out in the country somewhere, maybe pull back up one of those old oil lease roads where the brush hid us, and bleed a little off the truck into some propane tanks. You know, the kind you all use on your gas grills. Doogie took it from there. He kept a little anhydrous for himself and sold the rest to whoever needed it to make meth and then split the cash with me. I saved it all, hid it away in an old Maxwell House can in the garage. It was more money than I'd ever seen, and I was afraid to touch it, for fear that once I started spending it, I wouldn't be able to stop.

"You're a good man, Baby James," he said. "You and me? We're going places."

But we weren't. I knew that. No place but to hell in a handbasket, like my daddy always claimed. I had that money, but I was still eaten up on the inside.

Back in the winter, I'd started to talk to April. For a while, no one knew, not even Maizy, but days when I was out on my route, I'd just start in, and what I'd say went something like this: Honey, it's your daddy. April Renee, it's me. I'd tell her about the weather, just ordinary things like that: how much snow was on the ground, the way the air tasted like pennies, the whistle the wind made through the truck's window seals—things she might have forgotten in the twenty years she'd been gone. Things that were easy for me to say.

I expected she was in a place where there was no winter. That's the blessing, I suppose—one sunny day after another. Sort of like when you take off in an airplane and it's raining until you get up so high you break through to sunshine. There you are, up in the clear blue, looking down on all those clouds, and you don't give another thought to the rain and muck you left below you. It's not yours anymore. That's heaven, I guess: sunshine and blue skies and a carpet of fluffy white clouds and the worries of the living tossed away.

"No, that'd be hell," Maizy said when I finally told it all to her. "Every day the same. Baby, I'm guessing there's snow in heaven, just enough to pretty things up once in a while, and those fall days when the leaves have turned and there's just enough of a snap in the air to make you feel all bright and new. I bet it even rains a little, one of those drizzly rains that April liked to go out and play in. Remember?"

I told her I did, but I was miserable because I'd forgotten how April liked to hold her arms out to her sides and spin around with her head thrown back and her mouth open, trying to catch raindrops. I'd forgotten how she sounded when she giggled. I tried to close my eyes and hear it, and even though I got close, I never could manage it, not really, if you know what I mean. You think the voices of the dead will stay with you forever, but that's not really the truth of it.

"April was lucky to have you as a daddy," Doogie said to me the next day, and just like that I was filled with shame because I hadn't been a good daddy at all. Not only had I made poor use of the money meant to help us through her sickness, now I'd begun to forget the things that made her April Renee.

This year there was a woman over in Sparta who convinced people that her little girl had leukemia. She doped her up, shaved her head, claimed she was taking her to the hospital for chemo, and then when the girl came out of the dope and didn't remember any of it, her mama told her it was because of the chemo medicine messing up her mind. She made that little girl believe she was dying, all for the money that came rolling in. There's no saving that woman. Me? I'd like to think there's hope.

Eventually I told Doogie that was the end of the anhydrous; he'd have to get it somewhere else.

We were out in the country, back up an old lane where blackberry bramble and persimmon saplings were filling in what had once been the path to someone's farmhouse. There wasn't a sound but the wind through the brush and leaves and a blue jay jeering.

"Baby James, you don't mean that," Doogie said.

But I did. I convinced myself I was on my way to better times. "It is what I mean," I told him.

He laid his hand on my shoulder and chuckled. "It's not that easy, my man." He gave me a shake. "You're in with me now. We both know too much about each other."

"Could be," I said. "But that's the end of it, Doogie. I'm done."

In the days that followed, I'd drive up to the Lutheran church where Maizy and I tied the knot, and I'd tell myself life could start over. It was quiet there at the church, this little old country church up on a hill, a gravel road running by, pastures of timothy grass waving out to the horizon. Crows called, and that was a sound that put me at ease, coming so clear and sharp, no other noise around to clutter it up.

I'd get to talking to April. I told her what I did with the money folks sent when she was sick, and I asked her to forgive me. All that money. All the time I spent scheming with it, looking forward to those checks coming in the mail. I told April all of it. How I ripped open those envelopes, tossed the "Wish you well" cards aside. I'm looking for a way to make it right, I told her, hoping that somewhere she was listening. April, I said, it's not too late for your daddy. Honest, I believe it's not. You just wait.

From time to time, a car went by, a plume of dust trailing out behind, that head-banger rock and roll music blasting from the CD player. Kids. Maybe cranked up on meth. Who knows? All it takes is some anhydrous, some lithium batteries, some brake cleaning fluid, some Sudafed cold medicine, and you're ready to set up shop. The Nazi Method, they call the recipe for cooking meth with anhydrous, because the Germans used it to keep their soldiers jazzed up during World War II. You can set up a lab anywhere: the woods, your house, a horse trailer. The cops even caught some kids cooking meth in a car in the high school parking lot. That's how it is these days, and I'm sorry to say I ever had a part in it.

Anyway, up at the church I thought about what sort of woman April would have been.

Like Maizy, I imagine: strong-willed, stubborn, on the lookout for anyone bent on doing her rotten, but soft inside—yes, I believe that in spite of our troubles—soft like Maizy, or at least the girl she was that first time I walked into the Mister Peanut and threw her into a spin.

She claims it was my voice. "All buttery," she said one night, not long after April died. "Gentle. I told my mama. 'Maizy,' she said, 'you can't go wrong with a soft-spoken man.'"

Maybe she's right; maybe the quiet voice speaks from a peaceful heart. But what I figure is this: you can't know what's inside folks—hell, you can't even know what's inside yourself—until something happens to rough you up, something like your little girl dying and leaving you years and years to think on it, to feel it in your throat and chest, to never stop imagining that one morning you might open your eyes and there she'll be. She's with you and she's not. It's the here-and-gone of her that leaves a wound too deep and sore to ever heal.

The few times Maizy and I tried to talk it out, it was no use. It was like opening a valve on an anhydrous tank if you don't know what you're doing. The ammonia leaks out, and you get burned. The anhydrous attaches itself to a moisture source: your eyes, your skin, your lungs. Ask any meth cook about everything that can go wrong: burns, explosions, suffocations. If you're going to cook with "annie," you best be on your toes.

"It hurts me to remember too much," Maizy said that time we were talking about April and what it must be like in her heaven. "I get to thinking about how you threw that money away—money those good people sent to help us out—and how it took me nearly a year to save enough to put a headstone on April's grave. A year, Baby. I'd go out to the cemetery and see that little mound of dirt. I don't know that I'll ever be able to forgive you for that."

The night the linden tree fell, Maizy and I didn't know it. We were both sleeping. It was only the next morning, when we woke up and came out to the kitchen and looked out the window, that we saw the tree down across our backyard. It fell on Maizy's flowerbed, squashed her snapdragons and gladiolus and purple coneflowers. There'd been no storm, no wind, no thunder and lighting. A ninety-foot tree just crashed to the ground, and we didn't hear it. My God, it must have shaken the house, but we kept on dreaming. "Didn't you know it?" Maizy's mama asked her when she came over to get a look. "No, Mama," Maizy told her. "I guess Baby and me were both dead to the world."

How could that be? Maybe when April died, we stopped paying attention to what might be out there waiting to surprise us. Dead to the world. I'm thinking of those zombies now, the ones from those B movies like *Night* and *Dawn*—Hollywood zombies, though Doogie Roy claims we ought to call them Pittsburgh zombies, since all the important zombie movies were made there. That distinction aside, I'm thinking about how zombies always seem to have some dim memory of their past lives. Once they rise and start to walk, they can't keep themselves from visiting the places they knew when they were among the living. At first they seem normal. Then you look in their eyes and you see how empty they are. It's gone—whatever it is that made them who they were—and now they're putting on a show, fooling people into thinking they're human.

One night, I came home from a quick run to the Toot-n-Totem for milk and Doogie Roy was sitting in my house. He was laying back in my recliner chair, his hands behind his head, his feet up. Maizy was on the couch, her arms crossed over her chest. It was almost midnight, and the TV was on but the sound was on mute. The picture flickered and changed. People waved their arms, stamped their feet, turned and marched out of rooms, but there was no way to tell what they were saying.

"What's the story?" I asked.

Maizy got up off the couch and tramped on down the hall. Our bedroom door slammed shut, and somehow that vibration shook the TV off mute, and a woman's voice said, "You sonofabitch."

Doogie couldn't stop laughing.

I kicked his feet off the chair. "What's so funny?"

"Everything," he said. "I mean it, Baby James. This whole damned mess."

The cops were on to him. Earlier in the evening, they'd been in the Mister Peanut, wanting to ask him some questions. He heard them up front, and he slipped out the back and made his way to our house.

I knew he'd told Maizy everything, about the meth and the anhydrous and how I'd been in on it. I knew that's why she was steamed. Hearing it from Doogie surely brought back all the bad memories of the time April was sick, and now Maizy was back in our bedroom, no doubt holed up with misery and the belief that her life with me would always be a sad life and maybe it was time for her to cut bait.

Doogie needed to get out of town. Get set up somewhere else, he said. "If they put me away on a dope charge. Me? With my record? Baby, I'm never coming back." What he wanted was money. "Just a stake. You know, a start. Don't worry. I'll pay you back." He knew I had it, the cash he'd given me. "If the cops get me," he said, "they're going to ask questions. They're going to want to know where I got that annie."

"I believe you'd tell them," I said.

Said Doogie, "I expect I just might."

So there I was, caught by the short hairs. "Doogie," I said, "let me tell you I had plans for that money. I aimed to give it over to St. Jude's."

It wasn't the truth; I said it before I knew I was going to.

"That place you had April. That hospital for kids."

"In Memphis," I said. "I know you remember."

He closed his eyes. He balled his hands up into fists. I saw that tattoo again: 3 QTS. MILK, YOGURT, LESTOIL.

"I do," he said. "I surely do, Baby James. It was Sweethearts' Day, and there was ice on the roads, and I had Coco Joe. That was before they sent me up the first time and took Joe away from me. I still wonder where he ended up. But I remember that day. You bet I do. April and Joe and me and you and Maizy. I never told you this, Baby, but that's the closest I ever come to feeling part of a family. You understand?"

"I do, Doogie. Yes, I know what you mean."

"We got soldered together that day. You know it. Maizy does, too, even if she won't own up to it. We're all alike, shot to hell. We wouldn't know happy if it slapped us in the face. All of us. We're just getting by."

I asked him what he'd done with his share of the anhydrous money. "I know you were making a wad."

"Oh, it just goes. You know, Baby James. It just flies out of your hand."

It was then that Maizy came out of our bedroom, wrestling with a suitcase—one of those out-of-date boxy Samsonites that you have to carry, no wheels like the ones folks zip around with these days. A red vinyl suitcase with latches, the one Maizy carried on our honeymoon, the same one she packed when we took April down to St. Jude's to stay.

"Maizy," I said, and then for a few seconds I couldn't go on. It broke me, that suitcase, and the way she had to grip it with two hands and still it bumped against the wall. "Darlin'," I finally said. "Don't."

She got to the end of the hall, and she tried to swing the suitcase at me. I'm confident she was intent on doing me harm, but the Samsonite was too heavy, and she nearly toppled over.

I caught her. I held her to me the way I had all those years ago, when we'd first begun to get dizzy over each other. I held her the way I did the day April left us, and, like then, I felt Maizy holding me, too. I knew, from the way her arms wrapped around my waist and her face pressed into my throat, there was still a chance for us, and yet there was nothing to say—no words at all—to make this chance real and something we could work at. It was the merest shiver of air, a puny reminder of the way life had once been for us. Then Maizy pounded her fist against my chest.

"Oh, you sonofabitch," she said. "Making money off that junk, ruining all those people's lives."

The foot rest came down on my reclining chair, and I felt the floor shake when Doogie stood up. "People ruin their own lives," he said. "That's the true by and by of it, hard as it is to say. Some people just can't stop ruining them. People like me."

I wished there was something to say to make us all feel hopeful, but like I already told you, there weren't words enough.

So I asked Doogie what I'd always wanted to but never had. I asked him what the story was with his tattoo.

"Prison tattoo." He held out his arm and studied it. "That's what I was on my way to the IGA to get, the day the cops brought me in on grand theft auto. Three quarts of milk, some yogurt, and Lestoil. I had this old boy at Vandalia ink it on my arm, that list, so I could look at it and remind myself that someday I'd walk out of there and I'd have something to do. I'd have this errand to run." He put a hand on my back and one on Maizy's. "Little things. That's how we keep getting on."

I had to choose. Did I give that money to Doogie, or did I save it—maybe even stay good to my word and give it to St. Jude's—and take the chance I'd end up in Dutch with the law?

You can think your life comes down to making this choice or that, and sometimes I suppose it's true, but more often, it's not that way at all. You can't cut one choice out from all the others that have come before it or the ones bound to follow. Nothing is ever as clear cut as this or that. What I knew, standing there in my house that night with Maizy and

Doogie Roy, was I'd never get it right, this thing we call living. It was too late. Too many things said and done. Maybe I'd lost too much. Maybe I'd gotten hard in the heart and reached the point where I didn't give a good Goddamn what happened. But I was trying, just like I'd told April, to get straightened out, to remember what it was to love this life.

"I'm trying to get back," I said to Maizy. "Back to the way things were. There was you and me and April."

"That's where you're stupid," she said. "Nothing's ever going to be the way it was before April died."

It can be like that, life so full of loss you don't know what to say or where to turn. So I didn't do a thing. I just sat down there on the couch, dummied up, and there was Maizy with her suitcase and Doogie Roy, the two of them, waiting.

April, hon, I'm sorry I had to burn down the Mister Peanut—sorry I had to be that sort of man—but in the long run it was the thing to do. Even though your mama thought it was one more sign that we were on our way to ruin, it was right for her and me, and it was right for Doogie Roy. He didn't know it that night when he stood in our house expecting me to give him that money, but I hope, wherever he is, he knows it now. Maybe you'll find a way to tell him. Maybe someday, you'll send down a sign. He'll be driving by a burnt-out building and he'll see that yellow tape the fire department puts up—FIRE SCENE, it'll say, DON'T CROSS, and he'll understand there are limits to how many mistakes we can make in a life and still save ourselves. He'll know why I couldn't give him that money.

I had to burn down the Mister Peanut so Doogie would know I wasn't to be messed with, wasn't Sweet Baby James at all, but someone who, if he had to, could hurt people, innocent folks like the ones who owned the Mister Peanut, who didn't deserve a bad break.

Even now, I can barely believe it was me who said that night, "Come on, Doogie. Let's go for a ride. Then we'll see about that money."

He trusted me, just like we trusted the doctors when you were sick. What choice did we have? Sometimes, when you're down on your luck, you have to let people take you—you have to hope there's something better waiting on down the road.

Doogie got in my truck, and he said he knew he could count on me. He said I was his little buddy, and that almost broke me, but I made myself forget about Coco Joe and how you always took to him and that last day there at St. Jude's when he hopped up on your pillow and talked to you while you slipped away. I know, if you were here with me now, a grown woman, it'd embarrass you to hear me tell this story. I'll have to ask you to forgive me that.

And I'll have to hope you weren't watching that night when I pulled in behind the Mister Peanut, and I cut the engine, and I said to Doogie, "You've been cooking meth here, haven't you?"

"What's this?" he said. "The third degree?"

"No," I said, "it's the third sign." The first, like I've said, was that tattoo; the second was the linden tree.

"The third sign of what?"

"Of peace," I said, and it surprised me to say it. "Of letting go."

I made him help me. I told him it was the only way I'd let him have that money. I had the gasoline in a can in the bed of my truck. Doogie knew how to get into the Mister Peanut. It didn't take much. A can of gas, a match, and before the flames could lick through the roof, we were gone.

I drove Doogie out to his place in Goosenibble. The air stunk of the poultry house. I sat there waiting to catch the first whiff of smoke, to hear the alarm at the firehouse.

"You're not giving me that money, are you?" Doogie finally said.

"I can be a cruel sonofabitch," I told him.

"So can we all, Baby James."

"You tell the cops whatever you're a mind to."

I reached across him and opened the truck door; I sent him away to make up his mind.

That was the last time I ever saw him.

I went home to your mama. She was still awake, sitting on the couch, her knees up to her chin, looking for all the world like the girl I first fell in love with.

"It's late," she said. "We'll be worn out come time for work."

I sat down on the couch beside her. "The Mister Peanut's on fire," I said.

She was hugging a pillow, a look on her face like she was scared to death. "Trees falling," she said. "Places burning. What's next?"

She thought we were at the end of something. "Maybe someone's not living right," she said.

But who's to say? There was all that money, and I could be a fool cranked up on hope, pretending, even after I'd turned all that cash over to St. Jude's, that it was enough. But like Doogie said: it just goes, and there's never enough of it to stop all the heartache in the world and never enough of it to stop us from trying.

I reached over and took your mama's hand. We sat there, holding on, not saying a word, until, finally, the sun came in through the window and got into our eyes, and your mama said, "You ready?" And, April, I told her I was.

DUMMIES, SHAKERS, BARKERS, WANDERERS

THAT WINTER, MONA WAS IN THE HABIT OF RISING BEFORE DAWN. While Wright still slept, she went out to the barn to check on the Clydesdale mare. She liked stepping out into the cold, looked forward to those first breaths of icy air that stung her eyes and nose and stuck in her throat. She liked the sound of her boots squeaking over the packed snow, the glow of the pole light in the barnyard, the vapor of her breath hanging in the air. Most of all, she loved to hear the Clydes nickering in their stalls and to feel the solid bulk of them when she finally rubbed her hand over their withers and haunches and flanks.

Later, in the warmth of the kitchen, where by this time Wright would be drinking coffee, she would wait until he had heard the farm market reports on WVLN, and then, passing behind his chair, she would let her hand trail along his back, petting him, and she would tell him that the mare was fine.

"She's a tough old gal," he might say. "No quit in her." Then he would gulp down the last of his coffee and hurry out to his truck.

Just before Thanksgiving, he had been hauling the mare, Lucy, back from a breeder in Texas when the hitch had come loose and the trailer had toppled and Lucy had come out the back and gone sliding on her side down a snow-covered I-57. It had been a miracle, Wright told Mona, that no one had hit her. "Everyone was driving careful," he said.

"Hell, I was barely doing forty, taking it extra slow, and then a thing like that had to happen. I could shoot myself."

Their son, Gary, was still living with them then, and there was a month between Thanksgiving and Christmas when he was clean, the methamphetamine a nightmare fading. He talked about enrolling in some classes at the junior college, maybe even going to the U of I and getting a degree in landscape architecture, and Mona, caught up in his optimism, said yes, wouldn't that be fine. She refused to consider how precarious this time of grace might be—indeed by New Year's Gary would be using again. She preferred to watch him and Wright grooming the Clydes, the two of them paying particular attention to Lucy. Gary used the curry comb. He was tall and slender, and his long arms moved over Lucy with graceful sweeps and arcs that reminded Mona of a willow's branches lifting and falling with the wind. Lucy swung her face around and nuzzled him, and it was as if Mona was seeing this for the first time. After all the years of raising Clydes, she thrilled again to how gentle they could be. Wright used the hoof pick. He was patient and fastidious. He sweet-talked Lucy as he cupped an ankle in his hand, and she stood there, a foot lifted like a lady about to test the temperature of her bath. "Lucy girl." He flirted with her. "Who's my girly-girl?" Mona watched Gary and Wright moving among the Clydes, pampering them, and she let the sweetness fill her.

Now when Wright left each morning and she was alone, she dreaded the long day ahead of her, the Clydes the only bright spot. At least she had them to care for. Where Wright went those winter mornings, he never said. Later, she heard from friends that they had seen him in town at Turnipseed's Coffee Shop, or at the grain elevator, or at the city park slouched down in his truck, the engine running. It was clear to her that he really had nowhere to go those mornings and only left home so he would be away from her and their house, which was now a place filled with regret.

"Stop blaming yourself," she told him once.

"Can't," he said. "I'm the one who caused it."

"It's no one's fault." She repeated a line she could remember her mother saying. "Is just is."

But she didn't believe it, not in her heart of hearts. There she couldn't stop wishing that Wright had the courage to put the blame where it truly belonged—on her.

She had been the one, after all, who had said to Gary, that day after New Year's, "Either you get help or we put you out."

They had all been in the kitchen on an afternoon when a cold rain was falling. Gary was at the sink, drinking a glass of water. He was always drinking water when he was using, gallons and gallons it seemed. The meth dried out his mouth, and he was always thirsty. He tipped back his head and his Adam's apple slid up and down his throat. When the glass was empty, he wiped his lips with the back of his hand. He shook water drops from the glass and held it up to the light, turning it around with his long, narrow fingers.

"I bet I could eat this glass," he finally said. He put one side of the rim into his mouth, and Mona heard his teeth click against it. When he was on a run, cranked on meth, he got the idea that he was invincible. He had been in and out of the hospital after trying all sorts of foolish stunts: he had gashed his forehead in a car wreck, broken his leg while trying to climb the water tower, burned his hand because he had been convinced he could reach into fire, shot a nail from a pneumatic gun into his scalp because he wanted to let some air in and relieve the pressure in his brain. He took the glass away from his mouth and winked at Mona. "Tell you what, Moma." (He had always called her Moma, his mouth rounding with the long o sound, a pet name she was glad he had carried over from childhood.) "If I eat this glass—eat the whole damn thing—you and me, we'll call things square. I'll kick the meth. Go to that clinic in Champaign like you want. Otherwise, I'll walk out that door and go away so you won't ever have to be ashamed of me again."

"We're not ashamed of you," she said. "Tell him, Wright."

But Wright wouldn't answer. He just kept staring at Gary, who was still holding the glass.

"Well, Dad?" Again, Gary put his mouth around the rim of the glass.

That's when Wright swung his arm, the back of his hand knocking the glass away from Gary. It hit the wall and shattered. A trickle of blood leaked from Gary's lip. And Wright, something unleashed in him, hit Gary in the face with his fist. He caught him on the jaw, and Gary's head snapped back. He covered his face with his arms, but still Wright kept punching, his fists beating against Gary's wrists. Mona tried to pull Wright away, but he shook her off. He was grunting with the punches. Gary had started to whimper and squeal, the way he had as a boy when he had bad dreams. Mona was tugging at Wright's sleeve, his collar, his neck, anything she could get hold of. Gary was sinking down to the floor, his arms still crossed over his face. Wright leaned over, still trying to reach him with his punches. Mona had him by the shoulders, and they were off balance. They toppled over, and then there they were, the three of them in a heap. Wright was breathing hard. Mona's hair had fallen over her face. They untangled legs and arms. Gary uncovered his face and Mona saw the bruise on his jaw where Wright's first punch had landed. She reached out her hand to touch it, but Gary turned away.

Outside, the rain had turned to sleet and was peppering the kitchen windows.

"Look at us," Mona said. "Just look at us."

Gary grabbed onto the kitchen counter and pulled himself to his feet. Wright slumped over and covered his face with his hands. Gary grabbed his jacket from the peg by the door and went out into the sleet. That was the last time they saw him. He got into his Firebird and drove away.

They had no idea where he was, whether he was alive or dead, whether they would ever see him again. All Mona could do to get through her guilt for not being more forgiving, more tolerant, was to focus on the solid, knowable things around her: the snow and ice and cold, the Clydes, particularly the mare, Lucy, who was now so close to foaling.

One morning, Mona stepped outside just as the sky was beginning to brighten in the east. The bare limbs of the beech and hickory and sweetgum in the woodlot beyond the pasture's end were just starting to emerge from the darkness, and in the dim light they seemed to her a jumble of arms, frantically reaching.

More snow had fallen sometime in the night, and the wind had drifted the barn lot. She had to shovel snow away from the door before she could swing it open, and still the bottom scraped. She was thankful when she finally slipped into the feedway and breathed in its familiar aromas: straw and hay, oats and tack, manure and horse.

She went to the first stall and saw Lucy down on her side. The birth sac, its white balloon, sagged from between her hind legs, and Mona could see the foal's front feet inside the sac and then its nose. Her first instinct was to run back to the house and wake Wright—she had never tended to a foaling by herself—but then she saw that the foal, its head and chest visible now, had stopped moving. She knew there was no time for her to run for Wright; she would have to tear the birth sac before the foal suffocated.

When she did, she could see that the foal wasn't breathing. She tried to stay calm, to think what Wright would do. Then it came to her, the simplest thing: she took a piece of straw and tickled the foal's nostrils until they flared. She felt warm breath on her hand.

The foal surged and its hindquarters emerged. Mona held the rope of the umbilical cord and felt the pulsing of blood. Each pulsation stretched the elastic cord and felt as large as pullet eggs in her hand.

Confident that everything was as it should be, she backed out of the stall, knowing she had to get out of the way so Lucy could finally stand and break the cord and find her foal.

Mona felt something tearing at her heart, and she knew, then, that what she feared most, now that Gary had gone, was that she and Wright would become strangers, each of them wandering inside their own circle of guilt, unable to reach through to the other. She imagined bringing him out to the barn and showing him the foal, bright-eyed, wobbly-legged, full of promise and hope. It would be a single good thing, this gift, and maybe it would start a healing.

When Lucy finally broke the cord, Mona went back into the stall and dipped the stump in an iodine solution so bacteria wouldn't pass through it and leave the foal with navel ill or joint ill. "Good girl," she said to Lucy, who was nuzzling the foal, licking it clean. "Good Lucy girl."

Suddenly the foal's head jerked, and then its legs, and it began to bark again and again, the yip of a small dog—a terrier or a Pekingese, and Mona, watching, felt a chill pass through her. She knew she would have to wake Wright and tell him the foal had come, and instead of a gift it would be a sad, troublesome thing, because something neither of them could have seen coming had gone wrong.

"It's a dummy foal," the vet said. Wright and Mona were kneeling in the straw, trying to hold the shaking foal steady while the vet sedated it with an injection of Diazepam. "Dummies, shakers, barkers, wanderers," he said. "They're all terms for what I'm afraid you've got here, folks—NMS, neonatal maladjustment syndrome."

It was, he explained, a problem that came along from time to time. No one could predict when or even fully understand why. Some thought the condition resulted from sustained cerebral compression in utero or during delivery. Others blamed it on oxygen deprivation either during the latter part of pregnancy or during foaling.

"Darnedest thing," the vet said. He wore half-glasses on a cord around his neck, and they sat on the end of his nose as he finished the injection. "A real mystery. We'll do what we can and keep our fingers crossed. I'm sorry it's happened to you." He shook his head. "Here it is, one more thing for you to deal with."

"One more?" Wright said, and Mona heard the anger in his voice.

"I only meant..."

"I know what you meant."

The vet busied himself with inserting a feeding tube into the foal's stomach. For a good while, neither he nor Wright spoke. Mona kept her head bowed. How easily the vet had acknowledged their trouble, had made it known that their misery with Gary was common talk. She laid her hand flat against the foal's neck and felt the nerves twitching. Suddenly she was overwhelmed with a sense of how they were all connected, all the—what was it the vet had said? Dummies, shakers, barkers, wanderers. Maybe the best God could do was to align the universe so that all those who suffered could find one another.

"It's just rotten luck," she said, unable to bear the silence any longer. "Or maybe not." She stroked the foal's neck. "Maybe we're lucky."

She looked over at Wright and saw him staring at her with heat in his eyes. "How the hell to do you figure that?" he asked.

"Someone's got to be here to know this." The foal's eyes weren't moving. They set in a fixed stare as if they weren't eyes at all, but marbles or ball bearings. The barking had fallen back to an occasional whimper. "You know what I think? God doesn't…"

"Mona." The vet interrupted her. "It's all right to be angry. No one would blame you a bit."

She knew he thought that she had meant to say, "God doesn't give us more than we can bear," but what she had really been thinking was how the hurts of people were nothing without someone else to witness them. They were just howls in the dark. "God can't take in people's pains the way we do," she had meant to say. "That's what he expects from us: to bear witness, to know how close any of us are to anguish. That's our job."

"Maybe I'm angry," she told the vet. "Sure. Maybe a little. But I don't have time to dwell on that. Now, what do we have to do to save this foal?"

It would require keeping the foal warm and hydrated, the vet said. He would set up an IV to drip sodium bicarbonate into the left jugular vein, and antibiotics as needed. The feeding tube would handle the necessary nutrition. The most important thing now was to get some colostrum into the foal. Mona knew that this first milk from the mare was high in protein and natural antibodies that the foal's immune system would need. Since the foal couldn't suck from the mare, the vet would have to give them some frozen colostrum. "Thaw it at room temperature," he said. "If you microwave or heat it, you'll destroy the antibodies." He told them to turn Lucy out to the pasture so she wouldn't disturb the foal and set it to shaking and barking. "We'll keep it sedated and well-fed, and then hope for the best."

"What are our chances?" Wright asked.

"Fifty-fifty," said the vet.

Wright shook his head. "I'd like it if they were better."

In the kitchen, while they waited for the colostrum to thaw, Wright shelled peanuts from a bag he had brought home just before Christmas from the Trading Post Antiques store in Olney.

He had bought sacks of chocolate drops and peanuts, horehound drops and peppermint sticks, rock candy and divinity, the way he had when Gary was a boy—all this because Gary was clean and they were celebrating. Now the holidays were over and Gary was gone and there was all this loot. Wright pressed the peanuts between his thumb and forefinger and emptied the nuts out onto his palm.

"It's a hard thing," he said. "That foal. The vet's right. One more hard thing."

For a moment, Mona felt closer to Wright than she had in a good long while. His voice was toil-worn as if his words were stones he had to shove against to move, and she ached to see the slump in his shoulders. She knew they were nowhere near the end of their misery. She went to him and took his hands in hers.

She had no words for what she wanted him to know, only the heat of her skin, the squeeze of her hands. She let herself lean forward, bowed her head until it rested against his chest, and for a while, they were all body, neither of them speaking, relying instead on the silence, on the rise and fall of their breathing.

Then Mona heard the door open. She felt the icy air across her back and legs. When she turned, she saw Gary standing in the doorway, waiting, she imagined, for someone to tell him it was all right to come in. He was wearing an oversized flannel shirt, the tails hanging down to his knees. His eyelids were fluttering, and he was moving his head about, his eyes looking right, left, up, down like a bird on guard, ready to lift from the ground and fly at the first sign of danger. Mona knew right away that he was using.

"Man, it's cold." He wrapped his arms across his chest. "Man, I'm almost froze to death."

"You don't have a coat," Wright said. "Where's your goddamn coat?"

Gary unfolded his arms and held them away from his sides as if he were trying to carry something very large. He looked himself over, genuinely surprised that he had no coat. Then he looked up and grinned, that smile of pure amazement Mona remembered so well from when he was a boy and something surprised him. "No coat," he said. "How about that?"

"You'd think you were twelve," Wright said, and Mona, hearing the anger in his voice, knew they were at a point of danger.

"Better go out and check on the foal," she said to Wright. "Go on. I'll bring the colostrum out when it's thawed." She felt herself taking charge, knowing it was better to keep Wright and Gary apart until Wright had the chance to get comfortable with the fact that Gary had come home and that he was still in trouble with the meth. She touched Wright's arm. "Go on," she said. "Please."

Wright did what she asked. Without a word, he put on his insulated coveralls and went out to the barn.

Whatever happened from that point on, Mona knew that she would always be grateful that he had paid her this favor, the chance to be alone with Gary, to try one more time to say how much she loved him. She would speak kindly, not foolishly like she had that night when Wright had beaten Gary with his fists. She would start at the beginning—already the details were coming to her: the way he followed her though her flower beds when he was a boy, and she taught him the names, salvia, coreopsis, zinnia; the way Wright swung him up on his shoulders and galloped across the yard, neighing, while Gary shouted, "Heigh-ho, Silver," and the dog, Penny, a black lab, chased after them, her barks echoing. She would remind Gary of the time she had taken a snapshot of him and Penny sitting on the front steps. It was Easter morning, and he had on his first suit and a bow tie. His hair was combed off his forehead and held in place with some of Wright's Vitalis. He had his arm around Penny's neck and he was grinning, showing off the gap where he had lost a tooth. They had sent the photo away to a place that enlarged it and then made it into a jigsaw puzzle.

Mona still had it, and sometimes she got it out of the closet and put the pieces together, recalling that Easter morning when the sun had been bright and the grass green and there had been just enough of a breeze to ruffle the yellow cups of the daffodils atop their stems.

She would offer up all this, their simple story which, at its heart, was a story of love, as evidence that there had been a time—and could be again—when the three of them were happy. She would remind Gary of the way he had curried Lucy, his arms moving with such grace that anyone who watched him would know he still felt himself connected to the world. He hadn't drifted so far way that it would be impossible to save him.

All this she meant to say, but the only thing that came out of her mouth was a plea: "Let us help you. Gary, please."

She knew right away that she had made a mistake; her request was too urgent, too pressing, more of a command than an offer. It was the sort of finger-wagging, no matter how well-intentioned, that Gary had always bridled at.

"Help me?" He lifted his chin and his nostrils flared. "What makes you think you can help me?"

"I'm your mother." She said it plainly, trusting in the simple hope that flesh would answer to flesh.

"And you think you can fix me?"

She told him about the dummy foal and how it twitched and barked as if it were a thing lost to itself. She tried to tell the story without passing judgment on him and the way he was letting his life slip away to nothing.

"You were a good boy," she said. "You were my good boy."

"And now?"

"Here you are. The world gives us chances, opportunities. You came back for a reason."

"I came back because I'm in trouble. I'm in trouble, Moma. More than you know." He leaned toward her and lowered his voice. "They're on to me."

"They?"

"The aliens. They're on my tail."

He told the story in a whisper, afraid, he said, that they might be listening. His hushed voice soothed her. It was the sound of wind stirring leaves, of water lapping at stones, and because he was so forthright, so earnest, there was a nobility to his telling that would seduce anyone, Mona thought, no matter how doubting. Listening to him, no one could deny that he was in the midst of something extraordinary and yet completely human, and he was trying his best to explain it, to say it simply and directly and make it something that belonged to anyone who heard it.

"Do you know why they want me?" he said. "Because I'm magic. I can do magic things."

It was the meth talking; Mona knew that. Still she couldn't help thinking that a long way back she had prepared the way for Gary's fantasies. She had made his delusions possible. When he was a boy, she told him stories—goodness, where had they come from—stories about an octopus who played four violins at once, or a man so tall that when he walked his head bumped the stars and shook them from the sky. She painted a mural on his bedroom wall, the emerald city of Oz rising up beyond a field of poppies. In the backyard, she hooked an old playground slide to the branch of an oak tree, fashioned oversized bird's claws from Styrofoam and left them sticking out of the leaves at the slide's top so it looked like a giant bird, at any second, might come whooshing into view.

Had she made Gary's world too large and bright, led him to expect so much that the ordinary, even after he had become a grown man, was never enough? "Meth jazzes things up," he had told her once. "It makes everything king-sized." She remembered the names he had for it: Mr. Crystal, crank, tweak, go-fast. There had been times—she had to admit this now—when the drug's effects had seduced her, too, had brought her into Gary's euphoria, a small part of her charmed when he was just high enough to be jaunty and full of spirit. Of course, she felt guilty later, but there it was, a true thing.

"Come over here," he told her now, and, when she hesitated, he gave her a shy grin. He crooked his finger and motioned for her.

"Come on." He ducked his head, and she felt herself lean toward him. "Moma," he said. "I won't hurt you."

She never for a moment thought he would. She remembered how on Christmas Eve she had got out of bed for a drink of water and had come upon Gary in the kitchen, standing in the dark at the back door watching the snow drift down past the pole light in the barn lot. There was no wind, and the snow came straight down at a steady, lulling pace. "Waiting for Santa Claus?" she asked him, and he gave her a sheepish grin and told her no, he was just watching it snow. She stayed with him awhile, watching everything outside turn white, and she felt there was no need for words ever again; Gary had kicked the meth and they had put behind them the pleas and threats and desperate attempts. She was content to stand there with him in the middle of the quiet night.

That was the feeling that was coming over her now. She thought that if she went to him and did what he asked, everything would be all right.

He had picked up a juice glass from the counter and was holding it out to her. It was a slender, fluted glass with a dainty etching of fruit along its rim: grapes, an apple, an orange, a pear. "Take it," Gary said, and she held it in her hand, feeling its delicate design. It was the last glass left from a set that had been a wedding present; its mates had been cracked and chipped and broken over the years. Mona hadn't realized how much this last one meant to her until she held it now, and Gary looked at her and said, "I want you to drop it."

"Drop it?" she said. "Are you joking?"

"I'm magic, Moma. Remember? I'm your good boy."

She heard in his voice a mix of plea and challenge, begging her to accommodate him if she dared, and she sensed that if she turned away from him, he would think it the final betrayal, and she would lose him forever. She remembered what, just a few minutes before, she had told him about opportunities, chances. All they had to do was take them. "Drop it," she said, trying to get used to the idea. "All right."

He would close his eyes, he told her. "Here, hold it close," he said. "Right here. Right in front of my face." He pressed his elbows against his rib cage and held his hands apart. "Put the glass directly above my hands, and prepare yourself to be amazed." He closed his eyes. "Whenever you're ready. Don't tell me when you're going to drop it."

For a good while, she watched the way his eyelids quivered—just the slightest tremor, as if he could barely keep them closed, and she thought of all the times she had watched him sleep when he was a boy and given thanks for the mere fact of him. Now she could feel how eager he was for her to drop that glass, how badly he wanted her to do it. She held the glass by its rim, the raised lines of its etching—the roughness of them—her only tether to common sense. Drop the glass? How could she? But there was that flutter in Gary's eyelids urging her on. "Trust me," he finally whispered. "Just trust me." And she let the glass go.

She couldn't know, then, what was happening in the barn, that the foal had come out of the Diazepam and had begun to shake. She would know it in just a moment when Wright would run out into the barn lot and call her name. "Mona," he would say. "Mona, come quick."

For the time being, though everything happened in less than a second, she was fascinated with the feeling of there being nothing in her hands; the glass had been there, and then it wasn't, and she was completely powerless to stop whatever was going to happen next.

Later, she would consider with amazement how much could be held in a fraction of a second, how many journeys the mind could take. She imagined Lucy sliding down the highway on her side, her legs pawing at the air as she tried to right herself, the white feathering around her hooves blowing back in the wind. That and the way Wright had beaten his fists against Gary's slender arms, and the way the blood had felt pulsing through Lucy's umbilical cord, and the sound of the foal barking, and the delicate cups of daffodils on that long-ago Easter morning, and snow falling.

Then Gary's hands moved—she felt the air stir—and there he was, holding the glass.

For a moment, he kept his eyes closed. He held the glass in front of him, two hands grasping it as if he were a child and the glass was full and he was being careful to hold it steady. Mona thought it the most wonderful, the most frightening thing—the blind sense of motion, the quick movement of hands, the glass now safe.

She felt the way she had when she had tickled the foal's nostrils and it had begun to breathe—lucky, thankful to be free from disaster. "You caught it," she said.

Gary opened his eyes and looked down at the glass. "Magic," he said. Then he laughed, and Mona was glad for his laughing, for the risk they had taken and then come away clean. He laughed until his shoulders shook and his face was wet with tears, and he wasn't a man laughing at all, but a misery sounding, something raw and horrible just beyond ecstasy.

Mona held out her hands to him, wishing there were some way she could take it from him, all the terror. He lifted his arms—in a moment he would collapse against her, sobbing, his arms around her neck, and she would hold him up—but now he was only moving toward her, and the glass was falling from his hands to the floor where it shattered at their feet.

Months later, in summer, she would tell the story of the foal again and again. "It was the darnedest thing," she would say. "Yip, yip, yip. Just like a dog." But she wouldn't tell the part about Gary; that, she would hold to herself, considering it too precious to let out into the world. She would think of it all through the long months of his visits to the rehab clinic. "I can quit," he would say. "I just can't stay quit."

She would remember how he went out to the barn with her that winter morning, where they saw the foal shaking on the straw.

"Would you look at it?" Wright said, and he seemed so helpless. "Would you just look? Poor thing."

But Mona was seeing something different, something rich and unexpected—a blessing where she hadn't thought to find one.

For Gary had got down on his knees behind the foal and had laid his hands on it. He stroked its face and throat, rubbed his fingers over its lips and gums. He took his time, his hands slow and unhurried. He caressed the foal's ears, and Mona imagined the way they would feel—as sleek as the beards of irises, the blades of lamb's ears, the petals of roses. When she saw that the foal was beginning to relax—its head still now, its legs not twitching as badly—she felt something open inside her, some mercy. She felt so small in the presence of this astonishing thing, her ruined boy petting this dummy foal.

"What in the hell are you doing?" Wright asked.

"Loving it," Gary said in a whisper. "Letting it know it isn't alone."

He moved his hand over the foal's mane, combing his fingers through the hair. He stroked its withers and back. He rubbed its belly, taking care around the vet's incision for the feeding tube. The foal tipped back its head and nuzzled Gary's arm. Over the days to come, the sucking reflex would finally come to it, and it would nurse from Lucy. But now it was enchanted with Gary; his touch was the most wonderful thing.

All Mona could do was watch. Then, in a quiet voice, she asked Wright to please go to the house and fetch the colostrum, and he did.

While Gary held the foal against him, Mona squeezed the colostrum from its bag and into the feeding tube.

"There's broken glass all over the kitchen floor," Wright said, catching Mona's eye, asking her with his stare what had happened. She sensed an accusation in that stare, an unspoken belief that whatever followed would be her doing.

She wanted to say everything she was feeling, but she was dumbstruck. How could she begin to explain that moment in the kitchen when she had dropped the glass and Gary had caught it? How could she tell Wright what she now knew: love was nothing without surrender. She imagined Gary standing there, his eyes closed, his hands at the ready, listening for the faint, almost imperceptible sound of her fingers lifting from the glass and letting go.

"An accident," she said to Wright. "Just one of those things."

He didn't press her for anything more, and she was thankful for the fact that the three of them were together, gathered around the foal. They were kneeling in the straw the way the Clydes did sometimes in open pasture when they sensed a dip in air pressure, a rising of the wind, and they braced themselves for changing weather. The foal laid its head across Gary's legs and closed its eyes. Mona watched the rise and fall of its chest, its measured breathing responding to the gentle motion of Gary's hand. It was all so simple, she thought—this touching—and she wished they could stay there, never have to move, never have to rise up and face the rest of their lives.

She told herself there were days and days ahead of them—days and weeks and months and years—time enough for anything to happen. Anything, she thought, and a shiver passed over her. The word was so lovely, and yet so frightening. It lay against her, weighty and splendid, a promise alive and trembling at the heart of ruin, waiting for her to claim it.

ACKNOWLEDGMENTS

I'd like to thank the editors at the journals in which these stories first appeared:

"The Mutual UFO Network" and "The Dead in Paradise" in *Shenandoah*; "Love Field" and "A Man Looking for Trouble" in *Glimmer Train* and *The Best American Mystery Stories, 2015*; "Belly Talk" in *The Southern Review*; "Bad Family" in *The Nebraska Review*; "White Dwarfs" in *Another Chicago Magazine*; "Real Time" in *Cimarron Review*; "Drunk Girl in Stilettos" in *The Georgia Review*; "Dummies, Shakers, Barkers, Wanderers" in *The Kenyon Review*.